Charles Rogers

Memorials of the Earl of Sterling and of the house of Alexander

Vol. 2

Charles Rogers

Memorials of the Earl of Sterling and of the house of Alexander
Vol. 2

ISBN/EAN: 9783337150860

Printed in Europe, USA, Canada, Australia, Japan

Cover: Foto ©Raphael Reischuk / pixelio.de

More available books at **www.hansebooks.com**

Major General W. R. E. Alexander.

MEMORIALS

OF THE

EARL OF STIRLING

AND OF THE

HOUSE OF ALEXANDER

BY THE

Rev. CHARLES ROGERS, LL.D.

HISTORIOGRAPHER TO THE ROYAL HISTORICAL SOCIETY; FELLOW OF THE SOCIETY
OF ANTIQUARIES OF SCOTLAND; MEMBER OF THE HISTORICAL SOCIETY
OF QUEBEC; AND CORRESPONDING MEMBER OF THE
HISTORICAL AND GENEALOGICAL SOCIETY
OF NEW ENGLAND

VOL. II.

EDINBURGH
WILLIAM PATERSON, 67 PRINCES STREET
1877

EDINBURGH :
PRINTED BY M'FARLANE AND ERSKINE
(*late Schenck & M'Farlane*),
ST JAMES SQUARE.

CONTENTS.

*b

CHAPTER XXIX.

CHAPTER XXX.

CHAPTER XXXI.

CHAPTER XXXII.

CHAPTER XXXIII.

CHAPTER XXXIV.

APPENDIX.

MEMORIALS

OF THE

HOUSE OF ALEXANDER.

CHAPTER XIX.

FAMILIES OF ALEXANDER OF CAITHNESS; DRUM, DONEIS, BIGHEAD OF TORREIS, ABERDEEN; AUCHMULL, KINMUNDIE, GLASS, AUCHINOLL, ECHT, LOGIE-COLDSTONE, JACKSTOUN, BOYNE'S MILL, ABERDEENSHIRE; CHOPISWALLIS, CALSAYEND, KINCARDINESHIRE; AND OF GARLABANK, LEIS MILL, DUNDEE, MONTROSE, RAVENSBY, BALSKELLIE, AND WESTER PERSIE, FORFARSHIRE.

ACCORDING to tradition, several members of the House of Alexander obtained a settlement in Caithness under Campbell of Glenorchy, who in 1672 fought a battle with Sinclair of Keiss, at Artimarlach, near Wick. These settlers were the immediate followers of Campbell of Glenorchy, and accompanied him from Argyleshire.

On the 20th June 1632, Alexander Alexander or Elschinder, "portioner of Drum," in the county of

* A

Aberdeen, granted at Cosnaghtoune, an obligation to Lord Colville of Culross for £61 (Reg. of Deeds, vol. 467).

On the 4th July 1633, a contract of marriage was entered into between Alexander Alshender in Doneis, and Christian Chalmer, daughter of Charles Chalmer in Kintore, Aberdeenshire, the "tocher" being 500 merks (Reg. of Deeds, vol. 480).

On the 9th November 1633, John Alexander in Big-head of Torreis, granted at Insh, Aberdeenshire, an obligation for 100 merks to John Cruikshank of Cadden (Reg. of Deeds, vol. 479).

On the 25th November 1633, John Alexander, burgess of Aberdeen, and his sons, James and Patrick Alexander, purchased from James Gordon the lands of Auchmull for 3500 merks (Reg. of Deeds, vol. 494).

On the 7th August 1644, " Mr William Alexander " was served heir to his father, Robert Alexander, bur-gess of Aberdeen, in the lands of Ward of Kinmundie, in the parish of St Machar and county of Aberdeen (Special Retours, Aberdeen, xviii. 144).

Mr John Alexander, described as "advocate in Edinburgh," was one of the three husbands of Mary, daughter and heiress of George Jamesone, the emi-nent painter, a native of Aberdeen.   On the 15th January 1645, he petitioned the town council of the burgh to grant him a feu of a portion of ground, called the Hayfield, which George Jamesone, his father-in-law, had held in liferent. His request was acceded to, and the feu-duty fixed at "four pundis Scotis money yearlie" (Council Records of Aberdeen). By his wife, Mary Jamesone, Mr John Alexander had two sons, who attained considerable distinction. John Alexander studied the art of painting, chiefly in Florence, and on his return to Scotland in 1720, resided at Gordon Castle, under the patronage of the Duchess of Gordon, daughter of the Earl of Peterborough. He painted portraits, allegorical pieces, and historical landscapes. Many of the portraits of Queen Mary were executed by him. He began a picture of Queen Mary's escape from Lochleven Castle, in which the scenery round the lake is introduced, but he died before completing it. Cosmo Alexander, another son of Mr John Alexander and Mary Jamesone, became known as an engraver; he engraved a portrait of his maternal grandfather.

On the 7th March 1645, Mr John Alexander, advocate, and Richard and Alexander Alexander, and other citizens of Aberdeen, met to arrange measures for dissuading the Marquis of Montrose from marching his army into the city. John and Richard Alexander were among the delegates appointed to wait upon the marquis (Burgh Records of Aberdeen; Spalding's Memorials, vol. ii., p. 452).

Alexander Alexander, bailie in Aberdeen, was, on the 8th August 1672, admitted an honorary burgess of Stirling (Stirling Burgh Records).

Alexander Alexander, son of Alexander Alexander, bailie in Aberdeen, was a regent in Marischal College of that city. Obtaining licence from Alexander, Bishop of Edinburgh, he was admitted minister of Glass, Banffshire, before the 8th April 1679. Having two half-nets' fishing on the mid-chingle in the Dee, at Aberdeen, he purchased nets, hired servants, and had the fishing conducted by a relative. Finding at the expiry of two years that he had obtained a profit of only two shillings, he abandoned operations. The fishings proved more advantageous to his heir, who, in 1760, let them for a rent of £60. Mr Alexander was deprived by the Act of Parliament, 25th April 1690, which restored the ejected Presbyterian ministers. He resumed possession of the cure on a vacancy in 1693, and though his right was disputed, he contrived to retain the living till his death, which took place in 1713. By his wife, Margaret Collisone, he had a son, Alexander, proprietor of Auchinoll, and five daughters (Fasti Eccl. Scot., iii. 199).

On the 17th January 1657, Isobel and Margaret Alexander were served co-heiresses to John Alexander, merchant in Aberdeen, their father (Inq. Spec.).

Nisbet describes the arms of " Alexander Alexander of Auchmull, sometime bailie of Aberdeen," thus : " Parted per pale, *argent* and *sable*, a cheveron between two mullets in chief, and a crescent in base, all counter-changed ; crest, a hand sustaining a pair

of balances of equal scales ; motto, *Quod tibi ne alteri*"
(Nisbet's Heraldry, vol. i., p. 30).

Walter Alexander was admitted minister of the
parish of Echt, Aberdeenshire, 14th October 1666 ;
he demitted in 1694. By his marriage with Janet
Scot, he had a son, William, who became a teacher
in Aberdeen.   He was served heir to his mother
on the 28th September 1712 (Fasti Eccl. Scot.,
iii. 531).

Thomas Alexander, who had graduated at King's
College, Aberdeen, on the 4th July 1682, was, prior
to 1688, admitted minister of Logie-Coldstone, in the
county of Aberdeen.   He died on the 6th July 1715,
aged fifty-three.   His son, Alexander Alexander of
Jackstoun, was served heir to him on the 14th
January 1724.   He had a son, Thomas, who resided
at Inverernan, and a daughter, Margaret, who married John Forbes of Inverernan (Fasti Eccl. Scot.,
iii. 535).

On the 16th March 1694, John Alexander in
Boyne's Mill, parish of Forgue, Aberdeenshire, is
described as "eldest son of the deceased James
Alexander in Boyne's Mill." He declined service to
the lands (Reg. Mag. Sig., xvii. 464).

John Alexander in Chopiswallis, in the parish of
Fordoun, Kincardineshire, died in April 1577. In
his will, dated 23d August 1576, he appoints his
wife, Isobel Merchant, and his son, Charles Alexander, as his executors.   Thomas Alexander, "mes-

singer to the kingis maiestie," is a witness, and John
Alexander in Middletoun is a debtor on the estate
(Edin. Com. Reg., vol. x.).

On the 23d August 1620, Janet Alexander, spouse
of Alexander Alexander in Calsayend, parish of Con-
veth (Laurencekirk), and county of Kincardine, executed his will (Com. Reg. of St Andrews).

William Alexander in Collatown of Garlabank,
Forfarshire, executed his will on the 10th February
1580 (Edin. Com. Reg.).

On the 1st April 1577, John Alexander, brother's
son of the deceased David Alexander in Leis Myln,
Forfarshire, and his executor-dative, presented the inventory of his deceased relative, valued £226, 16s. 8d.
Scots (Edinburgh Com. Reg.).

James Alexander, merchant-burgess in Dundee,
died in November 1605. In his will, dated the 6th
day of the same month, he names as his executors,
his wife, Elspeth Galloway, and David Alexander,
litster-burgess of Dundee. His " frie geir " is valued
at 1019 lib. 14s. He mentions his " lawfull bairnes,"
William, Christian, and Euffame Alexander, and, as
one of his debtors, " Archibald Alexander in Banff "
(Edin. Com. Reg., vol. xli.).

John Alexander in Montrose was, on the 18th May
1665, served heir to his father, John Alexander,
miller in Montrose (Inq. Spec.).

On the 23d December 1648, David Alexander was
served heir of James Alexander of Ravensby, his

father, in the **lands** and village of Carnoustie and others, in the parish of Barry and county of Forfar (Inq. Spec., Forfarshire). David Alexander acquired the adjacent lands of Balskellie **by a** charter, **dated** 25th January 1667 (Charters **in Chancery**). **On the** 21st December **1676, James** Alexander, **son of** David Alexander, obtained service in the lands of Balskellie, and in the village and lands of Carnoustie (Inq. Speciales, Forfarshire). The family is mentioned by Nisbet (Heraldry, vol. i., p. 25).

Thomas Alexander in Wester Persie, Forfarshire, died intestate **in June 1580**. His testament-dative and inventory were given **up** by his brother, David Alexander in Wester Persie, on behalf of John, Marion, and Isobel Alexander, children of the deceased (Edin. Com. Reg., vol. x.).

CHAPTER XX.

WILLIAM ALEXANDER, "indweller in Leyth," died " of
the pest" in December 1587. The inventory of his
effects was produced by "Cristane Braidie, his relict
spous," together with his will, dated 12th December
1587. The latter presents the following clause:

"I, the said Mr William, leivis to my said spous and my
sone William, and to the langest leivar of thame tua, to nocht
failzieing, Williame my sone, the rest to be gewin to my said
spous, to wit, the hail wair quhilk trusting for goddis caus
that my brether, to wit, Thomas and Henrie, James and
Alexander, sall on na maner of way be allowit to defraude my
said spous, . . . and vmquhile sone, to wit, William . . ."

The goods of the deceased were valued at £279, 8s.
Scots. Among the debtors on the estate were John
Alexander, portioner of Pitsgobir (Pitgogar), and
Gauin Alexander, "his sone and appeirant air," and

Andro Braidie in Striveling (Stirling) (Edin. Com. Reg., vol. xix.).

Robert Alexander, merchant, Leith, was, on the nomination of Sir William Alexander of Menstry, appointed searcher at that port. The office was claimed by a son of Bernard Lindsay, the former occupant of the post, whereupon the following royal letter, dated 7th January 1627-8, was addressed to Lord Napier, the Treasurer-Depute :

"Right, &c. Haveing been informed how, by the death of Bernard Lindsay, the place of Searcher at Leith doth vake at our disposition, whereupon we were pleased to grant a guift to one Robert Alexander, Merchand there, according to the guift granted by us thairupon, But since informed that one —— Lindsay, a sone of the said late Bernard, doth pretend an interest therein, Wee have thought good that you trie the estate thereof and certifie us back again of the same or otherwise if you shall find just cause that the said Robert should discharge that place. Wee likewayes require you to use your best means for causing settle him tharin according to our said guift" (Register of Letters).

On the 27th February 1652, James Alexander, brewer in Leith, and Janet Reid, were married (South Leith Parish Register). They had a daughter, Margaret, baptized 10th October 1658, and a son, William, baptized 27th September 1660 (Baptismal Register of Edinburgh). On the 14th June 1688, William Alexander, indweller in Leith, executed his will (Edin. Com. Reg.).

James Alexander, advocate, was, on the 2d May

1685, served heir to David Alexander in Leith, his
elder brother (General Rétours, xxxviii. 64).

Robert Alexander is mentioned as a merchant-
burgess of Edinburgh in 1597 (Edinburgh Baptismal
Register).

John Alexander, merchant-burgess in Edinburgh,
died on 13th June 1616. His testament was "made
and gevin up by himself, with his awin tung, speik-
and at Perth, the 12 day of June 1616." He names
Susanna Alexander, his daughter, as his only executor. His assets amounted to 153 lib. 6s. 8d. (Edinburgh Commissariat Reg.).

Robert Alexander, merchant in Leith, died in
1629, and on the 17th July of that year his son, who
bore the same Christian name, was served as his
heir (General Services, x. 346). On the 26th March
1635, a bond for £2000 Scots, in favour of the late
Robert Alexander, indweller in Leith, by Sir William
Alexander of Menstry, with "Walter Alexander,
gentleman usher to the prince," as one of the cautioners, was registered at Edinburgh at the instance of
Elizabeth Alexander, daughter of the deceased Robert
(Register of Bonds).

The testament-dative and inventory of umquhil
George Alexander, merchant-burgess of Edinburgh,
who died in November 1589, was given up by Marion
and Catherine Alexander, his daughters, on the 19th
January 1610. His goods were valued at £770, 16s.
8d., and as one of his debtors was named David

Alexander, merchant-burgess of Edinburgh (Edin. Com. Reg., vol. xlvi.). David Alexander is, on the 15th February 1590, described as "merchant-burgess of Edinburgh" (Register of Deeds, vol. xxxvi., 317). He had sasine of a mill at Stirling (Stirling Reg. of Sasines), and on the 6th June 1616 obtained a charter of a hundred merks out of the lands of Wester Spott, Haddingtonshire (Reg. Mag. Sig.). He died on the 31st December 1616. In his will, dated 14th August 1611, he mentions his wife, Isobel Allan, his son, "Mr Robert Alexander," and his daughters, Elizabeth, Elspeth, Barbara, Katherine, and Janet; also his two sisters, Christian and Margaret. As one of the guardians of his children he names "Sir William Alexander of Menstrie." His movable estate is valued at £3102, 10s. Scots (Edin. Com. Reg., vol. l.).

Elizabeth, eldest daughter of David Alexander, married first, in 1618, James Cochrane, merchant-burgess and one of the magistrates of Edinburgh, receiving from him in liferent the five-merk lands of Luchscillis, in the barony of Monkland and county of Lanark (Gen. Reg. of Sasines, vol. ii., p. 176); she married, secondly, John Winram, merchant-burgess of Edinburgh, and is named as a widow 7th July 1642 (General Retours, vol. xvi., 247).

On the 29th January 1607, Robert Alexander, writer in Edinburgh, made complaint against a person who was indebted to him, and refused to pay (Reg.

Mag. Concilii).   He was, on the 20th March 1617, served heir to David Alexander, his father (Gen. Retours, vol. vi., 184, 258).

On the 4th December 1619, Elizabeth Alexander, wife of Bailie James Cochrane, and Katherine Alexander, wife of John Small, merchant-burgess of Edinburgh, were served heirs-portioners of Mr Robert Alexander, their brother (Gen. Retours, vii. 181, 182).

On the 22d December 1631, Sir James Ker of Crailing granted an obligation to William Stirling, writer in Edinburgh, as tutor for Elizabeth Alexander, daughter of the late Robert Alexander, writer and keeper of his Majesty's signet, for 1000 merks (Gen. Reg. of Deeds).

On the 21st December 1635, Mr Harie Shaw, minister at Logie, granted a bond for £60 to John Alexander, Writer to the Signet, Edinburgh. A witness to the transaction was James Alexander, merchant-burgess in Stirling (Register of Deeds, 489).

Alexander Alexander was long employed as "servitor" or amanuensis to the Earl of Stirling. With a view to his obtaining the office of a macer in the Court of Session, Lord Stirling had recommended him to the Privy Council. As the recommendation, though proceeding on the royal authority, had been overlooked, the command as to his appointment was, on the 24th July 1630, thus emphatically renewed :

" (CHARLES I.)

" Right, &c. Whereas wee wer long since pleased to signifie

oʳ plesure that Robert Chreichtoun and Alexander Alexander
should be preferred to the first vacking offices of Maesarie,
whereof notwithstanding they have been disappointed (as we
are crediballie informed), contrarie to our royal intentions. Now
least others should unseasonably importune us to have these
two offices, or least the said Robert and Alexander be furder
disappointed of what wee intend for them, Our pleasour is that
you tak notice of oʳ royall intentions herein. And if any such
offices doe vaik at oʳ guift by death, demissioune, deprivatioune,
or other wayes, that you hearken to none that have been or
shalbe suittors unto us or you for the same (seeing according to
oʳ first intention), wee have resolved to grant the first place
soe vaiking unto the said Robert, & the next unto the said
Alexander, and to this effect that you both cause mak ane act of
counsell and sederunt. And for your soe doeing these presents
shalbe a sufficient warrant."

As the Council remained silent, the Lords of Session
were, in a royal letter dated 18th May 1632, next
reminded of Alexander's claims. They were requested
not to allow his employment abroad in the royal
service to interfere with his preferment (Register of
Letters). He obtained a macership soon afterwards.
He married Margaret, eldest daughter of John
Forsyth, resident at Westminster; she was, on the
18th January 1643, served heir to her grandfather,
John Forsyth, burgess in Forres (General Retours,
xvii. 146). Alexander Alexander's will is dated 7th
April 1646 (Edinburgh Com. Reg.).

On the 16th November 1636, William Alexander,
merchant-burgess of Edinburgh, granted to Thomas
Winram a tak or lease of "thrie baithis on the south
side of the hie street of Edinburgh" for six years, at

the yearly rent of "thrie hundreth merkis Scots money" (Reg. of Deeds, vol. 516).

Thomas Alexander, writer in Edinburgh, died in November 1690, and his testament-dative was delivered up by his widow, Janet Waterston. His goods were valued at £133, 6s. 8d. (Edin. Com. Reg., vol. lxxix.).

Early in the eighteenth century, William Alexander (probably of Edinburgh) described as "nearest heir-male to the title of Earl of Stirling," married Elizabeth, eldest daughter of the Rev. Andrew Lumisden, minister of Duddingston, and latterly non-jurant Bishop of Edinburgh, by his wife, Katherine, only child of John Craig, son of the celebrated Sir Thomas Craig of Riccarton. By his wife, William Alexander had a son and daughter, who both died without issue (Analecta Scotica, vol. ii., pp. 32, 41).

During the sixteenth century, a branch of the House of Alexander was settled in the county of Peebles. In the Edinburgh Commissariat Register are recorded the wills of Andrew Alexander in Kirkurd, dated 5th February 1574; and of Thomas Alexander in Linton, dated 16th April 1575. In the same register appear the will of Janet Alexander, spouse to Alexander Forester, cooper in Blyth, in the parish of Linton, who died in October 1586, "her free gear" amounting to 231 lib. 10s.; the will of William Alexander in Gravelpits, in the parish of Linton, dated 14th January 1588; and the will of

James Alexander in Gravelpits, of the same parish, and his wife, Margaret Russell, in parish of Linton and sheriffdom of Peebles, of whom the former died on 8th November 1597, and the latter on the 8th December of the same year, leaving a son, Richard.

A branch of the family settled in the town of Peebles. On the 14th February 1711, Patrick Alexander, described as " dweller in Kirkburne," had a son, William, baptized (Peebles Parish Register). On the 18th December 1729, William Alexander, merchant in Peebles, and Margaret Crichton, were married (Peebles Parish Register). Robert, a son of this marriage, became a merchant at Moffat, Dumfriesshire. By his wife, Susan Nicol, sister of the Rev. William Nicol, minister of the Scottish Church, Swallow Street, London, he had an only child, William. Deprived of both his parents in childhood, William Alexander was educated in Edinburgh, where he afterwards settled. His son, the Rev. William Lindsay Alexander, D.D., born at Edinburgh on the 24th August 1808, studied at the Universities of Edinburgh and St Andrews, and in 1828 was appointed classical tutor in the Lancashire College, Blackburn. He was in 1835 elected pastor of an Independent church in Edinburgh, an office to which was added, in 1854, the Professorship of Theology to the Congregationalists of Scotland. Among other works, he has published, "Anglo-Catholicism not Apostolical," " Christ and Christianity," 1854; " Life of Dr Wardlaw," 1856; "Christian Thought and Work," 1862; "St Paul at Athens," 1865. He has contributed the articles "Moral Philosophy," "Scripture," and "Theology," to the eighth edition of the "Encyclopædia Britannica;" edited the third edition of "Kitto's Biblical Cyclopædia;" and is a member of the committee for revising the translation of the Old Testament.

In his "History of Peeblesshire," Mr William Chambers of Glenormiston mentions Charles Alexander, farmer at Easter Happrew, in the parish of Stobo, who, at the close of the eighteenth century, was distinguished for his skill as an agriculturist (Chambers's Peeblesshire, p. 236).

John Alexander, a scion of the House of Menstry, graduated at the University of St Andrews in 1603 (Act. Rect. Univ. St And.). In 1610 he was appointed rector of the united parishes of Hoddam, Luce, and Ecclefechan, in the county of Dumfries. He erected a parish church on a central site at his private cost (Chalmers' Caledonia, 1824, 4to, vol. iii., p. 197). He was one of fifty-five ministers who, on the 27th June 1617, subscribed a protest on behalf of the liberties of the Church. On the 21st October 1634, he was nominated a member of the commission for the maintenance of Church discipline (Fasti Eccl. Scot., i. 620). On the 6th January 1636, he granted to Sir Richard Murray, Bart. of Cokpute, on behalf of his wife, Isobel Barclay, and their son, William, a renunciation of an annual rent of 400 merks "furth of the lands of Cokpute," to which he had right by a contract made at Manchester on the 5th November 1632 (Register of Deeds, vol. 489). He and his wife obtained a charter, on the 28th November 1642, of the lands of Over Isgill, in the county of Dumfries (Reg. Mag. Sig., lib. lvii., No. 162).

On the 13th February 1643, a charter under the Great Seal was granted to James, Lord Johnstoun of Lochwood, and Mr John Alexander, rector of Hoddam, equally between them and their heirs, of the lands of Glendonyng, comprehending half the lands of Corlaw, Wester Ker, Fellcolme, and Felbrae, within the lordship of Eskdale and shire of Dumfries, as principal, and the other half of Corlaw, lands of Curcleuche, etc., in warrandice, which lands formerly belonged to the said James Johnstoun of Westraw, and were resigned by him for this new infeftment (Reg. Mag. Sig., lib. lvii., No. 232).

Mr John Alexander, minister of Hoddam, died on the 14th July 1660, in his seventy-eighth year. In the Register of the Privy Seal for 1664, are narrated certain proceedings between Isabella Barclay, his widow, and their son James, and the Rev. James Craig, admitted minister of Hoddam in 1661, in regard to the possession of the manse.

Mrs Isabella Barclay, relict of Mr John Alexander, minister of Hoddam, died 2d July 1682, aged eighty-two. The family consisted of three sons, James, John, and William, and a daughter, Barbara (Fasti

* B

Eccl. Scot., vol. i., p. 620). James, the eldest son, acquired the estate of Knockhill, in the parish of Hoddam. In 1701 he settled £1195, 6s. 4d. Scots on the poor of the parish.

John, second son of Mr John Alexander, was some time session-clerk at South Leith, an office which he demitted on the 13th July 1682 (S. Leith Sess. Reg.). In 1680 he published a quarto volume, entitled "Jesuitico-Quakerism Examined; or, a Confutation of the Blasphemous and Unreasonable Principles of the Quakers, with a Vindication of the Church of God in Britain." This work was dedicated to Sir Robert Clayton, Lord Mayor of London; and it bears to have been examined and approved by John Hamilton at the appointment of the Lord Bishop of Edinburgh. In 1683 John Alexander was ordained minister of Kirknewton. He was in the same year translated to Durrisdeer, in the county of Dumfries. Having adhered to Episcopacy, he was ejected by the people in 1689. He died at Edinburgh on the 16th July 1716, in his eighty-eighth year. He married, first, Isobel, third daughter of James, Bishop of Galloway; and, secondly, Margaret Angus, who died at Edinburgh subsequent to the 13th September 1723.

William Alexander, doctor of medicine (probably the youngest son of Mr John Alexander, minister of Hoddam), obtained sasine of the lands of Gillespie and Craignarget, in the parish of Old Luce, on the 16th September 1709.

The estate of Kirkland, in the parish of Dalry and stewartry of Kirkcudbright, belonged, in the latter part of the seventeenth century, to Thomas Alexander. He acquired, by marriage, the lands of Macketstown, Glenhowl, and others in the same parish. He is now represented by James Alexander of Corrieden, in the parish of Balmaclellan and stewartry of Kirkcudbright. His younger brother, William, is owner of the lands of Macketstown and Glenhowl.

On the 28th May 1684, Hugh Alexander of Barrachan, in the parish of Mochrum, is mentioned as having for his wife, Janet, daughter of John M'Culloch of Myreton, in the same parish. They appear to have had an only child, Margaret, who seems to have married James M'Culloch, and to have had two sons, John and Robert.

Migrating from the Carrick district of Ayrshire, a branch of the family of M'Alexander effected a settlement in the district of Glenluce, Wigtownshire. Engaging in the nautical profession, members of the family traded with the opposite shore of Ireland, where some of them effected a settlement. · John M'Alexander, owner of a coasting vessel at Chapelrossan, near Glenluce, where he resided about the middle of the eighteenth century, adopted the modern name of Alexander, which is borne by his descendants. By his wife, Elizabeth Murray, he had three sons, John, William, and Hugh ; also four daughters.

William, the second son, born 21st February 1763,
was pastor of the Congregational churches at Prescot
and Leigh, Lancashire ; he died on the 23d January
1855, in his ninety-third year.   His memoirs have
been published by his son, the Rev. John Alexander,
minister of Princes Street Chapel, Norwich, and
author of several religious publications.

CHAPTER XXI.

IN the year 1413, Richard Alexander is one of the several arbiters appointed to decide upon a question between John Stewart of Darnley and Sir John Ross of Hawkhead, relating to the lands of Hullerished (Memorials of the Maxwells of Pollok, vol. i.). As Paisley at this period consisted of not more than twelve houses, it is not improbable that from this Richard was descended John Alexander, who, in 1488, when the village of Paisley was erected into a royal burgh, was created a burgess. He is described as owner of a house and land on the west side of the "Paisley Tak and Unhouss" (Charter by Abbot George Schaw to Andrew Payntor, 1490). In 1491 David Alexander was placed on the roll of burgesses (Burgh Records of Paisley). He succeeded John Alexander, and possessed the same property in 1498 (Charter by Robert, Abbot of Paisley, to Richard Brigton). In 1508 Gilbert Alexander became a burgess of Paisley (Burgh Records). In the MS.

Rental Book of the Monastery of Paisley (Advocates Library, p. 153), the following entry occurs in the rental of John Hamilton, commendator, made in October and November 1525 : " Annui redditus ville de Paslay, The Pryor croft, Jhone Alex^{r.} & Gilbert Alex^{r.,} xiij^{s.} iiij^{d.} " Gilbert Alexander married Agnes Inglis, by whom he had a son, William, who is mentioned as his heir in 1542 (Family MSS., vol. i.).

In the Rental Book, at pages 185 and 187, are these entries : " Anno M° etc. xxvij (1527) Brablo syd, Jhon Alex^{r.} elder, xiij acris . . . ane akyr j^{bl} bere ; " (circa same date), " Corsflat, xvij acris, Jhone Alex^{r.} ane akyr 1^{b.} bere."

John Alexander, son of John Alexander, possessed, prior to 1541, the house and land known as the " Paisley Tak." He is, in a charter of that year, granted by John, Abbot of Paisley, to John Dowhill, described as " the late John Alexander." In 1579 John Alexander of the Paisley Tak is named in a deed preserved in the family. In the same year, Robert Alexander, with his wife, Janet Mathie, purchased, at the cross of Paisley, " the Pasley Tak," situated on the east side of the house and land possessed by John Alexander (Charter in possession of the family of Ballochmyle). Robert Alexander is described as " chamberlain " to my Lord of Paisley * in 1597, when he was created a burgess

---

* Lord Claud Hamilton, third son of James, Earl of Arran and Duke of Chatelherault, created Lord Paisley in 1585. James, his eldest son, was first Earl of Abercorn.

of the burgh (Burgh Records). He had a son, John, who married, in 1598, Elizabeth Carswell, by whom he had two sons, Robert and James, and two daughters, Catherine and Janet. Both the daughters were married.

James, second son of John Alexander and Elizabeth Carswell, was one of the two bailies of Paisley, and a Commissioner of War. He had two sons, James and Claud. The latter became a solicitor in Paisley.

Robert, elder son of John Alexander and Elizabeth Carswell, was born in 1604. He was a solicitor in Paisley; in 1647 he was elected a magistrate. He purchased, in 1648, the estate of Blackhouse, near Ayr; in 1665 the estate of Boghall, Ayrshire; and in 1670 the lands of Newtoun, Renfrewshire. He married first, in 1633, Marion, daughter of Claud Hamilton of Blackhole, by his wife, Janet Orr, who died in 1648; and secondly, Janet, daughter and co-heiress of David Henderson, burgess of Paisley, by his wife, Isobel Algeo. In an infeftment, dated 3d June 1662, are named "Robert Alexander of Blackhouse, and Janet Henderson his spouse." In the chancel of Paisley Abbey a tombstone was placed by Robert Alexander, to denote his right of sepulture in that sacred edifice. It is inscribed with his initials and the initials of his two wives, with their respective shields.

By his first wife, Robert Alexander of Blackhouse

had several children. Of these, two sons, James
and Claud, and two daughters, Janet and Marion,
survived him. Janet, the elder daughter, married
James Dunlop of Dovecot, and had issue. Marion,
the younger daughter, married, in 1678, John Maxwell of Brediland, and had issue. Of Robert Alexander's second marriage were born two sons, Robert
and John. John settled in Carolina.* He died on
the 8th October 1699, and his testament-dative and
inventory were, in January 1707, "made and given
up by Robert Alexander, one of the Principal Clerks
of Session." Among those indebted to him appears
the name of William, Lord Ross, who had originally
granted a bond to his father, the late Robert Alexander of Blackhouse (Edin. Com. Reg., vol. lxxxiii.).

Robert, third son of Robert Alexander of Blackhouse (by his second wife, Janet Henderson), married
Janet, daughter of Alexander Smith of Reidstoun, by
his wife, Margaret, daughter of Major Hugh Buntein
of Kilbryde. By her he had two daughters, Janet,
who married her relative, Robert Alexander of Blackhouse; and Margaret, who married Robert Alexander
of Newtoun.

James Alexander, designed " of Boghall," eldest
son of Robert Alexander of Blackhouse, was born in
1634. He entered the University of Glasgow, where
he graduated in 1653. Obtaining licence as a pro-

---

* Robert Alexander, Member of Congress for Carolina during the war of independence, may have been grandson of John Alexander, the original settler.

bationer in 1655, he was the same year ordained minister of Kilmalcolm, Renfrewshire.   For his adherence to the Presbyterian polity, he was deprived by Act of Parliament, 11th June, and of the Privy Council, 1st October 1662.   Accused of preaching and baptizing irregularly, he was summoned to Ayr in March 1669 ; he died of fever in the same year about the age of thirty-four (Fasti Eccl. Scot., vol. ii., p. 250).   He married Mary, daughter of John Maxwell of Southbar, descended from Adam Maxwell, fifth son of the first Lord Maxwell of Caerlaverock, by Elizabeth, daughter of William Cuninghame of Craigends ; she died in 1670.   By her he had a son, John, and four daughters, Elizabeth, Mary, Jean, and Anna.   His daughter Jean was, in September 1689, married to William Greenlees, one of the magistrates of Paisley (Reg. Abbey Parish of Paisley).

John Alexander, only son of Mr James Alexander, succeeded his father in the estate of Boghall in 1669, and his grandfather, Robert Alexander, in the lands of Blackhouse in 1687.   He married Janet, daughter of Alexander Cuninghame of Craigends, by his wife, Janet, daughter of William Cuninghame of Achinyards, and had two sons, Robert and William, and a daughter, Anna.   Anna Alexander married Peter Murdoch, who, in 1731, was Lord Provost of Glasgow.

Robert Alexander, eldest son of John Alexander of Blackhouse and Boghall, married Janet, daughter of his grand-uncle, Robert Alexander, by whom he had a daughter, Jean, who married John Lockhart of Lee.

William Alexander, second son of John Alexander of Blackhouse and Boghall, succeeded to the paternal estates on the death of Robert, his elder brother. He became a banker in Edinburgh, and was elected Lord Provost of that city in 1752, and its parliamentary representative in 1754. A continuation of his line will be found under the section, " Family of Alexander of Airdrie and Cowdenhill."

Claud, second son of Robert Alexander of Blackhouse, by his first wife, Marion Hamilton, was born in 1645. By a disposition, dated 24th September 1669, he received from his father several subjects in the town of Paisley.* In 1671 his father granted him the lands of Newtoun (Reg. Mag. Sig., lib. lxii., 288). A zealous supporter of Presbyterianism, he became obnoxious to the Government, and was imprisoned at Edinburgh. According to Wodrow (vol. iv., 215), he was, on the 3d August 1686, liberated " under a bond of a thousand pounds sterling, to live regularly, and answer when called to anything that is to be laid to his charge."

In 1677 Claud Alexander of Newtoun married Jean, third daughter of William Ralston of that ilk, and his wife, Ursula Mure of Glanderstoun, by whom he had two sons and two daughters. In the Poll Tax

---

* This disposition, in the handwriting of the granter, is now in the possession of Mr David Semple, writer, Paisley.

Rolls of Renfrewshire for 1695, he is entered thus : "Claud Alexander of Newtoune for himself, 4 lib. 6sh.; Jean Ralstoune, his spouse, 6sh. ; Robert, Claud, Ursula, and Marion, Alexander's children, each 6sh., with three servants."

Marion, elder daughter of Claud Alexander of Newtoun, was born in March 1683. She married, in 1709, Alexander, eldest son of Gavin Cochrane of Craigmuir, brother of William, first Earl of Dundonald. Ursula, the younger daughter, born February 1688, married, in 1706, John Russell of Braidshaw, ancestor of Sir William Russell, Bart. of Charlton, Gloucestershire. Claud, the younger son, born 26th February 1690, perished at sea.

Robert Alexander, elder son of Claud Alexander of Newtoun, born in April 1681, succeeded his father in the estate of Newtoun in 1703. He married his cousin Margaret, daughter of his uncle, Robert Alexander, by whom he had a son and daughter. The daughter, Jean, married Robert Neilson of Paisley, by whom she had issue.

Claud Alexander, only son of Robert Alexander of Newtoun, was born in 1724, and succeeded to Newtoun in 1738. He married, in 1746, Joanna, daughter of Alexander Cuninghame of Craigends (descended from the noble House of Glencairn), by his wife, Anne, daughter of Sir John Houstoun, Bart. of that ilk, and grand-daughter of John Drummond, Earl of Melfort. Claud Alexander of Newtoun died in 1772, leaving five sons and six daughters. The daughters were—Catherine ; Margaret, born 1753 ; Anna, born 1754 ; Wilhelmina, Lockhart, and Lilias (Baptismal Register of Abbey Parish, Paisley). Wilhelmina Alexander is celebrated by Burns in his song, " The Bonnie Lass o' Ballochmyle." The poet had, by the banks of the Ayr, chanced to encounter Miss Wilhelmina. There was no conversation or sign of recognition, but the poet afterwards despatched to her a copy of his song. She did not acknowledge it, but her nephew, the proprietor of Ballochmyle, has placed a bower on the spot where the poet saw her. Miss Wilhelmina Alexander died unmarried in 1843, at the age of eighty-eight.

Lockhart, fifth daughter of Claud Alexander of Newtoun, married her cousin, Claud Neilson, and had issue.

Boyd, third son of Claud Alexander, born January 1758, entered the service of the East India Company. He purchased the estates of Southbar and Boghall, Renfrewshire. In 1796 he was chosen M.P. for Renfrew, and was returned as representative for Glasgow in 1806. He married his cousin, Camilla,* daughter of Boyd Porterfield of that ilk, by his wife Christian, daughter of Alexander Cuninghame of Craigends. He died without issue in 1825. Alexander, fourth son of Claud Alexander, born August 1766, died

* Camilla Alexander was great-great-granddaughter of William Boyd, first Earl of Kilmarnock, whose great-grandson, the fourth earl, was beheaded on Tower Hill for joining in the rebellion of 1745.

unmarried.   John, the youngest son, entered the
army, and became major in the 56th Regiment.   He
married his cousin Jean, daughter of Robert Neilson,
and died without issue.

Robert, eldest son of Claud Alexander, was born
in 1747.   He, in 1772, succeeded to Newtoun, which
he afterwards sold; he died without issue.   Claud,
second son, born 1753, entered the Civil Service of
the East India Company, and became paymaster-
general of the Company's troops in Bengal.   From
the old family of Whitefoord he purchased the estate
of Ballochmyle, Ayrshire, in 1783, and there established his seat.   He married, in 1788, Helenora,
daughter of Sir William Maxwell, Bart. of Spring-
kell, by his wife, Margaret, daughter of Sir Michael
Shaw Stewart, Bart. of Blackhall and Ardgowan.
He was father of three sons and five daughters.
Margaret Stewart, the eldest daughter, died in 1861;
Catherine Maxwell, second daughter, died in 1834;
Anna Joanna, third daughter, died in 1859; Helenora,
fourth daughter, died young.   Mary, the youngest
daughter, married, in 1834, Joshua Stansfield Cromp-
ton of Azerley, Yorkshire; she died in 1867, leaving
issue.

Claud, eldest son of Claud Alexander of Ballochmyle, became an officer in the 1st regiment of Guards.
He succeeded to Ballochmyle in 1809, and married
Elizabeth, daughter of Colonel Keatinge, by his
wife, Lady Martha Brabazon, daughter of Anthony,

eighth Earl of Meath.   He died without issue in
1845, and was succeeded by his brother, William
Maxwell Alexander of Southbar.   This gentleman
died unmarried in 1853, and was succeeded in his
estates by his brother, Boyd Alexander.

Boyd Alexander of Ballochmyle and Southbar,
born in 1796, married, in 1828, Sophia Elizabeth,
daughter of Sir Benjamin Hobhouse, Bart. of
Westbury, Wiltshire, and sister of John, Lord
Broughton, G.C.B., by whom he had five sons and
one daughter, Helenora Margaret Angela.   She married, in 1857, John Archibald Shaw Stewart, second
son of Sir Michael Shaw Stewart, Bart. of Ardgowan,
and died in 1865, leaving issue.

John Hobhouse Inglis, second son of Boyd Alexander of Ballochmyle, was born in 1832, and succeeded his father in the estate of Southbar.   In 1844
he joined the Royal Navy, in which he obtained the
rank of captain.   He served in the East and West
Indies and the Crimea; also in the Japanese war, in
which he was severely wounded.   Captain Alexander
was a Companion of the Bath; an aide-de-camp to
the Queen, and an officer of the Legion of Honour.
He married Isabella Barbara, daughter of T. C.
Hume, Esq., and had issue, two sons, Boyd William
John, born 1862, and Edwin St Clair, born 1865; also
three daughters, Sophia Isabella, Evelyn Mary, and
Cora Sybil.   Captain Alexander died in November
1875.

Boyd Francis Alexander, third son of Boyd Alexander of Ballochmyle, was born in 1834. He served with the Rifle Brigade in Turkey, India, and Canada. He was twice wounded in the Indian Mutiny, and was mentioned in despatches, and promoted to the rank of major in the army for his services. He is now lieutenant-colonel. He married, in 1865, Mary, daughter of David Wilson of Castleton, Surrey, by whom he has had four sons, Boyd and Robert, born 1873 ; Herbert, born 1874 ; and David, born 1876 ; and two daughters, Marion and Helenor. In 1871 he purchased the estate of Swifts, Kent.

William Maxwell, fourth son of Boyd Alexander of Ballochmyle, was born in 1836. He was some time in the Civil Service of the East India Company, and served as a volunteer at Agra in the Indian Mutiny. He married Emma, daughter of the Rev. William Thorp.

Michael Stewart, youngest son of Boyd Alexander of Ballochmyle, was born 1839, and died in 1855.

Claud Alexander, now of Ballochmyle, was born 15th January 1831. He succeeded his father in the estate of Ballochmyle in 1861. He is a. deputy-lieutenant of Ayrshire, a colonel in the Grenadier Guards, and has obtained the Order of the Medjidee. With his regiment he served in the Crimean war. At the general election in 1874 he was elected M.P. for South Ayrshire. In 1863 he married Eliza, daughter of Alexander Speirs of Elderslie, M.P.,

Lord-Lieutenant of Renfrewshire, by whom he has a son, Claud, born 24th February 1867.

The families of this branch use the following armorial bearings : Alexander of Boghall and Blackhouse bears, "parted per pale argent and sable, a chevron betwixt a writing-pen fessways in chief, and a crescent in base, all counterchanged ; above the shield, an helmet befitting his degree, mantled gules, doubled argent ; next is placed on a torse for crest, a hand holding a quill proper ; the motto in scroll, ' Fidem Serva.' Matriculated 26th July 1673 " (Lyon Register).

Boyd Alexander of Southbar, M.P. for Renfrew, matriculated in 1784, bears, "parted per pale argent and sable, a chevron ; in base a crescent, and in chief a writing-pen counterchanged ; all within a bordure, parted per pale gules and or. *Crest*—A dexter hand holding a writing-pen, both proper. *Motto*—' Fidem Serva ' " (Lyon Register).

The arms of Claud Alexander of Ballochmyle, matriculated in 1788, are : " Parted per pale argent and sable, a chevron ; in base a crescent, and in chief a fleur-de-lys, all counterchanged ; within a bordure parted per pale gules and or. *Crest*—An elephant proper. *Motto* — ' Perseverantia vincit ' " (Lyon Register).

CHAPTER XXII.

FAMILY OF ALEXANDER OF AIRDRIE, LANARKSHIRE, AND COWDENHILL, DUMBARTONSHIRE.

WILLIAM ALEXANDER, second son of John Alexander of Blackhouse and Boghall, was, on the 13th June 1733, admitted a burgess and guild brother of Edinburgh. He was elected Lord Provost of that city on the 3d October 1752, and was re-elected to the office on the 2d October 1753 (Burgess and Town Council Records of Edinburgh). In 1754 he was chosen one of the Parliamentary representatives of the city (Anderson's History of Edinburgh, pp. 609, 610). According to the Rev. Dr Somerville, Lord Provost Alexander conducted business as a banker in Edinburgh. He often received a solitary letter by the London mail, a fact which Dr Somerville quotes in illustration of the limited business then conducted in the Scottish capital (Somerville's Life and Times, 1741-1814). Lord Provost Alexander died in July 1763. He married Marione Louisa de la Croix, a member of a Huguenot family which fled from Rochelle on the revocation of the Edict of Nantes, by whom he had three sons, Robert, William, and Alex-

* c

ander John, and a daughter, Jean. Having died intestate, his testament-dative and inventory were made and given up by Robert and William Alexander, merchants in Edinburgh, his sons and executors. His substance was declared to consist of stock in the Royal Bank of Scotland, amounting to £6792 (Edin. Com. Reg., vol. cxx.). Inscribed in a mortuary enclosure attached to Roslin Chapel, presented to him by a member of the House of St Clair, are these words : " In this ground are interred William Alexander, Provost and M.P. for Edinburgh, who died 1763 ; also his daughter Jean, and sons Robert and Alexander John Alexander.   Repaired 1840." *

Robert and Alexander John, sons of Lord Provost Alexander, died without issue.   William, the second son, was born in 1729.   After a period of residence in France, he proceeded in 1783 to the United States. Till 1811 he resided at Staunton in Virginia, when he removed to Kentucky, where he died in 1819, at the age of ninety.   He married, first, Christian, only daughter of John Aitchison of Rochsolach and Airdrie, in the county of Lanark ; and secondly, Agatha de la Porte, belonging to an ancient family at Montpellier.   Of his first marriage were born two sons and six daughters.   Bethia, the eldest daughter, born 27th March 1757, died in 1839, unmarried ; Marianne, second daughter, born 12th December

* Mrs Marione Louisa de la Croix, relict of William Alexander, died on the 1st January 1773.

1758, married General Jonathan Williams of Philadelphia, nephew of Dr Franklin; she had a son,
H. J. Williams, of Chesnut Villa, Philadelphia,
and a daughter, Mrs Thomas Biddle, deceased;
Christine, third daughter, born 24th August 1762,
died unmarried in 1845; Jane, fourth daughter, born
5th June 1765, died 1843; Isabella, fifth daughter,
born 17th October 1768, married John Peter Hankey,
merchant, London, by whom she had three sons,
John Alexander, *General* Henry, and *Captain* William, and a daughter, Julia, who married the Hon.
Seymour Bathurst; Joanna, sixth daughter, born
10th June 1771, died in 1783.

By his second marriage, William Alexander was
father of four sons, John Regis, Andrew, Charles, and
James, and a daughter, Apolline Agatha, who married Thomson Hankey, Esq., M.P. for Peterborough,
and one of the directors of the Bank of England.

John Regis, eldest son of William Alexander by
his second marriage, married, first, Marianne Campbell, secondly, Eliza Dudley; he died in 1874, leaving
issue. Andrew Alexander married Mira Madison,
daughter of the governor of Kentucky; he died in
1834, leaving issue. Charles, the second son of the
second marriage, married Martha Madison, and has
two sons.

William, born 18th May 1755, eldest son of William Alexander of Airdrie, was called to the bar by
the Society of the Middle Temple on the 22d Nov-

ember 1782. He was nominated King's Counsel in 1800, and a Master of Chancery in November 1809. In 1824 he was appointed Lord Chief Baron of the Exchequer, an office which he held till January 1831, when he was succeeded by Lord Chancellor Lyndhurst. He was sworn of the Privy Council on his elevation to the bench, 19th January 1824, and the same day received the honour of knighthood. As an equity and real property lawyer, he enjoyed professional celebrity. He succeeded in 1837 to the estate of Cloverhill or Cowden, in the parish of New Kilpatrick, Dumbartonshire, on the death of Andrew Hunter Spreul Crawfurd, his second cousin. He died on the 29th June 1842, at the advanced age of eighty-seven. His remains were deposited at Roslin Chapel.

Robert Alexander, second son of William Alexander and Christian Aitchison, was born 7th January 1767, and emigrated to the United States in 1786. He first settled in Virginia, and removed to Kentucky in 1791. There he purchased the extensive estate of Woodburn, in the county of Woodford. He died in February 1841. By his wife Eliza, daughter of Daniel Weisiger of Frankfort, Kentucky, whom he married in 1814, he had three sons and two daughters. Lucy, the elder daughter, born 18th September 1822, married James B. Waller of Chicago, by whom she has had two sons and seven daughters. Mary Bell, the second daughter, born 29th July 1830, married, in 1859, Henry Charles Deedes, Esq., formerly of the Indian Office. William Alexander, the eldest son, born in 1816, died in 1817.

Robert, the second son, born 25th October 1819, was educated at Oxford, where he graduated as Bachelor of Arts. He succeeded to the estates of Airdrie and Cowdenhill on the death of his uncle, Sir William Alexander, in 1842, when he added to his patronymic the names of Spreul Crawfurd Aitchison. He died unmarried 1st December 1867.

Alexander John Alexander, third son of Robert Alexander of Woodburn, Kentucky, born 7th October 1824, succeeded to the estates of Woodburn, Airdrie, and Cowdenhill, in 1867. He married, first, 6th May 1851, Lucy, daughter of David Humphreys of Woodford, Kentucky, by whom (she died 25th September 1858) he had David, born 19th February 1852, died February 1860; Mary, born 6th October 1853, died January 1860; and Robert, born July 1855, died 9th December 1859. Alexander John Alexander of Woodburn married, secondly, 5th October 1871, Lucy, daughter of Humphrey Fullerton of Chillicothie, Ohio, by whom he has had Robert Aitchison, born 27th August 1872, died 15th October 1872; Elizabeth, born 19th September 1873; and Alexander John Aitchison, born 5th August 1875.

CHAPTER XXIII.

FAMILIES OF ALEXANDER OF CANDREN, PAISLEY, REN-
FREWSHIRE, AND OF THE COUNTIES OF WEXFORD,
GALWAY, AND ROSCOMMON.

AMONG the descendants of Richard Alexander of
Paisley (see *supra*, p. 21) was John Alexander, who is
mentioned in 1553; also his son, Alexander (Ballochmyle Family Papers). Robert Alexander is described
in 1595 as farmer at Candren, near Paisley. His son
Robert was a tanner at Causeyside, on the banks of
the river Cart. According to the Registers of Paisley
Abbey Parish, families of the name of Alexander
continued to reside at Candren and at Causeyside,
Paisley, till the beginning of the present century.

In 1599, John Alexander, elder, was member of a
jury at the service of an heir; and in 1600, John
Alexander, younger, was one of a jury at another
service. Robert Alexander, elder, in Candren, is
mentioned in 1610.

John Alexander the younger was father of four
sons, Robert, William, John, and James, and a
daughter, Janet. Robert, the eldest son, engaged in
merchandise at Paisley, and was elected a bailie of

the burgh.   In the record of the baptism of Robert, lawful son of Claud Alexander, younger, in Paisley, 21st May 1680, he is named as co-witness with Robert Alexander, in Blackhouse, and is styled "Robert Alexander, merchand, late baylie of Paysley" (Register Abbey Parish, Paisley).   He married Janet Snodgrass, and had issue (Poll Tax Roll, Paisley, 1695).

William Alexander, second son, was a merchant-burgess of Paisley, and also held office in the magistracy.   He married, July 1670, Margaret Hamilton of Paisley (Register Abbey Parish, Paisley).

John Alexander, third son, settled in Dublin as a lime agent.   He died in 1671, leaving a widow and a daughter Avia, who married William Hartley, with issue (Grant Book, Probate Court, Dublin).

James Alexander, fourth son, practised in Dublin as a solicitor (see "Family of Alexander of Dublin").

Janet Alexander, daughter of John Alexander the younger, married John Spreul, merchant-burgess and magistrate of Paisley.   Bailie Spreul purchased lands from the community of Paisley in 1672, one of the cautioners for the price being his brother-in-law, Robert Alexander, merchant (Burgh Records of Paisley).

Bailie Spreul had, by his wife Janet Alexander, two sons—James, who became an apothecary in Paisley, and John, of whom hereafter.   James Spreul, apothecary in Paisley, married, 21st January 1674, Anna, daughter of John Spreul, town-clerk of Glasgow. Their daughter married John Shortridge, merchant, Glasgow, and had a son John, who became a magistrate of that city. He married Hannah Park of Paisley, and succeeding to the entailed property of his maternal ancestors in the Trongate of Glasgow, assumed the surname of Spreul.

The family of Spreul merits particular notice owing to its connection at several points with the House of Alexander.

Walter Spreul of Cowden, " seneschal of the Lennox," had, in the reign of Alexander III., a grant from the Earl of Lennox of the lands of Dalquharn in Dumbartonshire. In that county the family remained till 1622, when William, Lord Cochrane of Cowden, father of the first Earl of Dundonald, purchased from John Spreul the lands of Cowden. John Spreul, a younger son of the proprietor of Cowden, was in 1507 vicar of Dundonald, and Professor of Philosophy in the College of Glasgow. He was subsequently appointed rector of the university and a canon of the cathedral (Rental Book of Diocese of Glasgow, printed for the Grampian Club). He purchased the lands of Ladymuir, Castlehill, and Blackairn, in the diocese of Glasgow. In 1555 his lands came into the possession of his nephew, John Spreul, burgess of Glasgow. The grandson of this person, John Spreul, was Provost of Renfrew early in the reign of Charles I. His son, who bore the same Christian name, was town-clerk of Glasgow, and afterwards a Principal Clerk of Session (Nisbet's Heraldry, vol. i., p. 427; and vol. ii., appendix, p. 24).

John Spreul, eldest son of John Spreul, town-clerk of Glasgow, was trained to legal pursuits. He married Isobel, only child of Hugh Craufurd of Cloberhill, Dumbartonshire, and, succeeding to the lands, assumed the surname of Craufurd. In 1716 John Spreul executed a deed of entail, by which he destined the lands of Cloberhill and Drumchapel (which he called Cowden, the name of the old family estate) to his heirs-male, whom failing, his heirs whomsoever. Of his marriage were born eight daughters, and on his death, without male issue, the estate devolved on the issue of his youngest daughter, Agnes, wife of —— Hunter, whose grandson, Andrew Hunter Spreul Crauford, succeeded to the estate. On the death of this gentleman in 1837, Sir William Alexander, Chief Baron of Exchequer, grandson of the eldest daughter of the entailer, succeeded to the estates.

John Spreul, merchant in Paisley, who married Janet Alexander, was descended from the old family of Cowden. In the Burgh Records of Paisley is the following entry: " 19th Decr 1600.—qlk day Gabriel Spruell was decernit to deliver to Robt Stewart ane stane cheis, price y^t xiijs. iiijd., or then ane buik callit the Howis of Alex$^{r.}$" Gabriel Spreul died in

April 1603, and the book called "The Howis of Alexander" is known only by the preceding entry. When a youth, attending the grammar school of Paisley, the persecuted William Muir of Caldwell lodged in the house of John Spreul, and it is probable that he then embraced those Covenanting principles, on account of which he suffered persecution (Wodrow's History, vol. ii., pp. 28, 29, 73, 75; vol. iii., pp. 439-441). A zealous upholder of Presbyterianism, he was selected for punishment by General Dalziel in 1667, but contrived to effect his escape (Wodrow's History, vol. iv., p. 252). His son John, who afterwards became an apothecary in Glasgow, was taken prisoner at Paisley by Dalziel's soldiers in 1667, in consequence of his refusing to divulge his father's hiding-place. In 1677 he was cited to appear before a court at Glasgow on the charge of nonconformity. Learning that a severe sentence was contemplated, he fled from the country. Leaving his business to the conduct of his wife, he first proceeded to Holland, and afterwards resided at Dublin with his uncle, James Alexander. After the battle of Drumclog, he returned to Scotland in June 1679; but on the defeat of the Covenanters at Bothwell Bridge on the 22d of that month, he again sought refuge abroad. Returning to Scotland in 1680 with the view of carrying his wife and family to Rotterdam, he was, on the 12th November of that year, apprehended at Edinburgh, and examined before the Privy Council. As his answers failed to implicate himself or others, the Council decreed that he should be examined by torture. Though twice subjected to the frightful torture of the boot, he maintained his equanimity and upheld his honour. He was committed to the prison of the Bass in 1681, and there remained till May 1687, when he was liberated (Wodrow's History, vol. iii., pp. 252-262; vol. iv., pp. 412, 413).

John Alexander, of the family of Candren, was born at Paisley in October 1690 (Family Information). He proceeded to Ireland, and settled as a tanner and coal merchant at New Ross, county Wexford. He married Catherine,* daughter of Colonel Knight Clifford, co-heiress of the estate of Cahirglissane, county Galway. He died in 1769. In his will he expresses a desire to be buried "privately, without scarves." To his son James, as holding a commission in the army, he bequeathed "five shillings, not from any dislike." To his son Arthur he provided his freehold lease in Ross, with the stock of his tanyard, salt-work, and coal-yard in Ross; also his holdings in Carlow and Leighlen Bridge, and the interest of his dwelling-house and fields, called Tabbercreach. To his second son, Robert, he bequeathed £100, with the expression of a hope that having got a college education, he would consider this sum as sufficient.

* "*December* 16, 1727.—Licence granted by the archbishop for the solemnisation of marriage between John Alexander, of the parish of Hook, in the county of Wexford, gent., and Catherine Clifford, of the parish of Warburge, Dublin" (Book of Acts, Prerogative Court, Dublin).

To his "deare sister Madden" he bequeathed £5 to buy mourning (Will in Probate Court).

James Alexander, eldest son of John Alexander of New Ross, served as a lieutenant in the 83d Regiment.   He married Mary, daughter of J. Lovelace, by whom he had three sons, John, James, and Wentworth, and four daughters, Jane, Hannah, Margaret, and Grizel.   He died in 1791, and his will, dated 22d April 1789, was proved to his son John on the renunciation of his executors.   Described as "James Alexander of Harristoun, in King's County," he bequeathed to his eldest son, John, that part of the lands of Cahirglissane, in the barony of Kiltarton, county Galway, which came to him by his mother, subject to the payment of £10 yearly to his "beloved wife, Mary Alexander."   To his daughters, Jane, Hannah, Margaret, and Grizel, he bequeathed £100 each, and to his son James £50. Failing the issue of his son John, he bequeathed the lands of Cahirglissane to his son James and his issue, whom failing, to his son Wentworth, and failing the issue of all his sons, to his daughters in equal shares. To his son Wentworth, he bequeathed his farm of Carrick, near Portarlington, in Queen's County.   He made a suitable provision for his wife, and constituted as his executors "his brothers, Arthur Alexander and the Rev. Dr Robert Alexander, both of New Ross."

James, second son of James Alexander of Harristoun, married, first, —— Cosswaith, and, secondly, —— Winskill, by whom he had two daughters. Wentworth, the third son, died without issue. John, the eldest son, married a daughter of Giles Mahon, Esq., by whom he had three sons, John, James, and Arthur. John died in infancy. James died in 1847, leaving two daughters. Arthur Alexander, now of Maryville, county Galway, was born in 1810. He married, first, a daughter of B. Falkner, Esq., and secondly, a daughter of A. Johnson, Esq., without issue.

Arthur Alexander, youngest son of John Alexander of New Ross, succeeded to his father's estate; he died unmarried on the 7th January 1819.

Robert, second son of John Alexander of New Ross, is described in the will of his brother James, as the Rev. Dr Robert Alexander. He married a daughter of Mr Goddard Richards, by whom he had two sons and five daughters. George, the second son, born 17th March 1802, is unmarried. John, the elder son, born 4th March 1798, is LL.D. and rector of Carne, county Wexford. He has five sons and three daughters. Robert, the eldest son, born 28th December 1831, died 11th August 1835. The other sons are—John, born 2d September 1833; Stuart, born 5th April 1835; George, born 27th May 1839; Arthur, born 13th December 1843. John, the second son, is rector of Corclone. He married a daughter of John Jacob, M.D., and has sons and daughters.

George Alexander of Knockcroghery, county Roscommon, executed his will on the 9th November 1792. He bequeathed to his son John the lands of Seagh or Lismahoon; whom failing, to his son George and his heirs-male; or failing them, to his brother Edward and his heirs-male; and failing them, to his brother John and his heirs-male; whom failing, to his grandson, George Robinson. To his daughters, Dame Elizabeth Robinson and Mary Campion, he bequeathed his right to the lands of Knockcroghery. He bequeathed to his daughter, Jane Sandys, £300, and to his daughter, Susanna Dempsey, £300, also various sums to his grand-children. He appointed as executors his cousin George Hill of Spring Hall, county Galway, and his nephew, Samuel Alexander of Roscommon.

On the death of George Alexander of Knockcroghery, the validity of his will was disputed in the Court of Exchequer by his son John, but it was affirmed and proved to the executors on the 17th February 1794.

John Alexander of Knockcroghery, merchant, died in 1803. On the 4th July of that year his will, dated 18th June 1802, was proved to his widow. To his eldest daughter, Ann Jones, otherwise Alexander, he bequeathed £10, and to his son-in-law, Robert Galbraith, five shillings. The residue of his estate he divided between his wife, Elizabeth Alexander, otherwise Tennant, and his youngest daughter, Margaret Galbraith, otherwise Alexander.

Richard Alexander of Roscommon died in 1799 ; his will was proved on the 31st August of that year. To his daughter, Susanna Lynch, otherwise Alexander, he bequeathed the lands of Mechane, in the barony of Athlone, and to his son Samuel fifty pounds.

CHAPTER XXIV.

ACCORDING to the Register of Paisley, Reginald, or
Ranald, second son of Somerled by his second marriage, became a monk of Paisley, and granted to that
monastery "eight cows and two pennies for one year,
and one penny in perpetuity from every house on his
territories from which smoke issued;" he also enjoined
his dependants to afford protection to the members
of the monastery. Fonie, his wife, became a sister
of the convent, and granted to the monks a tithe of
her goods, whether in her own possession or on the
ocean. Donald, son of Reginald, also became a
monk, and his wife a sister of the convent, while both
made liberal grants to the members. Angus, son of

Donald, also described as a monk, granted to the convent, sometime before the year 1295, one penny yearly for every house in his territories, and half a merk of silver for his own residence (Reg. de Passelet, pp. 125-127).

In 1455 John of Yle, Earl of Ross and Lord of the Isles, confirmed to the monks of Paisley the rectory of the church of "Saint Kylkeran, in Kyntire," with liberty to dispose of it at their pleasure (Reg. de Passelet, p. 156).

From the Mull of Kintyre members of the House of Alexander obtained settlements in the counties of Ayr and Renfrew, under protection of the monks of Paisley, many of the first settlers being kindly-tenants of the monastery.

In the Obit Book of the church of St John the Baptist, Ayr, is mentioned, in the obit of Thomas Sorbie, who died 20th March 1438, the tenement of John Alexander, thus : " ten^m Johañis alexãdri " (Obit Book of Ayr, pp. 8, 46).

A charter was, on the 9th July 1450, granted by James II., under the Great Seal, confirming a charter by Colin M'Alexander of Dalcussen to Gilbert M'Alexander, his son and apparent heir, and to the heirs-male of his body; whom failing, to Alexander M'Alexander, brother of the said Gilbert, and the heirs of his body; whom failing, to the granter's heirs whomsoever, of the lands of Dalcussen, in the earldom of Carrick and shire of Ayr, for rendering yearly to

the Earl of Carrick, superior of the lands, a common
suit in the earl's court, with the customary service.
Among the witnesses to the original charter, which is
dated "at Peynmachey, 11th March 1449," are Alexander M'Alexander, laird of Creicnew, Fergus M'Alexander, and Duncan M'Alexander (Reg. Mag. Sig.,
lib. iv., 46).

In the Protocol Book of John Crawford, notary-
public of Ayrshire, 1542-1550 (No. 8 in General
Register House), a contract, dated 8th March 1549,
is recorded between Gabriel Sympill of Newlands, and
Robert Alexander, respecting the sale of certain subjects.   There is a further entry, dated 30th March
1550, between Ninian Mershall and Robert Alexander, with consent of his wife, Elizabeth Lang, in
connection with lands occupied by Robert Alexander
and his "forbears."

At the burgh of Ayr, on the 13th March 1589, an
action was prosecuted by Fergus M'Alexander of
Dalreoch, parish of Colmonel, Ayrshire, against
Robert Campbell, "burges of Air, and Mareoun Cun-
ighame, his spouse," anent a contract made on the
25th June 1588, between Campbell on the one part,
and M'Alexander on the other, whereby the former
sold to the latter a tenement in Ayr, at the price
of 400 merks.   M'Alexander complained that Campbell would not adhere to the articles in the contract,
nor register the contract.   Campbell made no appearance, and the Lords decerned the contract to be

registered (Reg. of Deeds, vol. xxxiv., fol. 317). On the 22d May 1634, Andrew M'Alexander of Dalreoch granted at Colmonel, to John Ramsay in Dalreoch, and Jonet Dultie, his spouse, an obligation for 260 merks (Register of Deeds, vol. 484).

At Maybole, on the 31st August 1669, Fergus M'Alexander, minister at the church of Barr, obtained service as nearest agnate or relative on the father's side, to Hew, Andrew, Margaret, Agnes, Jonet, and Elizabeth M'Alexander, children of the late John M'Alexander of Dalreoch. In this service it is certified that the heir exceeds the age of twenty-five years, and that he is immediate successor to the said Hew, Andrew, Margaret, Agnes, Jonet, and Elizabeth M'Alexander, should they chance to die; the children to be educated with Agnes Kennedy, their mother, till they be of lawful age (Reg. of Deeds, book xxix., 229). Fergus M'Alexander or Alexander was a bursar in the University of Glasgow in 1631, and there graduated in 1635. He thereafter ministered at Kilmud and Greyabbey in Ireland (Reid's Irish Presbyterian Church, vol. ii., p. 153), and being recommended by a committee of the General Assembly, 5th May 1647, was ordained minister of Barr, Ayrshire, in 1653. He was deprived of this charge by the Acts of Parliament, 11th June, and of the Privy Council, 1st October 1662. He was reponed in the living of Barr in 1687; he died on the 15th November following, and his remains were deposited in the parish church (Fasti Eccl. Scot., vol. ii., p. 98).

At the Tolbooth of the Canongate on the 4th February 1671, Hugh M'Alexander was served heir to John M'Alexander of Dalreoch (Reg. of Deeds, xxx. 144).

A branch of the House of M'Alexander possessed, in the sixteenth century, the lands of Corsclays, near Maybole. On the 20th March 1591, a charter under the Great Seal was granted to Thomas M'Alexander of Corsclays, of the forty-shilling land of Tumnochtie, of old extent, in the earldom of Carrick and shire of Ayr, formerly belonging to John Kennedie of Blair-quhane, sold under reversion by John M'Alexander, to which reversion the said Thomas was cessioner and assignee, and had thereupon obtained a decreet of redemption. Also of the merk land of Laggangill, and the merk land of Drummerling, of old extent, in the parish of Girvan, resigned by the said John Kennedie in favour of the said Thomas, and the two-merk lands of Corsclays, and the three-merk lands of Drummor, in the parish of Camneill, which formerly belonged to the said Thomas, erecting the said lands into a free tenandry, to be held of the king, paying therefor the rights and services due and wont (Reg. Mag. Sig., lib. xxxviii., No. 318).

On the 8th March 1632, Claud M'Alexander was, at Maybole, served heir to his father, George M'Alexander of Corsclays, and his mother, the late Catherine

M'Culloch.   George M'Alexander died in September 1622 (Reg. of Deeds, xiii. 42).

On the 28th December 1635, Robert M'Alexander of Corsclays granted a discharge for 500 merks to John Ferguson of Kilkenner, and Gilbert Ross, late Provost of Maybole.   One of the witnesses is John Alexander, the granter's son (Reg. of Deeds, vol. 455).   On the 21st October 1658, a service was "expede at the Tolbuith of the burgh of Ayr," to Robert M'Alexander, now of Corsclays, as heir to Robert M'Alexander of Corsclays, deceased (Reg. of Deeds, xxv. 127).   On the 26th August 1684, Robert Alexander of Corsclays complained that he was fined, by Crawford of Ardmillan, on the 7th of the preceding February, £2808, for withdrawing from ordinances, by a decreet passed in his absence, when he was sick (Wodrow's History, vol. iv., p. 52).

On the 2d August 1698, Mr Henry Scrymsour of Bowhill was served heir to umquhil Isabella Scrymsour, relict of Robert Alexander of Corsclays, his sister-german (Register of Deeds, xlvii. 348).

Gilbert Alexander in Derinconner, parish of Auchinleck, and sheriffdom of Ayr, died on the 19th November 1589.   His testament-dative and inventory were . given up by his son, John Alexander, by decreet of the Commissaries of Edinburgh.   It was dated 24th January 1592, and the movable estate was valued at 401 lib. 6s. 8d. (Edinburgh Commissariat Register, vol. xxiv.).

John Alexander of Darncholme, and his wife, Agnes Wylie, both died in the year 1596. Their joint will is dated at Darneholme on the 14th May 1596. They nominated as executors their son and daughter, Adam and Marion Alexander. Another son, John, received a legacy of 20 merks, and a daughter, Agnes, 20 merks. The "frie geir" of the deceased amounted to 190 lib. (Edin. Com. Reg.).

Robert Alexander in Mirriehill, parish of Stewarton, and county of Ayr, died in November 1631. His testament-dative was, on the 6th March 1632, given up by his relict, Janet Montgomerie, on behalf of Isobel and Margaret Alexander, their "lawful bairns." The "frie geir" amounted to 403 lib. 6s. Robert Alexander in Mirriehill is cautioner to the executors, and among the debtors are named Robert and Thomas Alexander (Glasgow Com. Reg.).

Marion Alexander, spouse to Archibald Templetoun, in Corse of Kilbryde, Ayrshire, died on the 15th August 1619. She bequeathed her "frie geir," which amounted to 53 lib. 11s. 8d., to her six children (Glasgow Com. Reg.). On the 15th June of the same year, Janet Alexander in Skirricraw, in the parish of Kilbryde, executed her will, leaving her "frie geir" to her grandchildren, Janet, Elspeth, and Margaret Syres (Commissariat Reg. of Glasgow).

John M'Alexander of Drummochrian, in the parish of Barr, is named in an obligation dated Ayr, 21st July 1636 (Reg. of Deeds, vol. 495). On the 28th

November 1636, Andrew M'Alexander, brother-ger-
man of John M'Alexander of Drummochrian, received
from Thomas Kennedy of Penquhane, an obligation
for £48 (Reg. of Deeds, vol. 498). John Alexander of Drummochrian was, along with others,
charged with being concerned in the rising at Bothwell, and was indicted to an assize on the 5th April
1681. He was forfeited, and being pronounced a
traitor, was sentenced to execution. His estate was
conferred on the Earl of Glencairn, who made it
over to John M'Levan of Grimmat, who held it till
1693. John Alexander was a second time indicted
for rebellion and reset of rebels, in July 1683
(Wodrow's History, vol. iii., pp. 250 and 466).

Connected with the family of Alexander in southern
Ayrshire, was the Rev. Robert Alexander, minister
of Girvan. Licensed by the Presbytery of Ayr,
1st August 1711, he was ordained minister of
Ayr in the following year. He died on the 8th
September 1736. By his will, dated July 1736,
he left £200 for maintaining a student in divinity
at the University of Edinburgh, to be presented by
the kirk session of Girvan to natives of the parish.
He married Janet, daughter of Hugh Hamilton,
merchant in Ayr, who died 23d February 1762
(Fasti Eccl. Scot., ii. 117).

On the 22d August 1603, Robert Alexander of
Bargarran, in the county of Renfrew, being in " deidly
seiknes," executed his will, nominating his wife as his

executrix.   He bequeathed the remainder of his property, after paying his debts, to be equally divided among John, James, Agnes, and Margaret, his "four bairnes."   His son John, to whom he left a special legacy of 40 lib., is described as "merchand burges of Glasgow."   His "frie geir" amounted to 109 lib. 6s. 8d.   His will was confirmed at Glasgow on the 5th April 1604 (Glasgow Com. Reg.).

In January 1634, died Robert Alexander of Hill of Dripps, in the parish of Cathcart, Renfrewshire. His testament-dative was, on the 13th January 1635, given up by his relict, Isobell Reid, on behalf of "James Alexander, minor, his lawful sone."   His "frie geir," was estimated at 733 lib., and one of the cautioners in the executory was Robert Alexander, merchant in Glasgow (Glasgow Com. Reg.).

In 1666, William Alexander in Dripps was fined £100, because in his parish of Cathcart he refused to assist the curate in enforcing attendance on Episcopal ordinances.   He was, in 1683, again fined £100 for refusing to become an elder under Mr Robert Fenwick, the Episcopal incumbent (Wodrow's History, vol. ii., p. 3, and vol. iii., p. 425).

On the 2d July 1631, George Alexander, merchant-burgess of Glasgow, received an obligation from John Laing, burgess there, for 110 merks; it was recorded at Edinburgh in September 1634 (Reg. of Deeds, vol. 479).

Margaret Alexander, wife of John Alexander, burgess of Hamilton, died 30th November 1598. Her testament-dative and inventory were given up by Jonet Alexander, her father's sister, "the frie gear" amounting to 962 lib. 2s. 8d. (Edin. Com. Reg.).

On the 2d January 1634, John Wood in Holmbarne granted an obligation to John Alexander, son of John Alexander, merchant-burgess of Hamilton, for £44 (Register of Deeds, vol. 497). John Alexander, burgess of Hamilton, was prosecuted for his adherence to the Presbyterian Church. Accused of resetting rebels, and "other treasonable crimes," he was sent to prison on the 24th July 1683 (Wodrow's History, vol. iii., p. 466).

William Alexander in Syd of Robertoun, parish of Lesmahago, and county of Lanark, died in December 1663. His testament-dative and inventory were given up by Marion Rob, his relict, on the 16th March 1663-4; the free gear amounting to 102 lib. 13s. 4d. (Com. Reg. of Lanark).

John Alexander, burgess in Linlithgow, died in October 1577. In his will, dated at Linlithgow, 29th October 1577, he mentions his brother James. His movable estate is valued at 160 lib. Scots. (Stirling Com. Reg.).

Alexander Alexander died at Strathbrock, parish of Uphall, Linlithgowshire, in August 1569. His testament-dative and inventory were, on the 3d November of the same year, given up by his brother David. His free gear was valued at 71 lib. (Edin. Com. Reg.).

Robert Alexander in Easter Town of Strathbrock died on the 9th December 1569. His testament-dative and inventory were, on the 23d December 1570, given up by John, Margaret, and Jonet Alexander, his "lawful bairns." His free gear was valued at 230 lib. 17s. 8d. (Edin. Com. Reg.).

James Alexander in Reidheuch, parish of Falkirk, died in December 1596. His inventory, valued at 741 lib. 6s. 8d., was given up by his brother, Robert Alexander in Beircrofts, on behalf of James, Patrick, Agnes, and William, "his lawful bairns" (Edin. Com. Reg.).

John Alexander in Falkirk died 22d June 1618 (Stirling Com. Reg.).

CHAPTER XXV.

A SURVEY of the province of Ulster, commenced in 1580, was completed in 1609 by Sir Thomas Ridgway, Vice-Treasurer of Ireland. Among the owners of lands or baronies, the family name of Alexander does not appear (Maps of Ireland, 1609; Petty's Census Returns; Hardinge on the Earliest Irish Census).

In April 1610, James I. issued a commission for the plantation of Ulster. The Commissioners, who were certain English and Scottish noblemen, were authorised " to agree and conclude as to the planting of the several counties, with power to grant warrants for letters-patent under the Great Seal " (Transcripts from the State Paper Office, 2d series, vol. i., 1603-1624, fol.).

The Commissioners divided the forfeited lands into portions of two thousand, fifteen hundred, and one thousand acres. Those who received the largest portions were bound, within four years, to build a castle and bawn—the latter being a walled enclosure with towers at the several angles. The castle was built in the interior of the enclosure, being intended to secure the inmates and their cattle from the incursions of plundering natives. Owners of the second class were called on, within two years, to erect a stone or brick house and bawn; and those of the third class a bawn only; while all were bound to plant British families on their possessions, and to provide them with defensive weapons (Reid's Presb. Church in Ireland, vol. i., *passim*).

On the recommendation of the Commissioners, letters-patent, dated 19th July 1610, were granted to Sir James Cuninghame of Glengarnock, Ayrshire, conferring on him and his heirs two thousand acres in the precincts of Portlagh, barony of Raphoe, and county of Donegal. This grant was declared to embrace "the quarters or parcels of land" designated Moragh, Dryan, Magherybegg, Magherymore, Tryan Carickmore, Grachley, and two portions of land called Eredy, while it was made a condition that the grantee should "alienate the premises to no mere Irishman, or any other person or persons, unless he or they first take the oath of supremacy" (Inq. Can. Hib. Rep., vol. ii.).

The lands of Glengarnock, in the parish of Kilbirnie, Ayrshire, and extending to 1400 acres, were acquired in 1293 by Reginald Cuninghame, second son of Sir Edward Cuninghame of Kilmaurs, through his marriage with the heiress, whose surname was Riddell. The lands and barony remained in possession of the family till 1613, when Sir James

Cuninghame of Glengarnock assigned the estate to his creditors (Cuninghame Topographised, pp. 168-178).

On the 1st May 1613, Sir James Cuninghame granted legal tenures on his lands in Donegal to thirty-nine persons who had made settlements thereon. That portion of the lands called Eredy was divided among nine settlers, one of whom was John Alexander (Inq. Can. Hib., vol. ii.).

The name Eredy closely resembles Eradall, one of the merk lands in South Kintyre, granted by James III. in 1484 to Tarlach MacAlexander of Tarbert (Reg. Mag. Sig., lib. x., 9). Sir William Alexander of Menstry, afterwards Earl of Stirling, maintained a correspondence with his relatives in Kintyre, while he and his predecessors were in habits of intimacy with the House of Cuninghame of Glengarnock. When he had obtained his first step in the peerage, he invited to visit him at Menstry his relative, Archibald Alexander of Tarbert, and procured him burghal honours at Stirling, while the chief of Mac-Alexander, in reciprocal friendship, acknowledged him head of his clan (vol. i., p. 147). Between the families of Alexander of Menstry and Cuninghame of Glengarnock, an intimacy had subsisted for generations. "John Cunynghame of Glengarno" was associated with Alexander Alexander of Menstry—great-grandfather of Sir William Alexander—and others, in a contract with John, Bishop of Dunkeld,

and Donald, Abbot of Coupar, the instrument bearing date 22d December 1547 (Acta Dom. Concilii
Sessionis, xxvi., p. 32).   By Robert Alexander of
Stirling, a scion of the House of Menstry, was granted
a loan of 200 merks to James Cuninghame, fifth Earl
of Glencairn, to whom Sir James Cuninghame was
related, alike by kindredship and marriage (Will
of Lord Glencairn, Edin. Com. Reg.).

To enable him to complete the purchase of his
lands in Donegal, Sir William Alexander granted to
Sir James Cuninghame a loan of £400 sterling, for
which, on the 26th February 1613-14, he obtained a
mortgage on the lands (Records of the Irish Rolls,
vol. v., p. 96).   As Sir James's creditors continued
importunate, Sir William Alexander proceeded, on
the 24th June 1618, to foreclose the mortgage, and
to take sasine of the lands (Records of Irish Rolls).
But this proceeding was only intended for his friend's
protection.

According to Pynnar, who, under the direction of
the Plantation Commissioners, made a survey of
Ulster in 1619, Sir James Cuninghame had, on his
estate in Donegal, erected " a bawne of lyme and stone,
and a small house in it, and in which the lady and
her daughter do now dwell."   Pynnar found near the
bawn "a small village, consisting of twelve houses,
inhabited with British tenants" (Survey of Ulster).

Sir James Cuninghame died in 1623, leaving a
widow.   This lady, a daughter of James, seventh

Earl of Glencairn, was pursued by her husband's creditors, from whom she was successfully defended, through the efforts of Sir William Alexander (Reg. of Letters). In 1629, Sir John Cuninghame, son of the original patentee, obtained the superiority of his father's lands, and had them erected into a manor, with power to create tenures (Morris's Calendar, Charles I., p. 453). Thereupon the original settlers, including John Alexander at Eredy, received new titles to their lands, and taking the oath of supremacy obtained denization (Irish Inquisitions, vol. ii., 1629).

The district of Laggan, lying between Lough Foyle and Lough Swilly, in county Donegal, was on the plantation of Ulster chiefly appropriated to Scottish settlers (Hill's Montgomery MSS., p. 183, *note*). In that district John Alexander of Eredy occupied several holdings. In the Subsidy Roll of the county of Donegal for 1662, he is, in the parish of Taghboyne, assessed for £4, 18s. In the Hearth Tax Roll[*] of Raymoghy parish for 1663, he is styled "John Allexander of ye Dukes[†] land." In Clonmany parish he is described as "John Allexander of Erithy" (Eredy), and in the parish of Raphoe as "John Allexander of Maghercolton." He is also named in the Hearth Tax Roll of the parish of Clonleigh.

---

[*] In 1662 the Parliament of Ireland passed an order that a tax for public purposes should be imposed "on the several hearths, firing places, and stoves," in the different counties. Lists were therefore made up, by certain commissioners, of all persons who owned fire-places, *i.e.*, occupied respectable houses throughout the kingdom. These lists are, for genealogical purposes, extremely valuable.

[†] The Duke of Lennox.

John Alexander of Eredy appears to have had several sons. In the Hearth Tax Roll of Clonmany parish for 1665, is named, as a householder, "John Alexander, jun." In Taghboyne parish Archibald Alexander is, in the Subsidy Roll for 1662, assessed for £13, 15s.; he is, in 1663, in the Hearth Tax Roll of Taghboyne parish, entered as "Archibald Alexander of Ballybiglimore."

In the parish of Clonleigh, in 1663, John Alexander is associated with a "William Alexander," and in the roll of that parish for 1665 he is named along with William Alexander of the parish of Raphoe. In the Hearth Tax Roll of the parish of Errigal, county Londonderry, in 1663, is named Robert Alexander at Dunvanaddy and Mevoy.

The district of Laggan, in which John Alexander of Eredy and his sons occupied lands, became a scene of contention. In this neighbourhood, in 1641, Sir Phelin O'Neill raised the standard of revolt. For its suppression the English Government granted commissions to the Viscount Montgomery (husband of Lady Jean Alexander), Sir James Montgomery, Sir William Stewart of Aughentane, and his brother Sir Robert. These were authorised to raise four regiments of infantry and as many troops of horse (Reid's Irish Presb. Church, vol. i., p. 344). The small army was entrusted to the command of Sir Robert Stewart and Sir Alexander, son of Sir William Stewart of Aughentane. Garrisons were provided to the forts of Omagh and Newton Stewart, while Sir Robert Stewart at once relieved the garrisons of Lymavaddy and Ballycastle. Sir Robert afterwards attacked O'Neill at Glenmakwin, near Raphoe, and destroying five hundred of his followers, inflicted on him a heavy discomfiture. Sir Alexander Stewart, along with Sir Thomas Staples and Colonel, afterwards Sir Audley Mervyn, vigorously followed up these successes. The rebels were worsted everywhere, till, at a decisive engagement at Clones, county Monaghan, on the 13th June 1643, Sir Robert Stewart subjected O'Neill to an overwhelming defeat.

The rebellion was renewed in 1649. On the 21st March of that year the Laggan troops recovered from the rebels the forts of Newton Cuninghame and the Corrigans, and proceeded to lay siege to Londonderry. But in the following August a party of Irish dragoons burned the fort of Corrigans and Manor Cuninghame and the town of St Johnstone, compelling the Stewarts to abandon the siege of Londonderry and return to the Laggan. In former, as well as present operations against the rebels, John Alexander of Eredy and his son John, had rendered important service, and so recommended themselves to the favour of Sir Alexander Stewart, younger of Aughentane, one of the commanders of the Laggan army. Probably on his recommendation, John Alexander the younger received compensation for the destruction of his property by the rebels in 1649. He is named

* E

tenth in a long list of persons so compensated, in a document issued on the 2d January 1668, by Sir Edward Smyth, Lord Chief-Justice of the Court of Common Pleas, Sir Edward Dering, Bart., Sir Allan Brodrick, and others, commissioners for the settlement of Ireland. The entry respecting him is in these words : " To John Allexander, forty-seaven pounds two shillings and ten pence " (Parchment Roll, Act of Settlement).

John Alexander, younger of Eredy, joined the army of the Laggan, in which he obtained the rank of captain. He resided some time at Londonderry, and latterly at Dublin. He died at Dublin in the year 1690. His will, dated 23d September 1690, was proved in the Prerogative Court on the 21st of the following February. The testator styles himself " Captain John Alexander," and appoints his wife, Susanna Alexander, his executrix and sole legatee. In the Register of the Prerogative Court, the testator is styled " Captain John Alexander nuper de London-derry," while the seal attached to his will displays a dexter arm embowed, the hand holding a dagger, the crest of his Scottish ancestors, the MacAlexanders of Tarbert.

Captain John Alexander was, according to tradition, twice married. By his first marriage he had a son, Alexander, so named in honour of his patron and military commander, Sir Alexander Stewart of Aughentane. His son, who obtained, on the Aughentane estate, the lands of Girlaw, in the barony of Clogher and county of Tyrone, married Jean Stewart of Killymoon, a near relative of Sir William Stewart of Aughentane, afterwards Viscount Mountjoy. This marriage, it is alleged, was distasteful to Lord Mountjoy, who desired for his relative a more aristocratic alliance. To his father, Alexander Alexander also became obnoxious, probably on account of his adherence to the Presbyterian Church, which his father had deserted. Before his death, his father is said to have forgiven him, but the will of Captain Alexander would not warrant the conclusion.

Alexander Alexander of Girlaw had by his wife, Jean Stewart, four sons, John, Hugh, William, and Alexander, and two daughters, Mary and Jane. Mary married Samuel Beatty, and Jane married Andrew Gray, both of the Eary, near Stewartstown.

Alexander Alexander, youngest of the four sons of Alexander Alexander of Girlaw, forfeited, by an imprudent marriage, the kindly feeling of his family. He lived at Cloon, near Lisbellan, in the county of Fermanagh, and had two sons, Andrew and Joseph, and a daughter, Mary. Andrew emigrated to America. Joseph lived at Cloon; he married and had two sons, George and Alexander. The daughter Mary married John Rutledge of Shanco, near Temple, county Fermanagh.

William, third son of Alexander Alexander, attained a very advanced age. He married Anne

Baxter of Glenoo, by whom he had three sons and a daughter, Margaret, who married James Dennis of Murley. William, the second son, resided at Drumbad; he died unmarried. James, the third son, resided at Tullynevin, and died unmarried. Daniel, the eldest son, married Margaret Burnside of Curlough, in the county of Fermanagh, by whom he had three sons and three daughters; he died about the year 1809, aged ninety-three.

Margaret, eldest daughter of Daniel Alexander, married James Wood of Tullynevin; Sarah, the second daughter, married Robert Howe of Magharaviely; and Ellen, the third daughter, married her relative, William Alexander.

John, second son of Daniel Alexander, emigrated to Philadelphia; he died unmarried. William, the third son, married Mary Coulter, by whom he had four sons, William, James, George, and Burnside, and two daughters, Mary and Jane.

Robert, eldest son of Daniel Alexander, married Anne Rutledge; he resided at Carrowkeel, county Fermanagh, and died in 1836, aged sixty-six. He married, and had four sons and two daughters. Ellen, the elder daughter, married John Hunter, and had eight children. Anne, the younger daughter, married Henry Bushel, without issue. John, the eldest son, married Jane Wilson; he now resides in Australia. Alexander, the second son, married Margaret Rutledge, without issue; he resides at Carrow-

keel in Fermanagh.   George, the third son, died
unmarried.   Joseph, the fourth son, married Jane
Rutledge, by whom he has had four children.

Hugh, second son of Alexander Alexander of
Girlaw, married Rachel, daughter of Robert Birney
of Gortmore, in the barony of Clogher, and Lucy,
daughter of Colonel Corry of Ahenis Castle, county
Tyrone, ancestor of the Earls of Belmore.   He was
father of two sons, and a daughter, Jane, who married
Samuel Smith, Nurney, county Carlow.   Robert,
the elder son, married Jane Small of Cess, in the
barony of Clogher, by whom he had four sons and
two daughters.   Mary, the elder daughter, married
John Lendrum at Mullaghmore ; Jane, the younger
daughter, married Robert M'Callum, Screeby, county
Tyrone.   Of the four sons, Robert, the second son,
settled in Philadelphia, where he married and had
children ; Hugh, the third son, settled in Scotland,
and died unmarried.   George, the fourth son, emigrated to America, and there died unmarried.

James, eldest of the four sons of Robert Alexander
and Jane Small, resided in Fivemiletown.   He died
on the 13th February 1811, aged fifty-four.   He married Sarah Lendrum, by whom he had three sons and
two daughters.   Sarah, the elder daughter, married
Richard Beatty ; Jane, the younger, married Oliver
Kidd ; George, the second son, died 26th November
1833, aged thirty-three ; James, the third son, died
in 1867.   Joseph, the eldest son, married Anne,

daughter of James Hogg of Grogey, county Fermanagh; he resided at Fivemiletown, county Tyrone, and there died in 1859. He left a son, Joseph, and a daughter, Jane, who resides at Dublin, unmarried.

Joseph Alexander, only son of Joseph Alexander and Anne Hogg, is a solicitor at Enniskillen, county Fermanagh. He married Ada Frances, daughter of John Hamilton of Milltown, county Donegal, and has a son, Percy Hamilton, and two daughters, Annie Josephine and Anna Jane Butt.

Joseph, second son of Hugh Alexander of Girlaw, married Sarah Gillespie of Screeby, by whom he had two sons and four daughters. Rachel, the eldest daughter, married Robert Frith of Coinagney; Mary, the second daughter, married James Ball of Drumgay, near Enniskillen; Sarah, the third daughter, married George Beatty of Cavenalich; and Jane, the youngest daughter, married Ralph Breen of Craene.

Thomas, eldest son of Joseph Alexander and Sarah Gillespie, married Jane Little, and settled near Frederickton, Oronoco, U.S. John, the second son, settled at Rahoran, Ireland. He married Susan Shorte, by whom he had two daughters, Margaret, who married Robert Elliott, and Sarah, who married Patrick Latimer. He prepared a pedigree chart of his family.

John, eldest son of Alexander Alexander of Girlaw, married Sarah Armstrong of Cloon, by whom he had five sons, Alexander, William, John, George, and

Robert. Alexander, the eldest son, resided on his mother's estate of Cloon, and died unmarried. John, the third son, married Elizabeth, daughter of John Cooke of Creive, by whom he had one son and six daughters.

William, only son of John Alexander and Elizabeth Cooke, resided at Breakly, county Tyrone, and died unmarried. Sarah, eldest daughter of John Alexander, died unmarried; Martha, the second daughter, married Robert Mitchell, Leitrim; Jane, third daughter, married James Cairns, Malinbarney, with issue; Elizabeth, fourth daughter, married William Alexander, Fivemiletown, county Tyrone; Eleanor, fifth daughter, married George Beatty, Tralee; Mary, the sixth and youngest daughter, married William Chirgar, and died in America.

George, fourth son of John Alexander of Girlaw, resided at Breakley, county Tyrone, and died unmarried. Robert, the fifth son, married Jane Paul of Kell, by whom he had two sons and a daughter, Sarah, who married John Baxter in Belfast. William, the elder son, married Ellen, daughter of Daniel Alexander, and had two sons and four daughters; Robert, the elder son, resided at Tempo, and William, the younger, settled at Furnish, county Tyrone. John, second son of Robert Alexander and Jane Paul, married Isabella Rutledge, and left a son, William.

William, second son of John Alexander of Girlaw, and on the death of his elder brother, Alexander, representative of this branch of the House of Alexander, resided at Girlaw. Engaging in manufactures, he attained considerable opulence. Proceeding to the district market at Fintona, he was waylaid, at a lonely spot near Fivemiletown, and there cruelly murdered. The murderer, whose object was plunder, contrived to escape.

By his wife, Martha Wilson of Cavenacross, county Fermanagh, William Alexander of Girlaw had four sons, John, James, George, and Hugh. George, the third son, resided at Breakley, and died in 1840, aged eighty. By his wife, a daughter of Captain Cairnes of Killyfaddy, he had four sons and two daughters. George, the eldest surviving son, resides in Philadelphia; he has had three sons, James, John, and William. Martha, the eldest daughter, married James Mills of Dromore, by whom she has had two sons, George and William, and three daughters, Eliza, Martha, and another.

Hugh, youngest son of William Alexander of Girlaw, died unmarried. James, second son, resided at Ardcloy, county Tyrone; he died in 1830, aged seventy-four. By his marriage with Jane Cooke, he had two sons, William and James, and two daughters, Eliza, who married James Burnside, and Anne Jane, who married Edward Cooke. James, the younger son, died unmarried; William, the elder son, married, first, Elizabeth, daughter of John Alexander, who died 13th October 1827; and secondly, Eliza Moore, who died 5th March 1835. He died 6th November 1866, aged seventy-four, leaving a son, John, and six daughters—Charlotte, wife of Thomas Clements, Lucinda, wife of John William Henry, and Eliza Anne, Jane, Margaret, and Maria, unmarried.

John, eldest son of William Alexander of Girlaw, entered Trinity College, Dublin, on the 7th October 1790. He became vicar of Drumrany, in the county of Westmeath, and died on the 9th January 1822. He married at Castle Knock, county Dublin, in 1794, Martha, daughter of Thomas Bellingham Ruxton of Carrickmacross, county Monaghan, afterwards of Armagh, and great-great-granddaughter of Captain John Ruxton of Ardee, county Louth ; she died at Kingstown, county Dublin, in 1846.

By his wife, Martha Ruxton, the Rev. John Alexander had ten children, of whom two sons died in infancy. Martha, the eldest daughter, married the Rev. Francis Short, rector of Corkbeg, county Cork, with issue ; she died 2d March 1844. Susan, second daughter, married Major John Dalzell of the 16th Regiment; she died in July 1875. Of her three children, one died in infancy. Her daughter, Emma, died unmarried. Her son, John Alexander Dalzell, is colonel in command of the 53d Regiment. Colonel Dalzell has been honourably mentioned in military despatches, and has obtained promotion for gallant conduct in the field. Twice married, he is father of a

daughter by his first wife.   Anne, third daughter of
the Rev. John Alexander, married her cousin, Robert
Pooler ; she died without issue.

Brickell, eldest son of the Rev. John Alexander of
Drumrany, was born in 1795.   Entering the army,
he became a captain in the 16th Regiment.   He
married Maria, daughter of John Hopkins, and
died, without issue, on the 9th May 1829.

John Ruxton Alexander, third son of the rector of
Drumrany, was born in March 1799.   Proceeding to
India as assistant-surgeon in the military service of
the East India Company, he became surgeon to the
Madras Horse Artillery ; he died of fever at Banga-
lore on the 28th April 1827.   By his wife, Elizabeth,
daughter of Colonel Smith of the Indian Army, he
had a daughter, Louisa.

Augustus Ruxton Alexander, fourth son of the
Rev. John Alexander, was born on the 22d September 1805.   Proceeding to India in the service of
the East India Company, he was posted to the 33d
Madras Native Infantry, of which regiment he became
Interpreter and Quartermaster.   He died of fever at
Bellary in India on the 16th May 1833.   Richard
Barlow, fifth son of the Rev. John Alexander, was
born at Drumrany in 1811.   He resided in Dublin,
and died at Windsor in October 1868.   He was
twice married without issue.

William, second son of the Rev. John Alexander,
was born on the 2d April 1796.   In 1815 he entered

the army, joining the 24th Hussars.   On the disband-
ment of that regiment subsequent to the war, he
obtained a cavalry cadetship in the East India Company's service; and, being sent to Bengal, joined the
5th Light Cavalry.   Appointed in 1838 to the command of the 4th Regiment of Irregular Horse, he joined
the army which proceeded to Affghanistan under
Sir John, afterwards Lord Keane.   For his services
at the capture of Ghuznee, he was honourably mentioned in despatches, promoted to a brevet-majority,
and granted a medal, and second-class order of the
Dooranee Empire.   At the battle of Maharajpore he
commanded the 5th Bengal Light Cavalry.   During the
first Seikh war, he took part with his regiment at the
battles of Moodkee, Ferozeshahur, and Sobraon.   In
the second Seikh war, he was, in the skirmish at
Ramnuggur, severely wounded; his right arm was
shattered, and had to be amputated on the field.   In
acknowledgment of distinguished service, he was
nominated C.B., promoted to a brevet-colonelcy, and
appointed commandant of one of the sanataria in the
Hills.   He died on the 2d October 1851, at the age
of fifty-five.

Colonel William Alexander married, in 1823,
Ann, eldest daughter of Lieutenant-General James
Kennedy, C.B.   Descended from the Earls of Cassilis,
James Kennedy was born on the 24th July 1778.
At an early age he entered, as a cavalry cadet, the
service of the East India Company.   He became

colonel of the 5th Bengal Light Cavalry, and attained the rank of lieutenant-general. He died at Benares on the 26th September 1859, having completed his eighty-first year. He married, 26th April 1804, Anna, daughter of Colonel Don, a cadet of the old Scottish family of that name. Born on the 28th March 1787, she has attained her eighty-ninth year. For many years she has resided at Benares, where she is celebrated for her beneficence. When the Prince of Wales visited Benares in 1876, His Royal Highness expressed a desire that Mrs Kennedy might be presented to him. He congratulated her on her venerable age, and on the respect and affection which she so largely enjoyed.

By his wife, Ann Kennedy, Colonel William Alexander was father of four sons and four daughters, of whom two sons and two daughters died young.

Anna Maria, elder surviving daughter, was born 13th April 1824. She married Amyand Powney Charles Elliot, captain in the 5th Light Cavalry, youngest son of the Hon. J. E. Elliot, and grandson of the Earl of Minto. She died 6th November 1857, leaving two sons and two daughters. Captain Elliot died in January 1869.

Ellen Henrietta, younger surviving daughter of Colonel William Alexander, was born on the 20th April 1830. She married, 4th October 1849, Colonel Henry Lane of the 5th Bengal Cavalry, son of Henry Snayth Lane of Broad Oak, Sussex. Colonel Lane succeeded to the paternal estate in 1866.   He is, by his wife, Ellen Henrietta Alexander, father of four sons and four daughters.   His eldest son, Henry Alexander, married, 8th April 1874, his cousin, Grace Elliot, by whom he has a son, born 27th March 1875.

Augustus Hay, younger surviving son of Colonel William Alexander, was born 26th January 1827; he entered the service of the East India Company as ensign of the 68th Regiment, and was afterwards appointed to a regiment of irregular cavalry.   Before the mutiny, he was appointed by the Earl of Dalhousie, Governor-General, to be second in command of the 3d Oude Irregular Cavalry.   Fighting with his regiment at Allahabad against the rebels, he fell mortally wounded.   He died on the 6th June 1857.   His remains were interred in the fort at Allahabad.   A brave soldier, his premature death was deeply lamented.

William Ruxton Eneas Alexander, elder surviving son of Colonel William Alexander, was born on the 27th August 1825.   Joining the Indian Army in 1842, he served in the Punjab, and was present at the battle of Goojerat.   He commanded the Ramgurh Irregular Cavalry during the campaign in Burmah, 1852-53, and was present with the land column at the relief of Pegu.   He took part in the capture of Meaday, and having led the attack on the stockade of Thomah, was much commended in the despatches.   In 1855 he, in command of the Ramgurh Irregular Cavalry, aided in suppressing the Sonthall insurrection.   In the following year he was vested with civil powers in the disturbed district.   For his services in subduing the revolt, he received the thanks of the Governor of Bengal, of the Commander-in-Chief, and of the Court of Directors.   During the mutiny of 1857, he commanded the regiment known as "Alexander's Horse," and greatly distinguished himself in an action fought on the 7th February 1858, when, at the head of a small party, he defeated and scattered a large body of insurgents.   He assisted in successfully resisting the attack on Agra in June 1857, and took part with Colonel Greathead's column in repulsing the rebel force from Gwalior in October 1857.   In 1862 he, in reward of service, received the officiating command of the 3d Bengal Cavalry.   In August 1867 he was appointed Colonel-Commandant of the 1st Bengal Cavalry.   Having retired from the army in April 1876, he received rank as major-general.

Major-General W. R. E. Alexander married, 11th September 1850, his cousin, Charlotte, daughter of Edward Macleod Blair, second son of Sir Robert Blair, K.C.B.   Head of the family of Alexander of Girlaw, he is a chief representative of the Irish branch of the House of Alexander.   His portrait fronts the title-page of the present volume.

CHAPTER XXVI.

WILLIAM ALEXANDER, one of the sons of Archibald
Alexander of Ballybiglemore, in the parish of Taghboyne, county Donegal (descended from the House of
MacAlexander of Tarbert, in Kintyre), occupied a
holding on the estate of Manor Cuninghame, in Taghboyne parish. He had four sons, Archibald, William,
Robert, and Peter. Peter Alexander, the youngest
son, settled at Londonderry; he was twice married,
with issue. Sometime after his death, his second
wife, Jane Scott, emigrated to Kentucky with several
children, who there settled.

William, second son of William Alexander at Manor
Cuninghame, emigrated to Philadelphia, and there
settled. He married a widow, and died without
issue. Robert, the third son, emigrated to Pennsylvania in 1736, where he became a teacher of mathe-
matics; he afterwards settled in Virginia.

Archibald Alexander, eldest son of William Alexander, was born at Manor Cuninghame on the 4th

February 1708. In 1736 he accompanied his brother Robert to America, settling at New Providence, in Pennsylvania. About the year 1747 he removed from New Providence to Augusta, now styled Rockbridge, in Virginia, where his brother Robert had already settled. He married first, at Manor Cuninghame, on the 31st December 1734, his cousin, Margaret, daughter of Joseph Parks, who occupied lands in the county Donegal;* she died in July 1755. He married, secondly, at Augusta, in 1757, Margaret M'Clure, of an Irish family.

By his first wife, Margaret Parks, Archibald Alexander was father of two sons, William and Joseph; and five daughters, Elizabeth, Anne, Hannah, Phebe, and Margaret. Joseph, the second son, was born at New Providence, Pennsylvania, on the 9th February 1742; he married Sarah Reid. Elizabeth, the eldest daughter, was born at Manor Cuninghame on the 28th October 1735; she married John M'Cleery of Timber Ridge, Virginia. Anne, second daughter, born at New Providence, Pennsylvania, 17th September 1740, married the Rev. Mr Carruthers. Hannah, third daughter, born at New Providence on the 21st April 1745, married Joseph Lyle. Phebe, fourth daughter, born at Augusta 12th August 1749, married John Paxton; Margaret, fifth daughter, born at Augusta 9th July 1751, died in infancy.

By his second wife, Margaret M'Clure, William

* Members of the family of Parks are still resident in the county Donegal.

Alexander was father of four sons and three daughters. John, the eldest son, born 28th July 1764, died in 1828; he married Sarah Gibson; James, second son, born 4th October 1766, married Martha Telford; Samuel, born 6th February 1769, married —— M'Coskie; Archibald, the fourth son, born 3d March 1771, married Isabel A. Patton.   Mary, the eldest daughter, born 4th July 1760, married John Tremble; Margaret, second daughter, born 1st February 1762, died unmarried; Jane, youngest daughter, born 1773, married the Rev. John Doak of Tennessee.

William Alexander, eldest son of Archibald Alexander and Margaret Parks, was born on the river Schuylkill in Pennsylvania, on the 22d March 1738. He settled in Virginia, where he engaged in agricultural and commercial pursuits.   He married, in February 1767, Agnes Anne, daughter of Andrew Reid, an opulent landowner, and by her was father of three sons and six daughters.   Andrew, the eldest son, married Miss Aylett; John, the third son, married Elizabeth Lyle.   Margaret, the eldest daughter, married Edward Graham; Sarah, second daughter, married Samuel H. Campbell; Phebe, third daughter, married William Carruthers; Elizabeth, fourth daughter, married Henry M'Cleery; Anne, fifth daughter, married Rev. William Turner; and Martha, sixth daughter, married Benjamin H. Rice.

Archibald Alexander, second son of William Alexander and Agnes Anne Reid, was born on the 17th

* F

April 1772.   Licensed to preach in October 1791, he was not long afterwards appointed President of Hampden Sidney Presbyterian College.   In 1807 he was chosen pastor of the third Presbyterian congregation of Philadelphia, where he ministered till July 1812, when he became First Professor in the Theological Seminary at Princeton, New Jersey, an office which he held till his death, which took place on the 22d October 1851.   He was D.D. and LL.D.   His more considerable works are his "History of the Colonisation of the Western Coast of Africa," 1846, 8vo; "History of the Israelitish Nation," 1852, 8vo; "Outlines of Moral Science," 1852, 8vo; and "Practical Sermons."   His memoirs have been published by his eldest son, the Rev. James Waddel Alexander, D.D. (New York, 1855).

Dr Archibald Alexander married, 5th April 1802, Janetta, daughter of the Rev. Dr James Waddel, of the county of Louisa, Virginia.   By this union he became father of six sons, and a daughter, Janetta, who survives, unmarried.

James Waddel Alexander, eldest son of the Rev. Dr Archibald Alexander, was, on the 13th March 1804, born at Hopewell, an estate situated at the junction of the counties of Louisa, Orange, and Albemarle, near the present site of Gordonsville.   Having attended an academy at Princeton, he entered the College of New Jersey in 1817, where he graduated three years afterwards.   Entering the ministry of the Presbyterian Church, he was, in 1828, elected pastor of the congregation at Trenton, New Jersey. He was, in 1830, appointed Professor of Rhetoric in the College of New Jersey, an office which he exchanged in 1844 for the pastorate of Duane Street Church, New York.   In November he was admitted Professor of Divinity in the Theological Seminary at Princeton; he returned to New York in 1851 to become pastor of the Fifth Avenue Church of that city.   There he ministered with remarkable acceptance till his death, which took place on the 31st July 1859.   He was D.D., and was much esteemed for his theological learning, and his remarkable power of illustrating and enforcing Divine truth.   In 1832-33 he edited the *Presbyterian* magazine.   Besides his memoir of his father, he published, " Christian Faith and Practice," " Thoughts on Preaching," and two volumes of pulpit discourses.   His " Forty Years' Familiar Letters " were published in 1870, in two octavo volumes.   He married, 18th June 1830, Elizabeth, daughter of George Cabell, M.D., by whom he had three sons, Henry, James Waddel, and William.

William Cowper Alexander, second son of the Rev. Dr Archibald Alexander, was born in the county of Prince Edward, Virginia, on the 20th May 1806. He studied at the Colleges of New Jersey and Princeton, graduating at the latter in 1824. Choosing the legal profession, he was called to the bar in

1827.   In 1837 he was elected a member of the legis-
lature of New Jersey.   A Senator of State from 1853
to 1860, he was four years President of the Senate.
Of the Peace Congress, for the purpose of averting
the civil war, composed of delegates from all the
states of the Union, he was an active member, and
often presided at the deliberations.   In 1857 he was,
in the democratic interest, candidate for the governor-
ship of New Jersey, but was defeated.   In 1859 he
became first president of the Equitable Life Assurance Society of the United States, and thereafter
resided at New York.   He died unmarried on the
24th August 1874.   He held a commission in the
army, and was known as Colonel Alexander.

Joseph Addison Alexander, third son of the Rev.
Dr Archibald Alexander, was born in the city of
Philadelphia on the 24th April 1809.   He studied at
the College of New Jersey, where he graduated B.A.
in 1826.   In the same year he was, by the common
council, elected clerk of the borough of Virginia.
After a period of public teaching, he was, in 1830,
appointed adjunct Professor of Ancient Languages
in the College of New Jersey.   In 1834 he was
nominated adjunct Professor of Oriental Literature
in the Theological Seminary at Princeton ; he was
elected professor in 1835.   In the same year, he was
licensed to preach by the Presbytery of New Brunswick, and at once obtained celebrity for the power
and unction of his pulpit prelections.   An accom-

plished philologist and general scholar, he contributed to the current periodical literature, important articles from his pen appearing in the *Princeton Review*, the *Biblical Repertory*, and the *Emporium*, a monthly magazine.   He published " Lectures on the Literature and History of the New Testament." His great work, a " Commentary on Isaiah," he commenced in 1836, and completed in 1846.   He died in January 1861.

Of the three remaining sons of the Rev. Dr Archibald Alexander, Archibald and Samuel Davies are unmarried.   Henry M. Alexander, the youngest son, is a counsellor-at-law at New York, in extensive practice.   By his wife, Susan M. Brown, Henry M. Alexander is father of five sons, Charles, Archibald, Samuel, Henry, and Maitland, and of a daughter, Janetta Waddel.

CHAPTER XXVII.

ROBERT ALEXANDER, probably a son of John Alexander of Eredy, and certainly a near connection of his house, is, in the Subsidy Roll of 1661, named under Errigal parish, county Londonderry, as "Robert Alexander de Meyboy," and is assessed for £3, the subsidy being £1, 12s. In the Hearth Tax Roll of 1663 he is entered as "Robert Alexander, Dunvanaddy and Mevoy." According to a well-authenticated tradition, he took part in the siege of Londonderry in 1649, and in acknowledgment of service, received from Colonel, afterwards Sir Audley Mervyn, a grant of land at Drumquin, in the parish of Ardstraw, county Tyrone.*

Joseph, son of Robert Alexander, was twice married. By his first wife he had two sons, James and

---

* For an account of Sir Audley Mervyn, see Transactions of Royal Historical Society, vol. iii., p. 421.

Thomas. James, the elder son, resided at Dromore, county Tyrone; his remains rest in the churchyard of that place, where an altar tombstone to his memory displays the armorial escutcheon of the House of Menstry.

Thomas, second son of Joseph Alexander, married Mary Osborne, by whom he had three sons, James, Francis, and Thomas, and a daughter, Rebecca. Thomas, the youngest son, was born in 1764, and died in December 1860, aged ninety-six (Tombstone Inscription in Dromore Churchyard). By his wife, Mary Skelton, he had a son, Thomas, who now resides at Dromore.

Joseph Alexander of Drumquin married, as his second wife, the heiress of Drumarnagross, county Tyrone; she bore him three sons, John, George, and Joseph. John, the eldest son, succeeded his mother in the lands of Drumarnagross. He married, and had seven sons, James, Joseph, Robert, John, Thomas, William, and George. James succeeded his father in the lands of Drumarnagross, and left a son, Joseph, now owner of the estate.

George, second son of Joseph Alexander by his second marriage, was physician at Fintona, county Tyrone. Joseph, the youngest son, practised medicine at Trillick in the same county.

Jane, wife of William Alexander, sixth son of John Alexander of Drumarnagross, is interred in the parish churchyard of Raphoe. She died on the 13th

January 1869, aged thirty-five (Tombstone Inscription).

Archibald Alexander is, in the Subsidy Roll for 1661, of the parish of Taghboyne, county Donegal, assessed for property to the value of £13, 15s. He is, in the Hearth Tax Roll of the same parish for 1662, styled "Archibald Alexander of Ballybiglemore." He was probably a son of John Alexander of Eredy, and brother of Robert Alexander of Meyboy, and afterwards of Drumquin. As a lay elder he represented the Presbyterian congregation of Taghboyne in the Presbytery of Laggan, from 1672 to 1681 (Presbytery Records). In the burial-ground at Balleighan, in Taghboyne parish, his tombstone is thus inscribed : " Here lyeth the body of Archibald Alexander, who deceased the 31st March, anno 1689." Having died intestate, his wife obtained "letters" for the administration of his affairs (Original in General Probate Office). She died in 1715, and is on her husband's tombstone thus commemorated : " Here lyeth the body of Elizabeth Mackey, wife of Archibald Alexander, who departed this life 30th January 1715, aged 78 years."

James Alexander, a younger son of Archibald Alexander, farmed a portion of the lands of Ballybigley, and died there on the 28th May 1743, aged seventy-five. His wife, Elizabeth Paterson, died 3d July 1740, aged sixty (Tombstone Inscription at Balleighan).

Joseph Alexander, eldest son of Archibald Alexander, married Margaret Jack. His marriage licence is, in the Diocesan Registry of Londonderry, entered thus : "November 17, 1686. — Licentia ad solem. matrimonii inter Josephum Alexander de Ballybiglemore in paroch. Taboyne in com. Donnegall et Margaretam Jack de Brookhall in paroch. Templemore."

Joseph Alexander, son of Joseph Alexander and Margaret Jack, died in the autumn of 1767. He had married Elizabeth Paterson, and in his will, dated 26th October 1763, he names four sons, James, Samuel, William, and Joseph, and a daughter, Sarah (Will in Probate Court). James, the eldest son, married Jane, daughter of Alexander Scott, by whom he had four sons, Joseph, Nathaniel, John, and Robert, and four daughters. Two of the daughters are unmarried, and, with their sister, a widow, reside at Ballybigley. Elizabeth, the remaining daughter, married John Alexander, son of James Alexander, farmer, Gortmesson, county Tyrone, and had issue, seven sons and one daughter. James, eldest son of the eldest daughter, is now farmer at Drumenon, Taghboyne parish ; he is married and has issue, one daughter. Joseph, second son of John and Elizabeth Alexander, is farmer at Imlich, county Donegal.

Joseph, eldest son of James Alexander of Ballybigley, died unmarried. Nathaniel, the second son, emigrated to St John, New Brunswick. He married and had sons and daughters. His only surviving son is Charles Crawford Alexander.

John, third son of James Alexander of Ballybigley, died without issue. Robert, the fourth son, proceeded to the West Indies, and there died without issue.

Samuel, second son of Joseph Alexander of Ballybigley, died in 1767. He had a son, James, and a daughter, Elizabeth. James Alexander was bank-agent at Omagh; his remains are deposited in the parish churchyard of Cappagh, county Tyrone. Elizabeth Alexander resides at Rathmullen, county Donegal.

John Alexander, printer, Strabane, county Tyrone, was descended from the families of Ballybigley and Crew. He died in 1801. In his will, executed 18th November 1798, he names his sons, John and Joseph.

Descendants of Archibald Alexander of Ballybigley settled at Londonderry. Robert Alexander of Bishop Street, Londonderry, who died in 1822, names in his will his sons, James and Samuel, and his daughters, Hannah and Elizabeth. James Alexander of Foyle Street, Londonderry, whose will was proved on the 3d November 1831, made bequests to his sons, John and James, and his daughters, Mary, Jane, Eleanor, and Elizabeth (Wills in Probate Court).

Also descended from Archibald Alexander of Ballybigley is the family of Alexander at Kinnekally, parish of Taghboyne. John Alexander, farmer at Kinnekally, died on the 7th October 1724. He married, first, Magdalene Kilgour, who died in July 1709 (Tombstone Inscription); and secondly, Mary. In his will, dated 26th March 1720, he names his sons, Robert, Joseph, and John. He also had a son Jacob. " Mr Thomas Alexander" is named as one of his executors (Will in Probate Court).

John Alexander, son of John Alexander, farmer at Kinnekally, died in 1785, aged seventy-nine. In his will, dated 1st October 1771, he names a son, James, and a daughter, Mary, married to John Gregg.

James Alexander, son of John Alexander at Kinnekally, died in 1829, aged eighty-five. His son James, who died in 1836 (Tombstone Inscription), left a son, John, who is now farmer at Drumbarnet, near Newton Cuninghame, county Donegal.

James Alexander, brother of John Alexander, farmer at Kinnekally, rented the farm of Altrest, in the parish of Donagheady. He had a son, William, and a grandson, James, whose son, Robert, is now farmer at Altrest.

Archibald Alexander, descended from Archibald Alexander of Ballybigley, settled at Ratteen, in the parish of Taghboyne. He married, and had a son, Andrew, who purchased the small estate of Crew, parish of Ardstraw, county Tyrone. He married Fanny Lockhart, by whom he had six sons, William, Samuel, Hugh, Joseph, Andrew, and Thomas. His tombstone in Ardstraw parish churchyard is thus inscribed : "Here lyeth the body of Andrew Alexander, who departed this life March the 5th, 1779, aged 73 years."

William, second son of Andrew Alexander of Crew, married, and had one daughter. Samuel, the third son, married, and had three sons and one daughter. David, one of the sons, now resides at Taghboyne.

Hugh, fourth son of Andrew Alexander, proceeded to the parish of Donagheady, and there purchased land. One of his sons now resides at Donemana, in Donagheady parish.

Andrew, fifth son of Andrew Alexander, purchased land at Donemana, where his son resides now.

Thomas, sixth son, emigrated to America.

Joseph, eldest son of Andrew Alexander of Crew, succeeded his father in his lands. He married Isabella Wauchope, by whom he had five sons, Charles ; Andrew, born 1799 ; Thomas, born 1800 ; Joseph, born 1802 ; and James, born 1804. He died in 1806 (Will in Probate Court).

Charles, eldest son of Joseph Alexander of Crew, was born 27th September 1797. He died some years ago, and was succeeded by his second brother, Andrew, who is married, with issue.

A descendant of the family of Ballybigley, Andrew Alexander, Presbyterian minister at Urney, county Tyrone, executed his will on the 14th October 1807, and died in the following year. To his wife, Elizabeth

Knox, he bequeathed "an undisputable right to the rents of Ballymanan, in the parish of Donaghmore, and county of Donegal." He mentions his daughter Elizabeth Alexander, unmarried, and his married daughter, Martha M'Conechy, and her children.

Descended from the House of Ballybigley, Thomas Alexander, "of the town of Lisslimnaghan, parish of Cappagh," county Tyrone, executed his will on the 1st October 1783, and died soon afterwards. He bequeathed his farm in liferent to his wife Isabella. Archibald Alexander is named as a legatee (Will in Probate Court).

A scion of the family of Ballybigley, Jacob Alexander acquired the lands of Greenville, parish of Ardstraw, and died 7th June 1822, aged seventy-eight (Tombstone in Ardstraw Churchyard). By his wife, Jane Eakin, he had a son, Joseph, and a daughter, Jane, who died 17th October 1822.

Joseph Alexander succeeded his father in the lands of Greenville. He married Isabella Turner, by whom he had a son, John George. He died in 1834. In his will, proved at Londonderry on the 12th December of that year, he leaves an annuity to his wife out of the lands of Bittany, in the parish of Cappagh, and the lands of Greenville, in the parish of Ardstraw. He mentions his son John George as a minor.

John George Alexander, only son of Joseph Alexander of Greenville, died prior to 1866. In the parish churchyard of Ardstraw a tombstone is thus inscribed : " Erected as a tribute to the memory of the late Jacob Alexander, Esq. of Greenville, and his family, by Francis O'Neill, executor of the late John George Alexander, Esq., pursuant to the directions of his will, May 1864. Also, the body of John Alexander, who departed this life the 20th day of January 1866, aged 86 years."

Joseph Alexander, of the parish of Upper Long-field, county Tyrone (a supposed descendant of the family of Ballybigley), died in 1832. By his wife, Jane Watson, he had six sons, Thomas, George, John, Joseph, Robert, and James ; and two daughters, Isabella and Elizabeth (Will in Probate Court).

In the Hearth Tax Roll of 1662, William Alexander is named in the parish of Clonleigh, county Donegal, while in the roll of 1665 his name disappears from Clonleigh, and is included in Raphoe parish in the same county (see *supra*). He was probably the father of James Alexander, Presbyterian minister at Raphoe from 1677 to 1704. To the charge at Raphoe, otherwise called Convoy,* James Alexander was ordained 12th December 1677 (Reid's Irish Presb. Church). Along with his brethren, Mr William Trail,† Mr Robert Camp-

---

* The parish of Convoy formerly constituted part of the parish of Raphoe, and though the meeting-house was at Convoy, the incumbent was styled minister of Raphoe (Note to Reid's Presb. Church in Ireland, vol. ii., p. 339).

† Mr William Trail was son of Mr Robert Trail, minister of Edinburgh, grandson of Colonel James Trail of Killelagh, in Ireland, and great-grandson of the laird of Blebo, in Fife. Born in 1640, he was ordained Presbyterian minister at

bell,* and Mr John Hart,† he was in 1681 subjected to a course of persecution.

Meeting at St Johnstone, on the 2d February 1681, the Presbytery of Laggan appointed the 17th day of that month to be observed for special fasting and prayer.   The Presbytery also framed a paper, to be read from the different pulpits, enumerating as causes of the fast, "apostasy and perjury, and breach of solemn covenants." Some expressions used in the paper being construed as reflecting injuriously on the Episcopal Church, Mr Alexander and his three colleagues were summoned before the justices at Raphoe. The justices met on Tuesday the 3d May, and, after an examination, the charge against the four brethren was dismissed.   Within a few weeks thereafter, the brethren were, on the same charge, summoned before the Privy Council, and by that body remitted for trial to the assize court at Lifford. The court of assize met in August, and the brethren, being found guilty, were sentenced to pay £20 each, and to subscribe an engagement against again calling a fast. Refusing to obtemperate the sentence, they

Lifford, Ireland, in 1672.   He afterwards proceeded to Maryland. Returning to Scotland at the Revolution, he was in 1690 admitted minister of Borthwick, Edinburghshire. He died 3d May 1714 (Fasti Eccl. Scot.).

* Mr Robert Campbell was ordained minister of Raymoghy, county Donegal, in 1671. He was called to the parish of Roseneath, Dumbartonshire, in 1689 (Fasti Eccl. Scot. ; Reid's Presb. Church).

† Mr John Hart was admitted to the second charge of Hamilton in 1653, and was translated to Taghboyne in 1656. He was ejected in 1662 under pretence of being accessory to a plot against the bishops. He died before 1689 (Fasti Eccl. Scot.).

were imprisoned at Lifford for eight months.   Their fines were afterwards remitted by the Court of Exchequer (Wodrow's MSS. ; Reid's Irish Presb. Church).

James Alexander continued to minister at Raphoe till his death, which took place on the 17th November 1704.   His salary was, on his appointment, fixed at £24 money, with twenty-four barrels of corn.   He died without issue.   By his will, dated 13th March 1702, he constituted his wife, Marion Shaw, his executrix and sole legatee (Will in Probate Court).

Mrs Marion Alexander or Shaw, relict of the Rev. James Alexander, died at Raphoe in 1711.   In her will she expressed her desire to be buried in the churchyard of Raphoe, "along with the corps of her dear husband."   She bequeathed her substance to her niece, Elizabeth Shaw, daughter of her brother, Mr James Shaw.   As overseers for the proper administration of her will, she named Mr Robert Campbell in Ray, Mr Alexander Nisbet in Tillidonell, and Mr Andrew Fergusson in Burt.

James Alexander of Raphoe (probably a nephew of the Rev. James Alexander) died in 1723.   In his will, dated 12th June 1723, he bequeaths his entire substance to his wife (Will in Probate Court).

In the churchyard of Raphoe, a tombstone, more than a century old, is inscribed, "Here lyeth the body of Elizabeth Alexander."   In the same churchyard an altar tombstone has the following legend:

"Erected to the memory of William Alexander, senior, who departed this life April 1856, aged 83 years; also of Robert Alexander, who died July 1861, aged 78 years. And also Jane Alexander, the beloved wife of William Alexander, junior, Dromore, who died 13th January 1869, aged 35 years."

CHAPTER XXVIII.

FAMILIES OF ALEXANDER OF BALLYCLOSE, COUNTY LONDONDERRY; MILFORD, COUNTY CARLOW; AND OF THE CITY OF LONDON.

In the Hearth Tax Roll of Errigal parish, county Londonderry, is named, in 1663, as resident at the village of Garvachy, " Andrew Alexander." " Robert Alexander de Meyboy " is entered in the Subsidy Roll of the same parish in 1661 (see *supra*). Andrew Alexander was, it is believed, a son of John Alexander, the original settler at Eredy, county Donegal; he was at the siege of Londonderry in 1649. He obtained the favour of Captain, afterwards Sir Thomas Philipps, who, with his elder brother, Mr Dudley Philipps, served with Sir Robert and Sir Alexander Stewart against O'Neill. Captain Philipps was appointed governor of Culmore Fort, near Londonderry, and obtained lands at Newton Limavady (Reid's Irish Presb. Church). From Sir Thomas Philipps,* or his son, styled Major-Colonel George Philipps,†

---

* Andrew Alexander is said to have espoused, as his first wife, a daughter of Sir Thomas Philipps, but on what we deem insufficient evidence.

† This person is described as author of the celebrated letter to Charles I., complaining of the London Companies' breach of charter in replanting the Irish

Andrew Alexander obtained a grant of land at Ballyclose, in the parish of Drumachose, near Newton Limavady.

Andrew Alexander latterly resided at Ballyclose, where he reared a convenient residence. A stone from one of the walls, bearing the founder's initials, with the date 1666, is placed in the wall of the present mansion. Through commercial pursuits conducted at Londonderry, Andrew Alexander attained considerable opulence. With many other adherents of the Revolution Government, he was, under the style of Captain Andrew Alexander, attainted in a pretended parliament, held by James II. at Dublin, on the 7th May 1689.

Andrew Alexander of Ballyclose married the daughter of —— Hilles, a landowner in the county of Londonderry. He had three sons, John, Thomas, and another.

Thomas Alexander occupied a holding in the parish of Errigal. Of that parish he was churchwarden in 1696-97 (Vestry Register).

John Alexander, the eldest son, sometime traded in Londonderry. He was resident at Ballyclose in 1717, for on the 16th June of that year he subscribed the register, certifying that Mr Gervais Temple, rector of Drumachose, had read common prayer in

Papists in place of English and Scottish Protestants, who had been settled on their lands. "He was attainted at a pretended Parliament on the 7th May 1689, as was his son, Captain Thomas Phillips of Limerick," and others (Graham's History of the Siege of Londonderry, *passim*).

the parish church, on the occasion of his admission to the cure (Diocesan Registry of Derry, No. 1, p. 410). He purchased the estate of Gunsland, county Donegal, and built a town residence at the Diamond, Londonderry. He married Anne White, a widow, daughter of John White of the Cady Hill, Newton Limavady, by whom he had three sons and one daughter, Martha, who married Alexander Kellie, with issue. He died 12th March 1747 (Family Tombstone at Newton Limavady). In his will, dated 21st January 1746, he makes bequests to his sons, John, Nathaniel, and William, and his daughter Martha; also to John Alexander, described as "his brother's son," and to Andrew Alexander, described as son of his brother Thomas (Will in Probate Court).

John, eldest son of John Alexander of Ballyclose, was born in 1695. He became a merchant in Londonderry. By his wife Sarah, daughter of Alexander Macaulay of Dromnagisson, county Antrim, he had three sons, Alexander, Andrew, and John; and two daughters, Margaret and Amelia. He died in 1766, aged seventy-one (Tombstone at Newton Limavady). Margaret, the elder daughter, married John Cranstoun of Belfast, in May 1794, with issue. Amelia, the younger daughter, married —— Williams, by whom she had three daughters.

Alexander Alexander, eldest son of John Alexander, served in the navy; he had an annuity from his younger brother Andrew. He died unmarried. Andrew, the second son, succeeded to the paternal estate; he married Rebecca Isabella, daughter of Colonel Alexander Stewart of Londonderry. He died, without issue, on the 1st July 1803, aged sixty-nine (Tombstone at Newton Limavady). By his will, executed 2d June 1803, he bequeathed his estate in trust to Robert Alexander of Dublin, and Henry Alexander of Boomhall, county Londonderry, for payment of his wife's annuity, and the conveyance of the rents thereafter to his brother, John Alexander of Belfast; on whose decease they were to convey his estate to Andrew Alexander, his brother John's youngest son; failing whom, to John Alexander, eldest son of his said brother; whom failing, to the right heirs of the said John Alexander (Will in Probate Court).

John, third and youngest son of John Alexander of Ballyclose, was born 26th January 1736. He resided at Belfast, where he engaged in merchandise. On the 29th May 1760, he married Anne, daughter of George Portis, Esq., collector of customs, Belfast, by his wife, Mary Ratcliffe, born 1741; she is, in the *Belfast Newsletter* announcing the nuptials, described as "a young lady of great beauty and merit, with a handsome fortune." John Alexander was father of four sons, John, George, Andrew, and Alexander. He died 23d December 1821, aged eighty-six.

George, the second son, died without issue.

John Alexander, eldest son of John Alexander

and Anne Portis, was born 27th February 1764.
He sold, in 1827, the estate of Ballyclose to Major
Alexander Alexander of Newton Limavady.   In
1790 he purchased the lands of Milford, county
Carlow, where he died, 16th August 1843, aged
eighty.   He married, 8th September 1801, Christian
Izod, daughter of Lorenzo Nickson, Esq. of Chapel-
izod, county of Kilkenny, by whom he had six
sons, John, Lorenzo William, George, James, Charles
Leslie, and Henry, and five daughters, Elizabeth,
Anne, Emily, Lucia, and Fanny.   Elizabeth and
Emily died young; Anne, born 1st August 1806,
married, 6th October 1828, John Cranstoun of Crane-
brook, county Tyrone; she died 10th April 1862,
without issue.   Lucia is unmarried; Fanny, born
1st February 1816, married, 19th October 1847,
the Rev. Charles Henry Travers, rector of Purley,
Berkshire.

Lorenzo William, second son of John Alexander
of Milford, born 22d October 1810, married, on the
25th June 1857, Harriet, eldest daughter of the late
Colonel Henry Bruen of Oak Park, county Carlow,
who long represented that county in Parliament.
He was father of one son, Henry Bruen, and two
daughters, Christian and Anne; he died 21st September 1867.

George, the third son, born 17th February 1814,
married, 28th February 1861, Susan, daughter of
J. H. Collins, barrister-at-law, by whom he has had

four sons, John Stephen, Frank, James, and Walter, and one daughter, Christian Izod.

James, the fourth son, born 8th March 1818, married, 12th July 1855, Lucia Margaret, eldest daughter of Sir William Clarke Travers, Bart. of Rossmore, county Cork, without issue.

Charles Leslie, fifth son, born 28th April 1820, is vicar of Stewkley, Buckinghamshire.

Henry, youngest son of John Alexander, first of Milford, is lieutenant-colonel, 1st Dragoon Guards.

John Alexander, eldest son of John Alexander, first of Milford, was born 26th July 1802. He graduated at the University of Dublin. He was High Sheriff of Carlow in 1824, and represented that borough in Parliament from 1853 to 1859. He married, 18th October 1848, Esther, eldest daughter of Matthew Brinkley, Esq. of Parsonstown, county Meath, second son of the Bishop of Cloyne, by whom he has had five sons, and one daughter, Harriet Lucia, who married, 8th July 1875, Captain Donnethorne of the Scots Greys. John, the eldest son, born 23d September 1850, studied at the University of Cambridge. He is now an officer in the Dragoon Guards. William Cranstoun, second son, born 5th November 1851, studied at the University of Oxford, and follows legal pursuits. Lorenzo, third son, born 28th August 1853, is a merchant in London. Charles Henry, fourth son, born 2d June 1856, is a cadet at Woolwich; and George, fifth son, born 20th June 1858, is an undergraduate in Trinity College, Dublin.

Nathaniel Alexander, second son of John Alexander of Ballyclose and Gunsland, and grandson of Captain Andrew Alexander, was born in 1689. He was admitted to the Corporation of Londonderry in 1740, and in 1755 was elected an alderman of the city (Corporation Records). He succeeded his father in the estate of Gunsland, county Donegal. He died 22d September 1761, aged seventy-two. His remains were deposited in the burial-ground of the Chapel of Ease, Londonderry (Tombstone Inscription). By his wife, Elizabeth, daughter of William M'Clintock of Dunmore, county Donegal, he had five sons, William, Robert, James, John, and Nathaniel, and six daughters, Mary Jane, Rebecca, Elizabeth, Ann, Jane, senior, and Jane, junior. The sons John and Nathaniel, and the daughters Elizabeth, Ann, Jane, senior and junior, died young.

Mary Jane Alexander, eldest daughter of Nathaniel Alexander, married, first, —— Weld, Esq., Londonderry, by whom she had two daughters, who died unmarried. She married, secondly, Hamilton Maclure, Esq., of Dublin, by whom she had one daughter, who married John William Foster, Esq. of Fane Valley, county Louth, and had sons and daughters. One of the daughters married, in 1819, Thomas, second Lord Plunket, Bishop of Tuam.

Rebecca Alexander, second surviving daughter of Nathaniel Alexander, married Josias Duprè of Wilton Park, Buckinghamshire, and had issue. A daughter married General Sir Terence O'Brien.

William Alexander, eldest son of Nathaniel Alexander, studied at the University of Cambridge, and was called to the bar, but afterwards became a merchant in the city of London. He died in 1774, and his remains were interred in St Laurence church, London. By his wife, Charlotte, daughter of Messenger Monsey, M.D., of Mulberton, in the county of Norfolk, who died in 1798, he had four sons and seven daughters. Charlotte, the eldest daughter, born in 1754, died in June 1829 unmarried. Elizabeth, second daughter, born 1758, died unmarried in September 1840. Anne, third daughter, born 1759, married William Dalton, and died without issue in 1840. Jemima, fourth daughter, born in 1764, married in 1789 the Rev. John Edmund Rolfe, vicar of Cranworth, Norfolk, first cousin of Admiral Viscount Nelson. Her son, Robert Monsey Rolfe, was called to the bar : he became successively Solicitor-General, Baron of Exchequer, Vice-Chancellor, and Lord Justice of Appeal. He was in 1850 created Baron Cranworth, and in 1852 was appointed Lord High Chancellor. He died in 1868. Rebecca, fifth daughter of William, died young, unmarried. Catherine, sixth daughter, married, in 1800, the Rev. J. B. Collyer of Hackford Hall, Norfolk, by whom she had two sons and three daughters. Charlotte Collyer, the eldest daughter, married the Rev. Dr Harris, by whom she had an only child. Robert, the second son, entered into holy orders, and died unmarried. John, the eldest son, became a barrister-at-law. He married Georgina Frances Amy, eldest daughter of Sir William Johnston of Johnston, Aberdeenshire, with issue. Mary, youngest daughter of William Alexander, died unmarried in 1844.

Monsey, eldest son of William Alexander, was born in 1756, and took orders in the English Church. When the Earl of Bristol was appointed Bishop of Derry, he became his lordship's chaplain. He afterwards obtained the incumbency of Moville, county Derry, and died in 1790. By his wife, Susanna, daughter of James M'Clintock of Tearntagh, county Donegal, he had an only child, Dorothea, who married, in 1816, the Rev. Alexander Staples, rector of Gowran, and had issue.

William, second son of William Alexander of London, engaged in merchandise in Dublin. He was drowned while bathing. In his will, dated 5th December 1791, he is described as "of St Mary's Abbey, in the city of Dublin." He made bequests of sums varying between £500 and ten guineas to numerous relatives, with this remark, "These bequests may possibly be construed as the effects of vanity, even so, I hope the crime is pardonable; but it really was always my opinion that such tokens as friendly farewells on our departure for a strange country, were gratifying to the feelings of both parties. I have only acted therefore in support of my opinion, and wish my time and circumstance would permit me to enlarge upon the subject."

To Henry Alexander of William Street he bequeathed the contents of his cellar, which he describes as "alas! but trifling." His will closes with these words : " I shall now conclude with sincere prayers for the health, happiness, and prosperity of my relations, friends, and acquaintances, in particular, and for the general peace and happiness of all the world" (Will in Probate Court, Dublin).

John Alexander, third son of William Alexander of London, died unmarried. Robert Alexander, the fourth son, was born in 1771. He held an appointment in the Civil Service of the East India Company, and was member of council at Madras. He married, first, Miss Williams ; and secondly, Grace, daughter of the Rev. St John Blacker, A.M., prebendary of Inver, in the county of Donegal; she died 19th October 1835. Robert Alexander latterly resided in Gloucester Place, London. He left two sons, James William and Robert, and two daughters, Charlotte and Mary. Charlotte, elder daughter, married John Muddelk, Esq. of Greenhill House, near Maidstone. Mary, the second daughter, married, 6th April 1837, the Rev. Sir Samuel Vincent Love Hammick, A.M., vicar of Milton Abbot, Devon,

and has issue, six sons and one daughter.   James
William, only child of Robert Alexander by his first
wife, died in India in 1836 without issue.

Robert Alexander, only son of Robert Alexander
by his second wife, resides at Downs House, Talding,
Kent.   He is unmarried.

CHAPTER XXIX.

ROBERT ALEXANDER of Boomhall was second son of
Nathaniel Alexander, alderman of the city of Londonderry, and grandson of Captain Andrew Alexander
of Ballyclose, county Londonderry. On his estate of
Boomhall, near Londonderry, he erected a family
mansion, at the spot where a boom was constructed
to prevent ships sailing towards the city during the
siege of 1689. At Londonderry he engaged in merchandise, and became prosperous. He died on the
27th March 1790, aged sixty-eight, and his remains
were deposited in the family burial-ground in the
Chapel of Ease churchyard, Londonderry (Tombstone
Inscription).

By his wife, Anne, daughter and co-heiress of

Henry M'Culloch, Esq. of Cladymore and Ballyarton, county Londonderry (who died 20th January 1817), Robert Alexander had five sons, Nathaniel, Henry, William, James, and Josias Duprè, and five daughters, Elizabeth, Jane, Anne, Rebecca, and Dorothea. Elizabeth, the eldest daughter, married Sir Andrew Ferguson, Bart. of The Farm, county Londonderry, by whom she had three sons and four daughters. Anne, eldest daughter, married Colonel William Blacker of Carrick, county Armagh; she died 3d January 1861 without issue. Sarah, second daughter, married the Rev. William Knox, son of the Bishop of Derry, and grandson of Lord Northland; she died in 1819, leaving three sons, William, Ferguson; and Thomas. Jane, third daughter, married John Montgomery of Benrarden, county Antrim, by whom she had a son, James, and two daughters, Barbara and Isabella. Eliza, fourth daughter, married John George Smyly, Q.C., by whom she had three sons and two daughters. Ellen, the younger daughter, married the Rev. Edward Newland. John, the eldest son, is a captain in the Londonderry Militia. Andrew Ferguson, second son, is rector of Aghadoey, county Londonderry, and canon of Derry Cathedral. William John is the third son.

Anne, third daughter of Robert Alexander of Boomhall, married Lieutenant-Colonel Alexander Scott, R.A., afterwards major-general; she died 18th September 1865.

Nathaniel, eldest son of Robert Alexander of Boomhall, was born on the 12th August 1760. Having studied at Harrow and at Emmanuel College, Cambridge, and obtained orders, he was collated precentor of Armagh in January 1796. In 1802 he became Bishop of Clonfert; and was in 1804 translated successively to the sees of Killaloe, and of Down and Connor. In 1823 he was appointed Bishop of Meath. He was D.D., and a member of the Privy Council of Ireland. He purchased the estate of Portglenone, county Antrim, and died at Dublin, 21st October 1840. He married in 1785 Anne, only surviving daughter of the Right Honourable Richard Jackson of Jackson Hall, county Derry, M.P., and heiress of her brother, Sir George Jackson, Bart. By her (she died in August 1837) he had seven sons and four daughters.

Anne, the eldest daughter, married — September 1813—the Rev. John Molesworth Staples, rector of Moville, second son of the Right Honourable John Staples of Lissan, county Tyrone, and brother of Catherine, first wife of Robert Alexander, Archdeacon of Down, and of the Marchioness of Ormonde, the Countess of Clancarty, and the Honourable Mrs Ponsonby. She died in 1869. Her second son is Sir Nathaniel Alexander Staples, Bart. of Dunmore, Queen's County.

Mary Jane, second daughter of Bishop Nathaniel Alexander, died unmarried.

Elizabeth Rebecca, third daughter, married John Armytage Nicholson of Balrath, county Meath; she died in 1860. Henrietta, fourth daughter, married Robert Smyth, Esq. of Gaybrook, county Westmeath.

Robert Alexander, eldest son of Bishop Nathaniel Alexander, was born in 1788. Having entered into holy orders, he became rector of Ahogill, and Archdeacon of Down; he succeeded his father in the estate of Portglenone. He married first, in 1813, Catherine, youngest daughter of the Right Hon. John Staples of Lissan, county Tyrone, by his second wife, the Honourable Harriet, daughter of Richard, third Viscount Molesworth; secondly, in 1832, Hester, eldest daughter of Alexander M'Manus of Mount Dens, county Antrim. The Ven. Robert Alexander died at Portglenone House on the 31st July 1840.

By his first wife, Archdeacon Alexander was father of four sons and seven daughters. Harriet, the eldest daughter, married John Wakefield, and died without issue. Ann, Louisa, and Mary, second, third, and fourth daughters, died without issue. Grace, fifth daughter, married Gilbert Nicholson of Glenmore, Drogheda. Catherine, the sixth daughter, married Molyneux Shaldham, Esq. Charlotte, the seventh daughter, is unmarried.

Nathaniel, eldest son of Archdeacon Alexander, succeeded to the estate of Portglenone. He was a deputy-lieutenant of Antrim, and sometime represented that county in Parliament.   He married Florinda, daughter of Richard Boyle, Esq., by the Hon. Alicia Handcock, daughter of Richard, Viscount Castlemaine.   He died in 1850, and was succeeded by his son, Robert Jackson Alexander, now of Port-glenone.

John Staples, second son of Archdeacon Alexander, died unmarried in India in 1843.   Robert, the third son, is unmarried.   George, the fourth son, died without issue.

Richard Jackson, second son of Bishop Nathaniel Alexander, died in 1810, unmarried.   James Alexander, the bishop's third son, was rector of Killegally, in King's County.   He married Alicia, daughter of Samuel Dopping of Lowtown, county Westmeath, and died in 1855, leaving a son, Nathaniel, who died in 1860.

Nathaniel, fourth son of Bishop Nathaniel Alexander, was a merchant in Calcutta, and acquired the estates of Craivagh, county Londonderry, and of Epsom, in the county of Surrey.   He married Charlotte, daughter of Noah Hickey, of the city of Dublin, by whom he had five sons—Nathaniel, born 1828, died 1865; Robert Hugh, born 1831; William James, born 1836; John Henry, born 1839; George Caledon, born 1842; and four daughters—Sophia Charlotte, born 1824, married the Rev. Charles Hay; Ann Isabella, born 1826; Mary Eliza, born 1830; and Henrietta Frances, born 1833.

Henry Alexander, fifth son of the Bishop of Meath,

was born on the 16th February 1803, and became a barrister-at-law.   He owns a considerable estate in the parish of Forkill, county Armagh, is a deputy-lieutenant, and was high sheriff of that county in 1856. He married, on the 14th August 1839, Lady Louisa Juliana, second daughter of Thomas, Earl of Ranfurly, by Mary Juliana, daughter of William Stuart, D.D., Lord Primate of Ireland, by whom he has six sons and five daughters.   Blanch Catherine Sophia Ann, the eldest daughter, was born in 1841; Alice Mary Juliana, second daughter, was born in 1843; Constance Henrietta Georgina, third daughter, born in 1845, married in 1867 Captain Colquhoun Grant, Judge of Hydrabad, Scinde; Emily Louisa Jane was born in 1850; and Edith Ellen, in 1864.

Granville Henry Jackson, eldest son of Henry Alexander of Forkill, was born in 1852, Henry Nathaniel in 1854, Claud Henry in 1856, Ronald Henry in 1858, Frederick Henry Thomas in 1860, Dudley Henry Blayney in 1863.

George, sixth son of Bishop Nathaniel Alexander, held an appointment in the Indian Civil Service. He married, in 1833, Rebecca, daughter of William Molloy of Rockvalley, county Tipperary, by whom he had one son, Nathaniel.

William Stuart, seventh son of Bishop Nathaniel Alexander, held an appointment in the Indian Civil Service.   He married Janet, daughter of Brigadier-General Charles Dallas, governor of St Helena, and niece of Sir Thomas Dallas, G.C.B., lieutenant-general, by whom he had three sons, William, who died in 1868, Nathaniel, and Charles.

Henry, second son of Robert Alexander of Boomhall, was called to the English bar. Purchasing Glentogher, an estate of four thousand acres, in county Donegal, he attained distinction for his agricultural enterprise. He represented the city of Londonderry from 1797 to 1801, and was sometime chairman of the Committee of Ways and Means. When his first cousin, afterwards Lord Caledon, was appointed governor at the Cape of Good Hope, he accompanied him as secretary to that colony. He died 6th May 1818. By his wife, —— Rivers, he had four daughters; the eldest is Mrs Rawlinson; the three others, Catherine, Mary, and Eliza, reside at Moville, county Donegal. Of his two sons, James was employed in the East India Company's service; he married Miss Harvey of Merlin Hall, county Donegal, and died in India. Robert is a general in the army, and resides at Blackheath, Kent.

William Alexander, third son of Robert Alexander of Boomhall, was a general in the army, and mayor of the city of Londonderry. He died on the 1st January 1824, aged fifty-six. He married Martha, daughter of Sir Robert Waller, Bart. of Lisbrian, and granddaughter of Samuel Waller * of Newport,

---

* Samuel Waller was a lineal descendant of Lieutenant-General Sir Hardress Waller, brother of Edmund Waller, the poet.

county Tipperary, and Ann, his wife, sister of Lord
Chancellor Jocelyn, by whom he had three sons
and one daughter, Catherine, who married George
Thompson of Clonskeagh Castle, county Dublin.
Waller, his second son, died unmarried in 1804.
William Ferguson, his third son, was an officer in
the Indian Army, and died 25th March 1833.

Robert Alexander, eldest son of General Alexander,
was born at Drogheda on the 17th September 1795.
He became rector of Aghadoey, and prebendary of
Derry; he died 11th May 1872. He married, 16th
October 1820, Dorothea, only child of Henry M'Clintock of Ballyarton, county Londonderry, by whom
he had three sons and five daughters. Mary, the
eldest daughter, born 6th June 1821, married, 17th
September 1845, William Keown Boyd of Ballydugan,
many years M.P. for Downpatrick, by whom she
has had eleven children. Richard, the eldest son, is an
officer in the navy; he married Florence, daughter of
Stephen Lushington, and niece of Sir Stafford North-
cote. Matilda, the second daughter, born 13th
August 1822, married Maximilian Hammond Dalison of Hampton, in the county of Kent, and has
eight children.

Elizabeth, third daughter of the Rev. Robert Alex-
ander, married, 10th January 1856, the Rev. Andrew
Ferguson Smyly, rector of Aghadoey and canon of
Derry, by whom she has had four children.

Katherine, fourth daughter, born in 1830, married

James Sinclair, second son of James Sinclair of Holly Hill, county Tyrone, by whom she has one daughter.

Dorothea, fifth daughter of the Rev. Robert Alexander, born in 1831, married, in 1856, Colonel Henry Keown, by whom she has had seven children.

The Right Rev. William Alexander, D.D., D.C.L., eldest son of the Rev. Robert Alexander, was born at Londonderry, 13th April 1824. He was educated at Tunbridge School, and at Exeter and Brasenose Colleges, Oxford. At that university he obtained the theological prize essay in 1850, and the university prize for a poem on a sacred subject in 1860. He also delivered an English ode in the Shelbrain Theatre, addressed to Lord Derby upon his installation as Chancellor in 1853. The bishop is D.D. by diploma, and received the honorary degree of D.C.L. in 1876; he has been select preacher and Bampton lecturer. He was appointed Dean of Emly in 1864, and was advanced to the bishopric of Derry and Raphoe in 1867. During the brief period of his career in the House of Lords, he delivered a speech upon the Irish Church, of which the *Times* said that "loud bursts of cheers greeted the bishop's animated address." The Bishop of Derry is the author of many separate lectures, discourses, poems, and charges. A long series of articles and reviews from his pen have appeared in the *Christian Remembrancer*, the *Contemporary Review, Good Words*, and, in

early life, in the *Dublin University Magazine*. In
1867 the bishop printed for private circulation,
" Specimens, Poetical and Critical." In 1872 he
published " The Leading Ideas of the Gospel :
Sermons preached before the University of Oxford;"
and in 1876, " The Witness of the Psalms to Christ
and Christianity " (Bampton Lectures). He married,
15th October 1852, Cecil Frances, daughter of Major
Humphreys, J.P., of Miltown House, county Tyrone.
Mrs Alexander is well known as author of " Moral
Songs," " Hymns for Little Children," " Hymns, De-
scriptive and Devotional," and other works ; her
noble lyric, " The Burial of Moses," has scarcely been
surpassed by Tennyson or Browning.

Robert Jocelyn Alexander, B.A., Brasenose College, Oxford, eldest son of Bishop William Alexander, while an undergraduate obtained the Newdi-
gate University prize for a beautiful and pathetic
poem on " The Last of the Red Indians." He was
born, June 11th, 1852, and married, in 1876, Alice
Rachel, daughter of J. J. Hamilton Humphreys.

Henry M'Clintock, second son of the Rev. Robert
Alexander, was born 7th October 1834. As a naval
officer, he has distinguished himself both in India and
New Zealand. He married, on the 22d October 1864,
Eliza Frances Charlotte, only daughter of Sir William
S. Wiseman, Bart., C.B.

Robert Waller, third son of the Rev. Robert Alexander, was born 4th April 1836. An officer in the

Indian Army, he was killed in action with the mutineers before Delhi on the 19th June 1857.

James, fourth son of Robert Alexander of Boomhall, proceeded to India, and there acquired a large fortune. Returning to Britain in 1811, he purchased the estate of Somerhill, Kent, and was appointed deputy-lieutenant for that county, and elected M.P. for Old Sarum. He married, first, Eliza, daughter of Captain Dundas; and secondly, on the 18th March 1813, Charlotte Sophia, daughter of Thomas Dashwood, and relict of the Hon. Charles Andrew Bruce, brother of the Earl of Elgin. He died on the 12th September 1848. By his first wife he had one child, Eliza Charlotte; and by his second marriage, two sons, Robert and James, and three daughters, Charlotte Sophia, Ann, and Jane. Eliza Charlotte, the eldest daughter, became in 1823 second wife of Sir Stratford Canning, G.C.B., British minister at Constantinople, afterwards Viscount Stratford de Redcliffe; Charlotte Sophia and Ann are unmarried; Jane, the youngest daughter, married General Sutherland; she died without issue.

Robert, eldest son of James Alexander of Somerhill, was born on the 10th February 1815. He married his cousin, Miss Fane, and died at his residence, near Oswestry, Shropshire, on the 23d October 1863.

James, second son of James Alexander of Somerhill, born 7th May 1823, married Ann, daughter of

Maximilian Dudley Dalison of Hampton, Kent.   He
is a banker in London, of the house of Alexander,
Fletcher, & Co.

Josias Duprè Alexander, fifth son of Robert Alexander of Boomhall, acquired a fortune in India.   In
1816 he purchased the estate of Stonehouse, Kent,
and was appointed a director of the East India Company, and elected M.P. for Old Sarum along with his
brother James.   He died 20th August 1839.   By his
wife, Mary, daughter of the Rev. Thomas Bracken, he
had two sons and eight daughters.   Of his daughters,
Lucy Emma, Ellen Louisa, and Fanny Selina, are
unmarried ; Charlotte Maria and Agnes Henrietta
died unmarried ; Mary Ann married James Pratt
Barlow, Esq. ; Eliza married, 22d January 1842,
Robert, son and heir of the Rev. Boughey Dolling
of Dollingstown, county Down ; Madeline married
Rev. A. Simpson.

Caledon Duprè, eldest son of Josias Duprè Alex-
ander of Stonehouse, was captain of the 1st Life
Guards.   He married Caroline, daughter of Willing
Ewing.

Josias Bracken, second son of Josias Duprè Alexander, married, 11th January 1848, Agnes Cecilia,
eighth daughter of Alderman Sir William Curtis,
Bart.

CHAPTER XXX.

JAMES ALEXANDER, third and youngest son of Alderman Nathaniel Alexander, was born at Londonderry
in 1730. He held several important offices in India,
and on his **return to** Britain was, in 1774, elected
M.P. for Londonderry, which he continued to represent till 1784. He was, on the 6th June 1790, created
Baron Caledon of Caledon, county Tyrone, in the
peerage of Ireland. In November 1797 he was
advanced to the dignity of Viscount Alexander, and
on the 29th December 1800 was created Earl of
Caledon. He married, 28th November 1774, Anne,
second daughter of James Crawfurd of Crawfurds-
burn, county Down (who died 21st December 1777),
by whom he had one son and two daughters. Lord
Caledon died 23d March 1802.

Lady Mabella, elder daughter of Lord Caledon,
born 7th August 1775, married, 5th July 1796,
Andrew Thomas, eleventh Baron Blayney, and became mother of the eighth and last Lord Blayney.

She died 4th March 1854. Lady Elizabeth, younger daughter of Lord Caledon, born 2d June 1776, died unmarried.

Duprè Alexander, second Earl of Caledon, only son of the first earl, was born 14th December 1777. He was Knight of the Most Illustrious Order of St Patrick, lord-lieutenant of the county of Tyrone, and colonel of the Tyrone Militia. His lordship married, 16th October 1811, Catherine Freman, second daughter of Philip, third Earl of Hardwicke, Lord-Lieutenant of Ireland, by whom he had an only son. His lordship died in 1839.

James Duprè, third Earl of Caledon, only son of the second earl, was born 27th July 1812. He was colonel of the Tyrone Militia, and captain in the Guards. He married, 4th September 1845, Lady Jane Frederica Harriet Mary Grimston, fourth daughter of the first Earl of Verulam, and had issue, three sons and one daughter. The earl died 30th June 1855.

Lady Jane Charlotte Elizabeth, only daughter of the third Earl of Caledon, is unmarried. Walter Philip, second son of the third earl, born 8th February 1849, is lieutenant in the Scots Greys. Charles, third son, born 26th January 1854, is an officer in the Tyrone Militia.

James, fourth Earl of Caledon, was born 11th July 1846, and succeeded his father 30th June 1855. His lordship is a captain in the Life Guards.

William Alexander, third and youngest son of John Alexander of Gunsland and Londonderry, and grandson of Captain Andrew Alexander, settled, before 1736, as a merchant in Dublin. He died in 1788. By his wife, Mary, daughter of —— Porter, of Vicardale, county Monaghan, he had two sons, William and Robert, and five daughters, Mary, Anne, Elizabeth, Sarah, and Jane. Jane died unmarried. Mary married William Jocelyn Shaw of Kentstown, county Meath. Anne married, 6th October 1764, Sir Richard Johnstone, Bart. of Gilford, county Down.

William, elder son of William Alexander of Dublin, was born on the 3d March 1743. Engaging in merchandise at Dublin, he became lord mayor of that city. For his public services he was created a baronet 11th December 1809. Sir William Alexander married, 1st August 1764, Catherine, daughter and heiress of John Folie Mapas of Rochetown, county Dublin, by whom he had two sons and two daughters.

Catherine, elder daughter of Sir William Alexander, Bart., married Robert Hamilton of Clonsillagh, county Dublin. Eliza, the younger daughter, married John Hamilton of Hacketstown, county Dublin.

William John, younger son of Sir William Alexander, Bart., served as an officer in the army. By his wife, Isabella, younger daughter of Robert Alexander of Seamount, he had four sons and three daughters. Harriet, the eldest daughter, married her cousin, the Rev. Godfrey Alexander. Elizabeth, the second daughter, is unmarried. Anne Catherine, the youngest daughter, married Captain Edward Barnes, eldest son of Sir Edward Barnes, late commander-in-chief in India; she died in 1876. Robert Henry, the second son, was killed in the retreat from Cabul in 1842; Henry, third son, died in India in 1856; Richard, fourth son, died in 1867.

William Alexander, eldest son of William John and Isabella Alexander, is a major in the army. He married, 10th September 1839, Mary, third daughter of the Right Hon. Edward Grey, Bishop of Hereford, by whom he has one son and six daughters. Major William Alexander is heir-apparent to the baronetcy.

Sir Robert Alexander, second baronet, elder son of the first baronet, was born 16th December 1769. He married 17th June 1796, Eliza, daughter and heiress of John Wallis, Esq., barrister-at-law, by whom he had three sons and two daughters. He died 1st December 1859.

Jane Anne, elder daughter of Sir Robert Alexander, married, 6th August 1833, Captain J. Nembhard Hibbert of Chalfont Park, Bucks. Catherine, younger daughter, died at London, unmarried, 15th April 1826.

Sir William John Alexander, third baronet, eldest son of Sir Robert the second baronet, was born 1st April 1797. Educated at Trinity College, Cambridge, he was called to the bar in 1825. Nominated Q.C. in 1844, he was afterwards appointed Attorney-General to the Prince of Wales. He died on the 31st March 1873.

Sir John Wallis Alexander, Bart., second son of Sir Robert Alexander, second baronet, was born 1st October 1800. He married, 18th May 1858, Lepel Charlotte Phipps, youngest daughter of Henry, first Earl of Mulgrave, and sister of Constantine Henry, first Marquis of Normandy; she died in 1859, without issue. John Wallis Alexander succeeded his brother in 1873 as fourth baronet.

Robert Duprè, third son of Sir Robert Alexander, married, 17th September 1833, Eliza, youngest daughter of B. B. Nembhard of Jamaica, by whom he has had two sons and two daughters. Robert Duprè, the elder son, was born on the 4th July 1834, and died in infancy. Raynsford Duprè, second son, was born 25th December 1835. Caroline Charlotte, the elder daughter, married Philip Villiers Reid, Esq., county Clare. Another daughter was born in September 1839.

Robert Alexander of Seamount and Garristown, county Dublin, younger son of William Alexander, merchant, Dublin, married, in May 1785, Henrietta Judith, daughter of Henry Quin, M.D., physician-general to the forces in Ireland, by whom he had eight sons and six daughters, of whom, three sons and three daughters died young and unmarried. Robert Alexander died at London on the 14th July 1827.

Anne, elder daughter of Robert Alexander of Sea-mount and Garristown, married the Rev. J. Nussey. Isabella, younger daughter, married Captain William John Alexander, second son of Sir William Alexander, Bart.

William James, eldest son and heir of Robert Alexander of Seamount and Garristown, married Gertrude, eldest daughter of Gustavus Handcock Temple, by whom he had two sons, Robert Quin and Gustavus, and a daughter, Mary. Gustavus and Mary Alexander died unmarried. Robert Quin Alexander, now of Garristown, married Miss Reilly, by whom he has two sons and five daughters. The daughters are unmarried.

Henry, second son of Robert Alexander of Sea-mount and Garristown, was a director of the East India Company, and M.P. for Barnstaple. He married, first, Elizabeth, daughter of Joseph Pringle, Esq., Consul-General of Madeira; secondly, on the 4th January 1843, Sabina Hester, eldest daughter of Thomas Taylor of Sevenoaks, Kent, by Lady Lucy Rachel, youngest daughter of Charles, third Earl of Stanhope. Of these marriages were born three sons, Henry Robert, William Charles, and Frederic, and three daughters, Harriet, Fanny, and Leonora. Henry Robert, the eldest son, married Elizabeth, daughter of Colonel Young, of the Honourable East India Company's service; he died in 1869.

The Rev. Charles Alexander, rector of Drumcree,

in the diocese of Armagh, third son of Robert Alexander, married Elizabeth, daughter of Edward Smith Godfrey of Newark, Nottinghamshire, by whom he had a son, Godfrey, and a daughter, Isabella. Godfrey Alexander is in holy orders, and is rector of Stoke Bliss, Herefordshire, and domestic chaplain to the Earl of Caledon; he married Miss Alexander Shaw. Isabella Alexander married Thomas **Rawlinson**, by whom she has two sons and two daughters.

Robert, fourth son of Robert Alexander of Seamount and Garristown, held an appointment in India. He died in April 1814, without issue.

Edward Alexander, fifth son of Robert Alexander, died in 1872 without issue.

CHAPTER XXXI.

FAMILIES OF M'ALEXANDER AND ALEXANDER, IN THE COUNTIES OF ANTRIM, ARMAGH, AND DOWN, AND OF ENAGH, CAW, AND KILFENNEN, IN THE COUNTY OF DERRY.

MEMBERS of the sept of MacAlexander of Dalcussen and Dalreoch, in the southern or Carrick district of Ayrshire, settled on the Scottish coast, and trading to the opposite shores, there planted their families. The distance from Stranraer to Larne in Antrim is thirty-nine miles. According to a tradition which obtains among the Irish families, an exodus of the sept of MacAlexander from Galloway to the coast of Larne, took place in the reign of Charles I.

In the Hearth Tax Rolls of the county of Antrim for 1666, the name of MacAlexander occurs frequently. In the Rolls of Ballymena parish are named John M'Alexander and Hugh M'Alexander. In the parish of Islandmagee, William M'Alexander and Alexander M'Alexander are named. In the Rolls of Ballyter appear the names of Robert M'Alexander, James M'Alexander, and John M'Alexander. In the same district are recorded James M'Alexander at Doagh, and John M'Alexander.

In 1701 John M‘Alexander in the diocese of Connor and county of Antrim executed his will; he refers to five sons, naming Samuel and Hugh; also three daughters (Will in Prerogative Court).

During the reign of Charles I. a family named Alexander, adherents of the Covenant, fled from Dumbartonshire,* and obtained a settlement in the parish of Kilwaughter, near Larne.   William Alexander of the parish of Kilwaughter is mentioned in the Hearth Tax Roll of 1666.   Mrs Janet Alexander, who resided at Kilwaughter, died in 1709, bequeathing to John Alexander, her brother, "one boll of oats" (Will in Probate Court).

In the Rent Roll of the Jointure Lands of Anne, Countess of Clanbrassill, William Alexander is named in 1689 as renting for one pound yearly the lands of Ardigon in the parish of Killileagh; and in the same year William Alexander is entered in a rental of £2, 5s. for subjects situated in the town of Killileagh. In the same Rent Roll, "Widow Alexander" appears in 1691 as paying £4, 8s. for premises in the town of Killileagh (Hamilton MSS., pp. 126, 127).

In the barony of Carey in the northern district of Antrim, John Alexander is in the Subsidy Rolls of 1661, and in 1666, assessed in six pounds sterling.

* A connection between the families of Alexander of Stirling and those of Dumbarton is indicated by the following minute: "At Stirling the 14th day of August 1606, the eldership of the Kirk being convenit; the bretherin thinkis meet that Cuthbert Cunningham, Provost of Dumbartom Colledge, sall pay *ad pios usus* fyve pundis money for the passage through the Kirk to burie the corps of umq¹ Janet Alexander, his spous" (Kirk Session Records of Stirling).

In 1730 " Margaret Alexander, widow," undertakes along with Thomas Alexander to administer the estate of Robert Alexander, who lived in the parish of Ahoghill and district of Connor (Connor Wills). On the 8th January 1735, Thomas Alexander of Ballyclare, in the parish of Ahoghill, executed his will (Will in Probate Court). He seems to have been succeeded as tenant at Ballyclare by James Alexander, who died in February 1770, aged sixty (Tombstone Inscription in Ballybinny Churchyard, county Antrim). The next tenant at Ballyclare (Size Hill Farm), was James Alexander, who is named in a rent roll in 1798 (Estate Register of the Marquis of Donegal). His tombstone in the churchyard of Ballybinny is thus inscribed : " In memory of James Alexander of Size Hill, who died on the 31st May 1810, aged forty years. Also his wife Elizabeth, who died on the 13th August 1843, aged sixty-nine years."

Thomas Alexander, tenant at Ballynure, cousin of the preceding, had a son James, now a physician at Belfast.

William Alexander of the townland of Ballyhound, in the parish of Carnmoney, executed his will on the 9th July 1775, bequeathing his property and effects to his wife and children (Will in Probate Court). In the same parish Hugh Alexander rented about 1750 the farm of Carntall on the Donegal estate. He had three sisters, who married and had families, of whom the greater number emigrated to America. He married and had four sons, Hugh, James Ramsay, John, and Thomas. John, the third son, rented the farm of Ballyalbaragh at Ballyclare. He died in March 1839. In his farm he was succeeded by his son Thomas, who survives (Family Information).

In the same district, James Alexander rented the farm of Cogry in 1775 (Estate Register of the Marquis of Donegal). In this farm he was succeeded by William Alexander, whose representative, John Alexander of Cogry, died in 1815, aged sixty-seven (Tombstone in Rashee Churchyard). Martha Alexander, his daughter, married Conway M'Nicol, who rented the farm of Cogry, and died in 1863.

John Alexander, farmer at Doagh, near Ballyclare, executed his will on the 2d February 1786. He bequeathed his movable estate to his grandchildren, Martha, Margaret, and Jane Alexander.

Samuel Alexander of Ballymena, who rented the farms of Ballynaskie and Clogher, executed his will on the 13th December 1790, and died in 1792. He divided the farm of Ballynaskie between his sons, John and James, and made bequests to his son Patrick and his daughter Jane (Will in Probate Court).

Robert Alexander, in the parish of Glenavy, in the county of Antrim, died in 1776; his will is dated 10th April of the same year. He made bequests to his sons, Robert and David; to his daughters, Mary, otherwise Courtney; Jean, otherwise M'Canbry; and Elizabeth, otherwise Durham; also to Robert, James, John, William, and Elizabeth Alexander, the children of his son Thomas (Will in Probate Court).

In a bond, dated 20th August 1788, Jane Alexander, widow of Robert Alexander, of the parish of Glenavy, undertakes to pay to the Lord Bishop of Down and Connor, or his successors, the sum of £1000. Henry Alexander is named in the bond (Bond in Probate Court).

From the family of Alexander of Ballyclare sprung those families of the name who now reside at Larne and Carrickfergus. John Alexander, merchant in Larne, died in 1809. In his will, dated 10th June 1807, he bequeathed a portion of his substance to his sons, James and William (Will in Probate Court).

The Rev. Nathaniel Alexander, minister of the Presbyterian congregation at Crumlin, in the county of Antrim, belonged to the family of Alexander of Ballyclare. From 1788 to 1802 he successfully conducted an educational institution. He was married, but died without issue. From the family of Alexander of Ballyclare also descended the Rev. Thomas Alexander, minister at Cairncastle, county Antrim. Son of Robert Alexander, farmer at Knockcairn, near Crumlin, county Antrim, he was born on the 1st January 1770. He studied at the University of Glasgow; and being licensed to preach by the Presbytery of Templepatrick, was, in 1793, ordained assistant minister of the Presbyterian congregation at Cairncastle. In 1829 he joined the Unitarian or Remonstrant Secession from the General Synod of Ulster. Resigning his charge in 1840, he latterly proceeded to London, where he died on the 26th May 1851. He married the only daughter of the Rev. Mr Lewson, his predecessor at Cairncastle, by whom he had five sons, John, Robert, Thomas, Lewson, and Henry, and one daughter, Jane. John and Robert died without issue; Thomas, who resides at Iowa, United States, has five children. Lewson is settled in Belgium, and has five children; Henry is minister of the Unitarian congregation at Newry (*Christian Unitarian Magazine*, vol. iv., pp. 332-338, 336-372, and Private Information).

A branch of the family of MacAlexander of southern Ayrshire emigrated to Ireland from Glenluce, Wigtownshire, in the reign of Charles I. Thomas Mac-Alexander from Glenluce settled at Tanderagee, near Gilford, in the county Armagh. He married, and left a son, William, who, studying medicine, practised as a physician at Rathfirland, county Down. He married Elizabeth Todd, by whom he had four sons, John, William, Thomas, and James, and two daughters, Jane and Margaret. John became a physician, and practised at Rathfirland; he and his brothers, William and James, died without issue. Thomas, the third son, married Isabella Chambers of Rathfirland, and left two sons, John and William, and two daughters, Eliza and Martha. The elder daughter, Eliza, married William Rae of the island of Bermuda; Martha, the younger daughter, is wife of the Rev. H. Osborne of Holywood. John, the elder son, formerly of Phillistown House, Trim, in the county of Meath, is now resident in Canada. William, the second son, is a graduate in medicine, and a staff-surgeon in the army* (Family Information).

In the Hearth Tax Roll of the barony of Onealand and parish of Shankill, county Armagh, for 1664, " Culbert [Cuthbert] Alexander " at " Munbreefe " is assessed two shillings for one hearth.

Fergus MacAlexander, of the family of Dalreoch, parish of Colmonel, Ayrshire, who was a bursar of the University of Glasgow in 1631, was appointed minister of the Presbyterian congregation, first at Kilmud (Kilmood), and afterwards at Greyabbey, in the county of Down ; he was subsequently admitted parish minister of Barr, in the county of Ayr, where he died in 1687 (see *supra*, vol. ii., p. 51).

William Alexander, a member of the Ayrshire family of Dalreoch, settled in the district of Londonderry. In the Cathedral Registry of Londonderry is the following entry : " Fergus, the son of William Alexander, bap. the 21 Aprill 1655."

---

* Dr William Alexander possesses as an heirloom a table cover about five feet square, woven with an earl's coronet in the centre, surrounded with the rose, shamrock, and thistle. A coronet is also woven into the four corners, with the letters E. W. A. inserted between the spikes of a purple crown.

A supposed member of this family, John Alexander, settled about the year 1666 in the vicinity of Lough Enagh, in the parish of Glendermott and county of Londonderry.   In 1686 he purchased the lands of Caw, about two miles to the eastward of Londonderry, on the east bank of Ross's Bay.

William, son of John Alexander of Enagh and Caw, succeeded his father in these lands.   He married, and had three sons, Samuel, John, and Robert.

Robert, the youngest son, emigrated to America. Refusing to join the party who contended for independence, he returned to Britain.   He afterwards sailed for America with letters of recommendation from Charles James Fox; but the vessel was lost at sea, and he perished with the other passengers.   He married Miss Wilmot, an American gentlewoman, and two of his sons became judges in the United States.

John, second son of William Alexander, owned lands in Kilfennan, Enagh, and part of Gransagh, in the liberties of Londonderry; he died in 1801.   In his will, which was executed on the 30th August 1800, he bequeathed to his nephew, John Alexander, son of his brother Samuel, that part of the lands of Kilfennan which he purchased from David Wilson; also the lands of Coshquean and Bonnymain, in the barony of Inneshowen, held in lease from the Marquis of Donegal; also his title and interest in the lands of Enagh, in the liberties of Londonderry; also part of the lands of Gransagh in the said liberties.   To his nephew, Samuel Alexander, to his brother, Samuel, and other relatives, he bequeathed moneys (Will in Probate Court).

Samuel Alexander, eldest son of William Alexander of Caw, was born in 1725, and died in 1814, aged eighty-nine.   He married Sarah Ross, by whom he had three sons, Samuel, John, and William, and two daughters, Jane and Sarah.   William, the youngest son, died young.   Samuel, the eldest, succeeded his father in the estate of Caw, and died without leaving issue.

John, second son of Samuel Alexander, succeeded his brother in the estate of Caw.   He was born in 1770, and died in February 1852.   He married Hannah Richardson Murray, descended from Colonel Adam Murray, distinguished on the Royalist side at the siege of Londonderry, by whom he had three sons, Samuel, John, and Adam Murray, and two daughters, Hannah and Sarah Jane.

John, youngest son of John Alexander, became a doctor of medicine, married, and left a daughter.

Adam Murray, second son, was born in 1809.   He became a barrister-at-law, and for many years officiated as judge in the Supreme Court of British Guiana. He died unmarried in 1874.

The Rev. Samuel Alexander, the eldest son, was born in 1808.   He is rector of Termon, diocese of Armagh, and county of Tyrone.   He married Charlotte

Frances Beresford, by whom he has had three sons, John Adam, Charles Murray, and Henry; also three daughters. John Adam Alexander, the eldest son, resides on the estate of Caw, and is a magistrate in the county of Derry. Charles Murray, the second son, is a captain in the Royal Tyrone Fusiliers, and possesses the estate of Enagh, under the will of his uncle, Adam Murray Alexander.

CHAPTER XXXII.

FAMILY OF ALEXANDER OF DUBLIN.

IN the reign of Charles I., Robert Alexander, son of John Alexander the elder, of Candren, Paisley, settled in Dublin. In the Subsidy Roll of that city, dated 1st February 1637-8, are named in "St Nicholas parish without the walls, Robert Grococke and Robert Alexander;" they are together assessed "in bonis" the sum of £3, 6s. 8d. Two nephews of Robert Alexander, John and James, sons of his elder brother John,* of Candren, Paisley, proceeded from Scotland to Dublin, and there settled.

John Alexander engaged in business as a lime agent (Book of Judgments, Public Record Office, Dublin). He died in 1671 intestate, and on the 20th December of that year, letters of administration were granted to his widow, Catherine Alexander, and William Hartley, his son-in-law, and Avia, his daughter, for the use of

---

* The relationship subsisting between the families of Alexander of Candren, Paisley, and James Alexander of Dublin, is confirmed by Wodrow, who, in describing the sufferings of John Spreul, Paisley (whose mother, Janet Alexander, was daughter of John Alexander of Candren, Paisley), remarks : "He was in Ireland with his uncle, Mr James Alexander, in May 1679, and came over to Scotland after the scuffle at Drumclog in June" (Wodrow's History of the Scottish Church, ed. 1829, vol. iii., p. 252)

Catherine Hartley, daughter of the said William Hartley and Avia Alexander. On the 22d December 1677, Catherine Hartley, styled " of Blind Key, Dublin," administered the affairs of her grandmother, Mrs Catherine Alexander (Grant Book, Probate Court, Dublin).

James Alexander settled in Dublin as an attorney. His name first occurs in the Public Records of Dublin in 1665. On the 6th December of that year, Ellen Gascoigne, widow, empowered and authorised James Alexander—styled " of the city of Dublin, gent."—to receive all sums of money payable to her from His Majesty's Exchequer, upon the Lord-Deputy's warrant, and to grant discharge for the same (Assignment Records, Dublin, vol. iii., 256). In the same records (vol. vi., p. 61) a power of attorney is granted to James Alexander by Lieut.-Colonel George Stewart,* dated 21st April 1668, wherein the colonel constitutes him his " true and lawful agent to aske, receive, and demand, all such sumes of money as are or shall grow due to the Company of Foot under his command."

On the 4th January 1671, James Alexander obtained from William Stewart † of Ballilan, in the barony of Raphoe and county of Donegal, authority " to receive

---

* Colonel George Stewart was son of Sir Robert Stewart. He sometime resided at Culmore, near Londonderry (Lodge's Peerage, edited by Archdall, vol. vi., p. 244).

† William Stewart was eldest son of Sir William Stewart, Bart., who was created Baron Stewart of Ramelton, and Viscount Mountjoy in 1682. He became a lieutenant-general in the army, and succeeded his father as second Viscount Mountjoy in 1692. He died 10th January 1727.

rents due to him by George Pryott of Edmontoune, in the city of Dublin, and to compound with the commissioners authorised for satisfying forty-nine officers of the thousand per lot for his part of the same" (Assignment Records, vol. vii., p. 89).

In 1680 and 1681, James Alexander appeared as attorney for Francis, Earl of Longford, Ambrose Aungier, John Gordon, James Hartley of Dublin, ironmonger, and Michael Gaynor of Black Castle, in a suit raised against them by Humphrey Perrott (Book of Judgments).

James Alexander held for ten years subsequent to 1672, the office of deputy-clerk of the Pells, in the Exchequer Court (Revenue Accounts).

Among the Irish Chancery Rolls for 1674, are four deeds, by which Henry, Earl of Clanbrassill,* and Alice his wife, conveyed lands in the county of Down to James Ross, John Blackwood, James Mure, and David Kennedy—James Alexander acting as attorney for the purchasers (Public Record Office, Dublin).

A zealous promoter of the Presbyterian Church, James Alexander received on the 7th November 1698, a mandate authorising him to draw the quarter's payment of £1200, granted to the Church as an annual boon by William III. (Assignment Records).

James Alexander married as his first wife, a

---

* James Hamilton, second Viscount Claneboye, was promoted as Earl of Clanbrassill, in the county of Armagh, on the 7th June 1647. He married Lady Anne Carey, eldest daughter of Henry, Earl of Monmouth, who married secondly Sir Robert Maxwell, Bart. Lord Clanbrassill died 20th June 1659.

daughter of Peter Blanchville of Blanchvilletown, in the county of Kilkenny. Sometime prior to 1676, Peter Blanchville was succeeded in his estates by his son Edmund, for on the 11th June of that year, James Alexander received from the said Edmund, on a payment of £500, a bond on "the castles, towns, and lands of Blanchvilletown, Blanchvilleskill, Blanchvillespark, Smithstown, Bennett's Bridge, Carlin, Severstown, Madogstown, and Church Claragh, in the barony of Gowran, and county of Kilkenny." The loan had not been redeemed when Edmund Blanchville was, on the 13th February 1688, forfeited for high treason. After certain proceedings, James Alexander, on the 10th August 1700, presented to the Trustees of the Court of Claims, a statement of claims against the forfeited lands. Among these is a claim for £200, for which, on account of Edmund Blanchville, he had become bound to Charles Agar, on the 24th September 1675. Certain of the bonds, he represents, had been "lost or mislaid in the late troublesome times, when the claimant carried away papers into England, about the month of January 1688, in a confused manner," and were held by the Court "to be comprehended within the benefit of the capitulation or articles of Limerick" (Decrees of Court of Claims).

James Alexander died on the 3d March 1701. The following document, purporting to be his will with a codicil attached, was on the 23d August 1701,

proved in the Prerogative Court of Dublin, by Richard
Fenner, his son-in-law, "without prejudice to Edmund
Alexander," the testator's son and a co-executor :

"I, James Alexander, of the cittie of Dublin, being this 25th
day of December in the year of our Lord 1699, in perfect health
and sound memory, praised be God for the same, but considering the uncertainty of this life, many younger than I being
taken away by sudden death or short sickness, do now deliberately make and write with my own hand, this as my last Will
& Testament, hereby revoaking and makeing void all former
will or pretensions either by word or writing, and this to be
taken as my last Will & Testament.   In the first place, I
comitt my soul to Almighty God, hoping through the merits of
my blessed Lord, Jesus Christ, to obtain mercy and pardon of
all my sins, &c., and my body to be decently buried as the
Freinds who shall be near me at the time of my death shall
think fitt.   And if it shall happen that I dy in or near the cittie of
Dublin, I desire to be buryed in ye same grave in St Clevan's
churchyard, where my last wife was buried, it being deep and
having most room, close to the left side of my first wife's grave,
and this to be done without any charge, but what is absolutely
necessary.   And for settling what little concerns I have in the
world, I desire my debts may be satisfied, as easily as my undernamed Executors can deall with my creditors, who are very few,
all that I can think of being only a bond * to David Kennedy
of Ballycultra, in the county of Down, which I think is under
one hundred or eighty pounds, which debt I design paying him

---

* This bond is referred to in the will of David Kennedy of Ballycultra, dated
22d April 1697, and proved in the Prerogative Court at Dublin.   In the schedule
of assets he has the following : "James Alexander of the city of Dublin, gent.,
by bond and judgment, dated March 3, 1693-4, payable the first —— 1694.
Judgment entered in the Common Pleas" (Records in Dublin Probate Court).
David Kennedy belonged to the parish of Dundonald, county Down.   He served
as captain under the Earl of Mount Alexander, in 1649, when the earl commanded in Ulster.   By Act of Settlement he obtained £1482, 1s. 4d. as arrears
of pay (MS. preserved among the Family Papers at Donaghadee, and Irish Record
Commission Reports, vol. iii., p. 296).

with a bond due to me by Sir Robert Hamilton,[*] with considerable interest. I think the penalty is now due. I hope Mr Kennedy will be reasonable in his demands, in regard he had Lodging & Dyett at my house severall times that he was in Dublin, which I leave to himselfe as he thinks fitt. Another bond for about seventy pounds to John Usher, Esq.,[†] who discounted with me for a debt of money that I lent to his brother Adam Usher,[‡] and which I think was about halfe of the principal that John Usher may clayme of me. This debt to Mr Usher was the relict of an old account between him & the Lord Glenawly,[§] and I do believe Mr Usher doth not expect more than I paid or lent his said brother, Mr Adam Usher, he never to this day having demanded or spoke of it to me, however he is a worthy good gent., & I leave it to his own discretion. And for what debts are due to myselfe, I have them all by way of Deb^r. & Cred^r. in my long book, and do desire that all my worldly substance may be equally divided amongst my four children—viz., my sons Edmond, Richard, & John, and my daughter Hannah, and if any of them dye before they be fitt to receive their portions, I desire that the portion of such child or children that shall so dye may be divided amongst those of them that shall survive, & because I am at an uncertainty about my son-in-law, Richard Fenner, whose portion I designed to be paid him out of the debt due to me upon the estate of Edmond Blanchvill, of the county of Kilkenny, Esq., the same seeming to be in hazard if the said Blanchvill be not restored, and if so, I desire that he may come in for a share as the rest of my children, besides

* Sir Robert Hamilton of Mount Hamilton, son of Sir Hans Hamilton of Monella, was created a baronet in 1682; he died in 1703 (The Hamilton MSS., Belfast, 4to, p. 162).

† John Usher of Monachan, Master in Chancery, eldest son of Sir Walter Usher of Portrane, county Dublin, by his wife Elizabeth, daughter of Sir William Parsons of Bellamont, Lord-Justice of Ireland (Burke's Landed Gentry).

‡ The Rev. Adam Usher, a brother of the preceding.

§ Hugh, Lord Hamilton of Glenawly, was second son of Malcolm Hamilton, Archbishop of Cashel. He entered the Swedish service, in which he became Master-General of Artillery. He was raised to the peerage in 1660. He died in 1724. James Alexander acted as attorney for Lord Glenawly, and was authorised to administer his affairs during his absence abroad (Assignment Records, Dublin).

one hundred sterling, with the interest thereof, that I left with the said Richard Fenner when I went out of this kingdom, beginning of the late warr, and which he lent out and took bond to Audley Mervin, Esq.,* and I do hereby appoint the said Richard Fenner, and my son Edmond Alexander, to be executors of this my last Will, praying & enjoyning that they take speciall care that my three younger children by my second wife, be well secured their portions till they come to age to make use thereof themselves. And it is also my earnest desire and request, that care may be taken for their education & learning, and that they may be put to such Trades or Callings as may be thought most suitable for them, & that in every respect they may be soe treated & regard had to them as if they had been all borne of one Mother. One thing furder I desire, that if any of the children of Walter Morison, late of Convent Garden, London, Taylor, be alive, that there may be Twenty pounds paid them, I having been formerly concerned for the said Walter Morrison, that I am conscious that I ought to give them so much. This is my Will, which I have now deliberately written with my own hand, and do sign & subscribe the same, the day & year aforesaid.   JA. ALEXANDER.

"Signed & sealed in the presence of
John Matthews, Elizabeth Jones, Deborah Gill.

"The above being my last Will, I have nothing to add at present, but the debt due by Blanchvill seeming now to be good from the Trustees, I order Mr Fenner in the first place to be satisfied all due to him; and the rest to my son Edmond; but if it prove otherwise then I have good reason to believe, it will do well yet, & in that case I desire that Mr Fenner and my son Edmond may come in for a share of the redyest money, also hoping other debts may prove good, out of which I leave and bequeath to my grandchildren by Mr Fenner, three hundred pounds to be divided amongst them, and if any of them dye, the share of such to go amongst those that survive as their Father

---

* Probably a son of Sir Audley Mervyn, the celebrated soldier and Speaker of the Irish House of Commons.

sees fitt, but if wee find good success in our affaire, then I intend to augment them.   In witness whereof I have subscribed these presents, this first day of March 1701.

" JA. ALEXANDER." *

John M'Clelan, husband of Hannah Alexander, daughter of James Alexander by his second wife, disputed the validity of the will, which became the subject of a protracted suit.   On the 20th September 1707, it is set forth in the Grant Book of the Prerogative Court that Marmaduke Coghill, commissary of that Court, had adjudged the will ineffectual, on the ground that Richard Fenner and Edmond Alexander had suppressed the truth in connection with it. A decree was consequently granted, that the affairs of the deceased should be administered by Hannah M'Clelan, *alias* Alexander, and Edmond, Richard, and John Alexander, lawful children of the deceased.

The children of James Alexander, by his first wife, the daughter of Peter Blanchville, were Susannah, Sarah, and Edmond ; and by his second wife, Richard James, John, and Hannah.

Susannah, elder daughter of James Alexander by his first wife, married, 10th January 1692, James Agar of Gowran Castle, in the county of Kilkenny, whose mother, Ellis Blanchville, was her mother's sister.† She had a son, James, and two other sons,

---

* Dublin Probate Court.

† Charles Agar, of an old family in the county of York, settled at Gowran Castle, in the county of Kilkenny. He died 14th February 1696. By his marriage with Ellis, daughter of Peter Blanchville of Blanchvilletown, county Kilkenny, he had a son, James, who succeeded him in his estate. On the death of

* K

who all died in infancy. She died prior to the 25th December 1699, the date of her father's will.

Sarah, daughter of James Alexander by his first wife, espoused Richard Fenner of the city of Dublin, whom she predeceased. She had four sons, James, Alexander, Edmond, and William; and three daughters, Elizabeth, who married —— Parry, Susannah, and Mary.*

Edmond, only son of James Alexander by his first wife, died unmarried in 1716. His will, proved in the Prerogative Court of Dublin by his nephew, James Fenner, on the 29th March 1716, proceeds thus :

"In the name of God, Amen, the 13th May 1706.—I, Edmond Alexander of the city of Dublin, being of sound and perfect memory (praise be to God for the same), and knowing ye uncertainty of this life, and being desirous to settle things in order, do make this my last Will & Testament, that is to say,—*First*, and principally, I commend my soul to Almighty God, my Creator, assuredly believing y^t I shall receive full pardon and free remission of all my sins, and be saved by the precious death and meritts of my blessed Saviour and Redeemer, Christ Jesus. And my body to be buried in St Cavanis Churchyard, near my mother & sister (if I dye in Dublin); if I dye in the county of Kilkenny, I desire to be buryed in the tomb at St Kenny's Church (belonging to my mother's family), in such decent manner as to my Executors hereafter named, shall seem meet and convenient. And as touching such worldly estate as

Susannah Alexander, his first wife, he married, secondly, Mary, eldest daughter of Sir Henry Wemyss of Danesfort, county Kilkenny (who died in 1771, aged 106), and had by her sons and daughters. James Agar, eldest son of Henry, his eldest son, was created Baron Clifden, 27th July 1776 ; the eldest son of his second son, James, was, on the 6th June 1790, created Lord Callan ; and Charles, third son of his eldest son, was appointed Archbishop of Dublin, and in 1806 was created Earl of Normanton.

* See will of Edmond Alexander, *infra.*

it has pleased God to bless me with, my will and meaning is, ye same shall be employed and be bestowed as hereafter by this my will is expressed; and, first, I do revoke, renounce, frustrate, and make void all wills by me formerly made, and declare & appoint this my last Will & Testament.

"*First*, I will y^t all those debts which I owe in right or conscience to any manner of persons whatever shall be well and truly paid by my Executors undernamed. Item, I give & bequeath to my sister, Hannah Alexander, *alias* M'Clelan, the sum of five shillings and five pence, to buy her husband a glass eye, and this with the consent of her three counsellors, Elizabeth, Richard, & Jenny Jones. Item, I give and bequeath to my brother, Richard Alexander, the sum of five shillings, to purchase his guardian a Rattle. Item, I give and bequeath to my brother, John Alexander, the sum of five shillings; I intended him ye best share of what I had, but as he has turned me from being his guardian, so I now do him with this five shillings to buy him more understanding in the future. Item, I leave Mrs Jones my pardon for her perjury about my Father's will, & hope she may heartily repent and make her peace with God. Item, I will that all my substance be equally divided amongst my dearest sister, Fenner's, children; y^t is, to James, Alexander, Edmond, William Fenner, & to Elizabeth Fenner, *alias* Parry, Susanna, and Mary Fenner, to be paid them at the age of one-and-twenty, & if any of them dye before they arrive at that age, ye share of such child or children to be equally divided amongst the remaining children of my sister Fenner. Item, I leave as a legacy to Mrs Elizabeth Tarnoll's of King's Steet, in Bloomsbury, in London, the sum of five pounds sterling, for her care of me in my sickness, besides a debt due to her. Item, I leave James Agar and his lady each a guiney to buy a mourning ring. Item, I leave Mr James Cowan a mourning ring, of a guinea value. I do appoint Richard Fenner and his son, James Fenner, to be executors of this my last will, &c.   EDM. ALEXANDER.

" *Witnesses,* { Peter Agar.
Richd Malloy.
Owen Sullivan."

(Dublin Probate Court).

Richard James Alexander, elder son of James Alexander of Dublin by his second marriage, acquired the small estate of Mawdlins, near Trim, in the county of Meath.   He married Margaret Hughes, and had issue, two daughters, Hannah and Mary. He died in 1725.   His will, dated 13th July 1725, was proved by his brother, John, on the 2d February 1726 ; it contains the following :

" That the settlement made upon intermarryage in favour of my dear child and daughter, Hanna Alexander, shall continue, as at present, in the hands of William Lingan, Esq., in the Castle of Dublin, save y^t in case of her death her hundred and fifty pounds shall descend to the survivor of my two daughters ; but in case of both their deaths, the same to remain still at interest for the use of my beloved wife, Margaret Alexander, *alias* Hughes ; but in case of the death of all three, to remain for the use of my dear brother and sister, Mr John Alexander and Hanna Maclelan, *alias* Alexander.   As for the lease of my house on Lesyrshill, Dublin, I leave it for the use of my dear wife, Margaret, and daughter, Mary Alexander.   Item, my proportion of ye fund lying in the hand of Mr Young, near St Catherine's Church in Dublin, the interest of which comes to three pounds per annum, I leave to be disposed of in the best manner for the use of said Margaret, my wife, and Mary, my daughter.   Item, the hundred pounds lying in the hands of Mr James Eagar [Agar] of Gowran, in the county of Kilkenny, to continue at interest for use of said Margaret, my wife, and Mary, my daughter.   Item, all my goods and chattels, etc., here at ye Maudlins, near Trim, with what money lyes in my brother John Alexander's hands, to be also equally for the use of my said wife Margaret, and Mary, my daughter ; but in case of the death of my daughter Mary, I order her moyety of all above mentioned to be divided between my wife Margaret, and daughter Hanna, and in case of the death of both the latter, for my brother and sister as before. I order my sister, Sara Hughes, upon account of attending me some time as an honest servant, five pounds sterling to put her to some honest employment, out of the product of my goods. I order my lawfull debts should be paid out of the bulk of my worldly substance as soon as possible; funeral charges, book debts due to Mr Anthony, Trim, to be paid by my brother John. Item, I leave the charge of both my children to my dear wife, Margaret Alexander, as long as she behaves herself towards them as a good mother, but in case of her second marryage, I leave the charge of my daughter Hanna to her uncle and my brother-in-law, Mr James Bath of Nettstowne. Lastly, I constitute my brother, John Alexander, and brother-in-law, said James Bath, executors of this my last will and testament, to see justice done in every particular. RICHARD JAMES ALEXANDER."

A codicil is added, in which the testator desires that the money lying in his brother John's hands be forthwith paid to discharge debt (Dublin Probate Court).

Hannah Alexander, only daughter of James Alexander by his second marriage, married John M'Clelan, of the city of Dublin.

John, youngest son of James Alexander of Dublin, became a student of Glasgow College, session 1700-1. In the Matriculation Register of that University he has, on the 3d March 1701, recorded his name thus: "Johannes Alexander, Scot. Hib." The affix *Scoto-Hibernicus* indicates that, though a native of Ireland, the signer was of Scottish descent.

By his father's will, John Alexander was, as a minor, placed, with his brother, Richard James, under the care of their half-brother, Edmond, and brother-in-law, Richard Fenner.   When the will was set aside, John M'Clelan, husband of Hannah Alexander, obtained, on the 9th April 1706, legal guardianship of his brothers, Edmond and John, who were still minors (Grant Book of Prerogative Court).

The decision respecting his father's will was keenly resented by Edmond Alexander, who proceeded forthwith to frame his own last will,* in which he evinced much bitter feeling towards his brothers and sister by his father's second marriage.   Respecting his half-brother, John, he affirmed that he had intended to bestow on him the best share of his substance, but as he had deprived him of being his guardian, he left him " five shillings to buy him more understanding."

From the University of Glasgow, John Alexander removed to Bristol, to assist in the theological academy kept by the Rev. Isaac Noble,† minister of the Presbyterian congregation at Castle Green in that city.   Having become a licentiate of the Presbyterian Church, he was, in 1712, settled at Gloucester on the invitation of a portion of the Presbyterians in that city, who withdrew from the old meeting on

---

* His will is dated 13th May 1706 (see *supra*).

† Rev. Isaac Noble was ordained minister of the Castle Green Presbyterian Church, Bristol, on the 28th May 1689.   He was a popular preacher, and had upwards of five hundred hearers. . Besides discharging the duties of the pastorate, he conducted a theological seminary, which was much resorted to by persons preparing for the ministry of the Presbyterian Church.   Mr Noble published a sermon which he preached at Gloucester on the death of the Rev. James Forbes, 3d June 1712.   He is frequently mentioned in the " Life of the Rev. John Reynolds," an eminent Presbyterian divine.   He died on the 27th September 1726 (Calamy's Life, vol. i., p. 365 ; and Wilson's Presbyterian Congregations in England, in Dr Williams' library, London).

the death of the Rev. James Forbes.* He continued
at Gloucester till 1718, when he was translated to
the pastorate of the Presbyterian church at Stratford-
on-Avon.   An academy, which he established at
Gloucester, he continued at Stratford-on-Avon so
long as he remained in that place.

In 1726 John Alexander proceeded from Stratford-on-Avon to Dublin to attend to his duties as an
executor under the will of his deceased brother,
Richard James. In that will he is described as " Mr
John Alexander," in allusion to his clerical office.
Having preached at Dublin, his pulpit talents recommended him to the Presbyterian congregation in
Plunket Street, who, on the 29th April of the same
year, invited him to undertake their pastorate. He
at first declined, but on a renewal of the call on the
29th March 1730, he accepted it (Kirk Session Records of Plunket Street Church). His translation
from Stratford-on-Avon was opposed by some of his
English brethren as being detrimental to the Presbyterian cause in England, but the translation was
proceeded with, and on the 12th November 1730 he
was inducted in his new charge. He died at Dublin
on the 1st of November 1743; his funeral was conducted at the expense of his hearers (Kirk Session
Records of Plunket Street Church). Mr John Alex-

* The Rev. James Forbes was a native of Scotland. He was persecuted for
nonconformity. He died at Gloucester on the 31st May 1712, aged eighty-three,
having ministered at Gloucester fifty-eight years (Wilson's Presbyterian Congregations in England).

ander is described by Dr Kippis as "distinguished for his skill in Oriental literature" (Biographia Britannica, Lond. 1780, vol. ii., p. 206).

Mr John Alexander married, on the 8th August 1732, Hannah Higgs of Old Swinford, the marriage being celebrated by licence in the parish church of Hartlebury, Worcestershire (Parish Church Register of Hartlebury). Of the marriage were born six children, two of whom died in infancy (Records of Plunket Street Church). Mr Alexander having died intestate, the Prerogative Court, on the 27th February 1743-4, authorised Benjamin Higgs of Dublin, his brother-in-law, to settle his affairs, and act as guardian to his children, Mary, John, Benjamin, and Hannah Alexander, minors (Grant Book Register of Prerogative Court of Dublin).

Mrs Hannah Alexander, wife of Mr John Alexander, died at Birmingham on the 5th October 1768, aged sixty-three (Inscription on Tombstone at Birmingham).

John Alexander, the elder son, was born at Dublin, on the 26th January 1736. In his "Biographia Britannica," Dr Kippis describes his career in the following narrative : "Mrs Hannah Alexander removed with her family from Dublin, and settled at Birmingham. She sent her son John to an academy at Daventry, in the county of Northampton, where he prosecuted his studies under the Rev. Dr Caleb Ashworth, an eminent Nonconformist minister. He was next taken to London, and there placed under the tuition of the distinguished Dr George Benson, under whose care he remained for several years. With his learning and personal behaviour, Dr Benson was so much satisfied that he gave him free board and lodging. Leaving the metropolis, he remained some time with his mother at Birmingham. In that town and neighbourhood he preached occasionally, and afterwards discharged the clerical duties at Longdon, a place situated about twelve miles from Birmingham. On Saturday, 28th December 1765, he retired to rest in perfect health between eleven and twelve o'clock, intending to officiate at Longdon the next day, but at six in the morning he was found dead in his bed— an event which was sincerely deplored by his friends, as both a private and a public loss. He was in his thirtieth year." * After his death, the Rev. John Palmer of London published " A Paraphrase upon the Fifteenth Chapter of the First Epistle to the Corinthians, with critical notes and observations, and a preliminary dissertation. A Commentary, with critical remarks upon the sixth, seventh, and part of the eighth chapters of the Romans, to which is added a Sermon on Ecclesiastes, ix. 10, composed by the Author the day

* The tombstone of the Rev. John Alexander at Birmingham is thus inscribed : "Sacred to the memory of the Rev. Mr John Alexander, who was eminently distinguished as a Christian scholar and divine, though cut off in his thirtieth year. He was born January 26, 1736 ; died December 29, 1765. Learn, reader, that honourable age is not that which standeth in length of time, nor that is measured by number of years ; but wisdom is the grey hair, and an unspotted life is old age."

preceding his death. By John Alexander. Printed at London, in quarto, for Buckland and others, in 1766."

In his posthumous work, Mr Alexander upholds the opinion that the soul is in a state of unconsciousness between death and the resurrection. To *The Library*—a miscellany published in London in the years 1761 and 1762—he contributed an ironical defence of persecution, and essays, entitled "Dulness," "Misanthropy," "The Study of Man," "Controversy," "The Misconduct of Parents," "Modern Authorship," "The Present State of Wit in Great Britain," "The Index of the Mind," and "The Fate of Periodical Productions."*

Benjamin Alexander, second son of the Rev. John Alexander, was born at Dublin in March 1737. He studied medicine, and practised as a physician in London. A copy of his thesis on obtaining his degree, is contained in the British Museum. Dedicated to William Hunter, M.D., the celebrated physician, it extends to twenty pages, 4to, and bears the following title: "Dissertatio Medicæ Inauguralis de Motu Musculorum, &c., pro gradu Doctoratus summisque in Medicina honoribus et privilegis rite ac legitime consequendis eruditorum examini submittit Benjaminus Alexander Londinensis ad diem 1 Decembris 1761 hora locoque solitis."

Dr Benjamin Alexander published at London, in

* Biographia Britannica, vol. ii., pp. 206, 207.

1769, in three quarto volumes, a work, entitled "Seats and Causes of Diseases investigated by Anatomy, in five books; containing a great variety of dissections, with remarks; to which are added very copious and accurate indices of the principal things and names therein contained. From the Latin of John Baptist Morgagni." Dr Alexander died in April 1768 (Register of Burials, Bunhill Fields Burying Ground).

Mary Alexander, elder daughter of the Rev. John Alexander, born in October 1733, died, unmarried, on the 28th April 1794. Hannah, the younger daughter, born January 1740, married, 26th September 1769, William Humphrys, merchant, Birmingham (Register of Marriages of Parish of St Martin, Birmingham). Mr Humphrys was of Irish descent. Edward Humphrys of Tententown, in the county of Carlow, in his will dated 16th April 1782 (proved 27th May 1786), mentions his brother, William, and his nephew, Alexander, and his son (Sir William Betham's MSS. in the Ulster Office, Dublin Castle).

Of the marriage of William Humphrys and Hannah Alexander were born two sons and five daughters, of whom a son, Alexander, and a daughter, Elizabeth, survived infancy. The remaining history of this branch will be found in the Appendix.

CHAPTER XXXIII

FAMILIES OF ALEXANDER, NOT OF SCOTTISH ORIGIN, WHICH OBTAINED SETTLEMENTS IN IRELAND : WILLIAM ALEXANDER, JUDGE OF ASSIZE ; GEORGE ALEXANDER, SECRETARY TO THE LORD JUSTICES ; ROBERT ALEXANDER OF LONDON ; FRANCIS ALEXANDER OF DUBLIN ; SIR JEROME ALEXANDER OF DUBLIN ; JACOB ALEXANDER OF NEWTON LIMAVADY AND ROE PARK—FAMILIES AT MAGHERAGH AND GORTINESSON.

In the Calendar of the Carew MSS. appears the following transcript from an ancient register: " 6 Edward II. Monday, in the morrow of the Annunciation, pleas of the Crown at Cassell, before Walter de Thornebury, Chancellor of Ireland, and William Alexander, appointed in place of Edmond le Bottiller, engaged in remote parts" (Calendar of the Carew MSS., p. 353). At the date herein indicated, being the 26th of March 1313, William Alexander obtained the place of judge in the Assize Court at Cashel in place of Edmond le Botiller, who held office as Lord Justice of Ireland. From the same register we have the following : " 7 Edward II. Monday, before St

Laurence the Martyr, pleas of the Crown and gaol delivery at Corche, before Walter de Thornebury, Chancellor of Ireland, and William Alexander."

Sir Henry Wallop, who, in 1582, was appointed one of the Lord Justices of Ireland, had, as his secretary, George Alexander, a native of England, whose honest and faithful services he commended in a letter to Secretary Walsingham on the 2d January 1585 (Irish State Papers). On the 3d June 1584, George Alexander obtained a royal grant of the preceptory of the Ardes, with the manor of Johnston and the tithes of the rectory and parish church of Rathmollen, in the province of Ulster, which, on the 7th July following, he conveyed to Matthew Smyth of Newry, in the same province (Original in Usher's Box, Public Record Office, Dublin).

The will of George Alexander, dated 27th October 1585, is preserved among the records of the Consistorial Court of Dublin. In this document, which is of great length, the testator intimates his connection with Bedfordshire. He bequeaths a portion of his substance to his father, Nicholas Alexander, and makes provision for his sisters, "Urseley and Marie." He also bequeaths articles of apparel as remembrances to a number of persons with Jewish names.

In the settlement or colonisation of Ulster, which began in 1609, the corporation of the city of London took a principal part. They obtained an allotment

of the whole county of Coleraine, since called Londonderry, on the condition that they would fortify the
towns of Londonderry and Coleraine, and expend
£20,000 in the plantation (Reid's Presbyterian
Church, i. 81).

On the 7th February 1634, Robert Alexander,
silk mercer in London, executed his will. He names
two sons, Robert and Richard, and two unmarried
daughters, Margaret and Gertrude. To Robert, his
elder son, he bequeathed his lands in Ireland, being
that portion of territory which belonged to him as a
member of the Company of Skinners (Will in Probate
Court of Canterbury).

In his will, executed on the 22d July 1627, Lord
Caulfeild, Baron Charlemont, bequeathed to Francis,
son of his late niece, Dorothy, wife of Doctor Alexander, £200 English, to be paid him at the age of
twenty-four, and in the meantime £20 a-year towards
his maintenance (Lodge's Peerage, iii. 127-134).
Baron Charlemont was so created in 1620. As Sir
Toby Caulfeild, he was, on account of his military
services, appointed by James I. governor of the fort
of Charlemont, and of the counties of Tyrone and
Armagh. He was subsequently appointed one of the
commissioners for distributing the escheated lands in
Ulster among British undertakers. On his death in
August 1627, he was, in terms of the patent, suc-
ceeded in his estates and title by his nephew, Sir
William Caulfeild, knight, son of his younger brother,

Doctor James Caulfeild (Lodge's Peerage). Of this last, Dorothy, the second daughter, espoused "Doctor Alexander," so named in Lord Caulfeild's will, and who was probably a physician, who had sought practice on the new plantation of the London Companies. That his Christian name was Andrew, and that he died in 1642, as stated by Dr Cotton, are assertions which we have failed to verify (Cotton's Fasti Eccl. Hib.).

Francis Alexander,[*] son of "Doctor Alexander" and Dorothy Caulfeild, died at Dublin sometime prior to the 6th November 1630, when his will was proved in the Prerogative Court of that city. From that document, which is dated 16th July 1629, we extract the following :

"Whereas Toby, late Lord Caulfeild, did, by his Will, bequeath unto me one legacy of Two hundred pounds sterl. remayning yett unpaid, as by his last Will appeareth, I doe heirby authorize my trustie & welbeloved friend, Thomas Wilson, gentleman, whom I doe hereby make my sole executor, to aske, demaunde, and receive of Sir William Caulfeild, knight, Lord **Caulfeild**, the said **sum** of Two hundred pounds sterling, and upon receipt thereof, to **dispose** of y^t, as by **my** Will following I doe dispose of **the** same. First, I will that my executor be carefull for mee to see those debts that I duly owe be, carefully satisfied and paid; and after **the** said debts paid, and my funerall rights satisfied, I will and bequeath unto my loving freind, **Nath.**

* The Christian name of Francis does not re-appear among either the English or **Scottish** families of Alexander, resident in Ireland. A "Francis Alexander, **Doctor** of Divinity," certifies as to the value of certain books belonging to the late Dean and Chapter of Winchester, in a legal instrument, dated 22d December 1651 (Royalist Composition Papers, First Series, vol. 74, p. 148, in Public Record Office, London).

Crosby of Dublin, gent., the sum of Forty Pounds sterling. Item, I will and bequeath unto Robert Dunn, shoemaker, the sum of Twenty Pounds sterl. Item, I will and bequeath unto Richard Kearney, sonne unto Edward Kearney, the sum of Five Pounds sterling, to be put forth to encrease for his advancement in learning. Item, I will and bequeath unto Alice Conner that attendeth me at this tyme, Twenty shillings. Item, I will and bequeath unto William Lalor, all my apparrell and some books, both printed and written. Item, I will and bequeath unto Ellen Kearney, wyfe unto Edward Kearney, the sum of fforty shillings sterl., for to make her a ringe off; and for the remainder of my state and goods, I give and bequeath fully unto my said executor, to his own use, in recompense of his care of mee, and in performing this my last Will and Testament."

Francis Alexander died unmarried, but it is extremely probable that an English family of the name which we find established in the vicinity of Londonderry in the latter part of the seventeenth century, were descended from the same stock which had produced " Doctor Alexander " and Robert Alexander, mercer in London.

Notably connected with Ireland in the seventeenth century was Sir Jerome Alexander, Second Justice of the Court of Common Pleas, and founder of the Alexander Library in Trinity College, Dublin. Descended from a Jewish family in the county of Norfolk, he was a barrister-at-law, and a pleader in the Court of Star Chamber. In that court he was accused of defacing certain depositions in a case wherein he was plaintiff, and one John Yates defender, and whereby the court was misled so as to give judg-

ment against Yates.   Consequent on this offence, he
was, on the 17th November 1626, amerced by the
council of the Star Chamber in a penalty of £500,
deprived of his status as a barrister, and sentenced
to imprisonment in the Fleet prison.   To avoid the
consequences of this sentence he escaped to Ireland,
where, by Edward, second Viscount Conway, he was
employed in connection with his lordship's estates
in the counties of Down and Armagh, and in other
duties connected with Ulster.   He afterwards practised in the law courts of Dublin, but the sentence of
the Court of Star Chamber materially impeded his
advancement.   In January 1633 he unsuccessfully
attempted to procure a pardon from Charles I.,
through a subordinate in the office of Sir John
Cooke, Secretary of State.   About the close of the
same year he obtained, through the influence of Lord
Arundel, Earl Marshal, the royal licence to repair to
England.   But his enemies were on the alert.   On
the alleged informality of his not presenting his
licence to the Lord Deputy before leaving Dublin, he
was committed to prison.   Petitioning the king, he,
on the 7th December 1633, received the royal pardon
—the penalty inflicted by the Court of Star Chamber
being discharged by his father-in-law.   The royal
pardon was granted on the express condition that its
recipient "should never practise as a councillor-at-
law in England."

Jerome Alexander now obtained extensive employ-

ment in the courts of Dublin. Countenanced by Lord
Conway, he proved of much service in suggesting
legislative measures for restoring tranquillity among
British settlers in Ulster. In a lengthened paper,
bearing date 1655, he proposed that a commission
should issue from the Irish Chancery, with the Surveyor-General as one of its members. That commission, he suggested, should determine the boundaries
of baronies forfeited by rebels and delinquents since
the 25th of March 1639, and should subdivide and
allocate the same according to a scheme agreed upon
by the Committee of Adventurers. From the date of
his obtaining the royal pardon he began to invest his
savings in the purchase of forfeited lands. On the
26th May 1634, Everage M'Evor and Rory M'Evor
conveyed to him the lands of Bally M'Broghie,
and others in the district of Killwarkie and county
of Down. On the 28th September 1635, he paid
£53, 6s. 8d. on several "alienations of land" made
to him in the county of Down. On 9th December
1636, he purchased the manor and mansion-house,
and site of the late dissolved Abbey of Kilcooley,
from the Earl of Ormonde. One of the most opulent
of the English settlers in Ireland, Jerome Alexander
was invited to London in 1660, and on the 18th
August of that year was knighted by Charles II. at
Whitehall. On the 30th November following he
received letters-patent appointing him to the office of
Second Justice of the Irish Court of Common Pleas.

Sir Jerome Alexander died on the 25th July 1670, and his remains were deposited in St Patrick's Cathedral. In his will, executed on the 23d March 1670, he bequeathed to the provost, fellows and scholars of Trinity College, Dublin, his books and MSS., along with the sum of £600 to found a library in connection with the college, to be called Alexander's Library; he also provided for the endowment of a keeper. He bequeathed to the collegiate authorities rents of a portion of his lands in Westmeath for supplying a sixpenny loaf of bread weekly to ten indigent persons, being Protestants, at the gate of the college. He also made provision for recompensing a clergyman selected by the college authorities, who should preach a discourse each Christmas in celebration of that feast.

By the authorities of Trinity College, Dublin, the directions contained in his will are substantially observed. Indigent persons are every Saturday at the college gate supplied with bread, soup, and meat, along with an allowance of money. They are for the most part persons who have served the students, and no religious test is imposed. The MSS. and books bequeathed by him are preserved in the college library. The MSS. are kept separately, the press marks being G 3, 1—15, and G 4, 1—14. The printed books are placed among the other books of the library. At the Revolution of 1688 Sir Jerome's bequest of books was considerably interfered with.

In 1702 the MSS. were revised, when it appeared that several were missing. Some of these were recovered in 1741 and 1742, when Dr Lyons made a catalogue of MSS. in the college. About that period the MSS. were rebound and rearranged, so that a catalogue printed in 1697 is now of little use (Catalogi MSS. Angliæ et Hiberniæ, etc., Oxon., 1697). The special direction respecting the sermon on Christmas has not been observed for many years; it has been merged in the general preachership.

Sir Jerome Alexander married Elizabeth, daughter of John Havers of London (who died on the 10th November 1667), by whom he had three daughters, Jeromina, Rose, and Elizabeth. Jeromina, the eldest daughter, married Humphrey Lanham, by whom she had two sons, John and Humphrey, who died young, and three daughters, Mary, Rose, and Elizabeth. Elizabeth married, first, Nicholas Browne, and secondly, John Button; by her first husband she had a daughter, Elizabeth. Rose, second daughter of Sir Jerome Alexander, was twice married. Her first husband was Rawlin Mallech of Cockington, Devonshire, by whom she had a son, Rankin, and a daughter, Anne. She married secondly, 23d March 1656, Thomas Gorges of Heavitree, Devonshire, M.P. for Taunton, by whom she had two sons, Alexander and Edward, and a daughter, Elizabeth. Mrs Rose Gorges or Alexander died 14th April 1671.

Elizabeth, youngest daughter of Sir Jerome Alexander, was, in her father's will, prohibited from marrying any person of Irish extraction of whatever rank, under the pain of forfeiting the whole of his landed estates, which were otherwise bequeathed to her. She married Sir William Barker, Bart. of Bocking Hall, in the county of Suffolk. The lands of Kilcooley Abbey, with its beautiful demesne of sixteen hundred acres, are still occupied by the descendants of Sir Jerome Alexander, the present owner being William Ponsonby Barker, who is descended from Mary, daughter of Sir William Barker, the third baronet (Transactions of Royal Historical Society, vol. ii.).

Jacob Alexander of Newton Limavady died in 1710. In his will, deposited in the Prerogative Court of Londonderry, he mentions his wife and five children, of whom three were sons. He also names his brothers, Samuel and John, his sister Rachel, and three others, Thomas, Debora, and Rebecca Alexander, connections of his family.

According to Sir William Betham,* Jacob Alexander married in 1692, Jane or Margaret, daughter and heiress of John Oliver of Newton Limavady, a magistrate appointed to administer the oath of allegiance. Of two of his three sons, James and John, the wills are recorded in the Prerogative Court at Dublin in 1786. In his will, dated 16th October 1764, James, the eldest brother, styles himself "of

* Betham Pedigrees in the Ulster Office, Dublin.

Newtonlimavady, merchant." He bequeaths the life-rent of his houses, lands, and tenements, in the manor of Limavady, to his wife Elizabeth, and, at her death, the moiety of his lands of Killane to his son James. If James does not choose to reside at Killane, he enjoins him to dispose of the lands and tenements to his brothers, Leslie and John. He settles an annuity on his son Oliver, who is described as residing in America. To his daughter Jane he bequeaths £150, should she marry with consent of his executors. He adds that, having given his daughters, Mary Ogilby, Elizabeth Orr, and Anne Law, at the time of their marriages, more than he could afford, he leaves each of them five shillings only. He constitutes his sons, Leslie, John, and James, his residuary legatees.

The will of John Alexander, a younger son of Jacob Alexander of Newton Limavady, is dated 21st April 1772. The testator, who describes himself as "John Alexander of Newtonlimavady," liferents his wife Elizabeth, daughter of William Ross of Newton Limavady, and his wife, Mary Leslie of Leslie Hill, county Antrim, in his moiety of the land of Killane. He bequeaths to his niece, Mary Ogilby, £50; to his niece, Elizabeth Orr, £50; to his niece, Anne Law, £50; and to his niece, Jane Alexander, £150. He bequeaths to his three nephews, Leslie, John, and James Alexander, the residue of his estate, real and personal, providing that if his nephew James, who has gone to the East Indies, should die before he returns home, his share should be possessed by Leslie and John.

John, second son of Jacob Alexander, died without issue. His elder brother James had four sons, Leslie, John, James, and Oliver, and four daughters, Mary, Elizabeth, Anne, and Jane. Mary married Dr Alexander Ogilby of Newton Limavady; Elizabeth married James Orr of Gortin, parish of Aghadowey, county Derry; Anne married the Rev. William Law, Presbyterian minister at Strabane, county Tyrone; and Jane married Dr Robert Ogilby of Newton Limavady. James, the third son, became a major-general in the service of the East India Company, and died at Calcutta in 1779, unmarried (Betham's Pedigrees, Ulster Office). In his will, dated 18th March 1769, he is described as "James Alexander, late of Philadelphia, merchant, but now of London, and bound on a sea voyage to the East Indies." He bequeaths his freehold lands and tenements in the county of Derry to his brothers Leslie and John. John Alexander married Hester King of Newton Limavady, and died without issue.

Leslie Alexander, eldest son and heir of James Alexander of Newton Limavady, married Anna Simpson of Armagh (Betham's Pedigrees). He had five sons, John, James, Leslie, Alexander, and Thomas, and three daughters, Elizabeth and Louisa, who died unmarried, and Jane, who married William Moody of Roe House.   Thomas, the fifth son, settled as a merchant in London, and acquired the estate of Frowick in Essex, and Ahilly in the county of Donegal.   He married Jane, eldest daughter of William Haigh of Westfield, Doncaster, and died in 1867, leaving four sons, Leslie William, born 1841, now of Ahilly, James, Thomas, and Edward Merydeth Edgworth, and three daughters, Anna Louisa, Rosetta, and Elizabeth Frances.

Alexander Alexander of Foyle Park, fourth son of Leslie Alexander, died on the 1st September 1832, aged forty-one.   His will was proved at Londonderry by his brothers, John Alexander of Newton Limavady, and Lesley Alexander of "the Old Jewry, London."   To his brother Leslie he bequeathed the lands in the Manor of Goldsmiths, lately purchased by him from the Ponsonby family. He bequeathed his estate and lands in the Half Barony of Coleraine to his nephew, Leslie Alexander, son of his brother John.   To his brother John he bequeathed the estate* in Newton Limavady, which he purchased from John Alexander of Belfast; also his lands of Ballymore and Largy, in the county of Derry, subject to an annuity of £150 to his brother James.   His property in Newton Limavady, which he purchased from Mr Ogilby of London, he bequeathed to his brother Thomas.

* Alexander Alexander purchased the estate of Ballyclose, Newton Limavady, from John Alexander of Belfast in July 1827.

Leslie Alexander, third son of Leslie Alexander of Newton Limavady, resided at London and Foyle Park, in the county of Derry, of which county he was a deputy-lieutenant. He married, on the 22d September 1835, Amelia Maria, daughter of Lieutenant-Colonel Bates of the 21st Light Dragoons, but died without issue.

James Alexander, second son of Leslie Alexander of Newton Limavady, acquired the estate of Deer Park, in the county of Derry.

John, eldest son of Leslie Alexander, married Margaret, daughter of Samuel Maxwell, of Armagh, and had issue four sons, Leslie, Alexander, Samuel Maxwell, and John, and two daughters, Anna and Jane.

Anna, elder daughter of John Alexander of Newton Limavady, married A. J. Stanton, M.P. for Stroud; Jane, the younger daughter, married Edward Frederick Christian Ritter, of London; Leslie, eldest son, served as a lieutenant in the 11th Hussars; and died unmarried; Alexander, the second son, died unmarried; John, the fourth son, owned the lands of Ballyclose; he died unmarried. Samuel Maxwell Alexander, the third son, is proprietor of Roe Park, and representative of his House. He is a magistrate for county Donegal, and a deputy-lieutenant of the county of Derry.

A person named Alexander, from the county of Kent, of Jewish origin, settled on lands near Strabane, in the county of Tyrone, during the Com-

monwealth.   One of his descendants, Joseph Alexander, rented the farm of Magheragh, in the parish of
Donagheady, county Tyrone, and there died in November 1781.   He had two sons, Robert and James,
and two daughters, Elizabeth and Martha.   In his
will, dated 21st November 1781, he bequeaths the
lease of his farm to his son Robert.   To his son
James he bequeaths £100, to his daughter Elizabeth, £100, and to his daughter Martha, and her
husband, Arthur Kelly, £20.   To his sister Martha
he bequeaths two guineas, and to his brother Thomas
his body clothes.   A descendant of Joseph Alexander
by his son Robert now occupies the farm of Magheragh.

James, second son of Joseph Alexander, tenant
at Magheragh, rented the farm of Gortinesson, near
Strabane.   He had two sons, Robert and John ; also
a daughter, Elizabeth, who married John Alexander,
of the Scottish family of Alexander.   Her son received
an appointment in the Indian Army on the recommendation of the first Earl of Caledon, who acknowledged him as a relative.

Robert Alexander, elder son of James Alexander,
succeeded his father in the lease of Gortinesson ; the
farm is now rented by his son Robert.

John, younger son of James Alexander, farmer at
Gortinesson, had a son, John, who married Elizabeth,
daughter of James Alexander, of the Scottish family
settled at Ballybiglemore, county Donegal.   Of this

marriage were born seven sons and one daughter. Joseph, the second son, rents the farm of Imlick-Corrigans, county Donegal. James, the elder son, is farmer at Drumenon, parish of Taghboyne, county Donegal.

To the family of Magheragh belonged the late Rev. John Alexander, minister of the Presbyterian congregation at Douglas Bridge, near Newton Stewart. His brother, William Alexander, rents the farm of Mount Castle, parish of Donagheady, county Tyrone.

CHAPTER XXXIV.

FAMILY OF ZINZAN OR ALEXANDER.

ACCORDING to the learned author of the "History of Reading," Berkshire, the family of Zinzano, supposed to be of Italian origin, settled in England during the reign of Queen Mary (Coates' History of Reading, p. 445). The first reference to any member of the House in England occurs in 1555. Sir John Norres, knight, of Yattenden, Berkshire, died 21st October 1564. In the inquisition on his obit, made at Abingdon on the 25th January 1564-5, it was found that, by deeds executed on the 25th April and 20th August 1555, he had settled certain lands at Ashampsted and Hampsted-Norres, Berks, on his illegitimate daughter, Anne Norres, *alias* Graunt, and her issue. At the date of inquest, Anne was wife of Alexander Zinzan, gentleman, residing at Ashampsted.

Robert, son of Alexander Zinzan and Anne Norres, preferred as a surname his father's Christian name. In May 1585, a warrant was directed by Queen Elizabeth to the officers of Exchequer, authorising a grant of £50 to Robert Alexander, styled "one of the Quirries [equerries] of the stable, to defray his charges in conveying certain horses from the Queen to the

King of Scotts, also for the charges of such as should accompany him" (Docquet Book of Exchequer).

In April 1594, a royal licence was granted to Robert Alexander and Richard Mompessons, equerries of her Majesty's stable, "that they, their executors, administrators, and assignes only, and none other, may bring into this realme of England annis seeds and sumacke, during the space of twentie yeares after the date of the same letters patent, paying to her Majestie the customes and subsedies due from the same" (Docquet Book).

Among the knights dubbed by James I. in the royal garden at Whitehall, on the 23d July 1603, was Sir Robert Alexander of St Albans (Nichols' Progresses of James I.). Sir Robert married the daughter of —— Westrode, Esq. of Hansacker Hall, Staffordshire, by whom he had four sons—Sigismund, Henry, Alexander, and Andrew ; also three daughters.

Sir Robert Alexander or Zinzan seems to have died in 1607, for on the 24th December of that year, Henry Zinzan, *alias* Alexander, his second son, received the office of brigandery to his Majesty, in succession to his father, Sir Robert Zinzan or Alexander (Patent Roll, James I., v. 17).

On the 8th May 1607, a warrant, subscribed by the Master of the Horse, was directed to the treasurer and other officers of his Majesty's household, authorising them to pay to Alexander Zinzan, and two others, described as " ordinary ryders of his Majesty's stable, an encrease of 15 lb. by the yeare during their lives, over and above their former allowance of 20 lb. yearly. Also to pay unto Andrew Zinzan the younger, now entertayned as a ryder of the said stables, 15 lb. by the yeare for his wages during his life, and to such person as shall succeed as an ordynary ryder of the said stable." John Pritchard was, on the 24th January 1626, appointed a rider of his Majesty's great horses, in place of Alexander Zinzan, deceased.

On the 28th April 1607, "Andrew Zinzan, *alias* Alexander, of the town of St Alban, and county of Hertford," is named in an indenture between himself and Henry Cutlar of Ayr, in the county of Suffolk. During the same reign, Andrew Zinzan, *alias* Alexander, received £66, 13s. 4d. per annum for riding the king's great horses.

Among the burials in St Lawrence's Register for 1625 is named that of "Mr Andrew Zinzan, *alias* Alexander." In July 1624, Richard Zinzan, *alias* Alexander, received an annuity of £66, 13s. 4d., and yearly livery, for riding the king's great horses in reversion after Andrew Zinzan, *alias* Alexander (Record of the Sign Manual, vol. xvi., No. 10).

Sir Sigismund and Henry Alexander or Zinzan, sons of Sir Robert Alexander, were associated as masters of sports at the accession of James I. In describing certain fêtes in honour of the king's arrival at Grafton, the seat of her father, George, Earl of

Cumberland, and which took place on the 27th June 1603, Lady Anne Clifford writes thus :

" From thence (Althorp) the Court removed, and were banquetted wth great Royaltie, by my Father, at Grafton, wher the King and Queene wear entertayned wth Speeches and delicat presents, at wch tyme my Lord and the Alexanders did run and course at ye field, wher he hurt Henry Alexander verie dangerouslie." *

In the Warrant Book of the Exchequer (vol. ii., p. 141), a Privy Seal warrant, dated 14th March 1608, authorises the treasurer to pay to Sir Sigismund Alexander, knight, and Henry Alexander, Esq., the sum of £100 in " frie guift." They afterwards received £100 annually " towards their charges for running at tylte." In certain of the warrants, the "tylte" is described as having been run on the 24th of March.

On the 10th February 1611, Henry Alexander, described as " one of the gent. equerries of His Majesty's Stables, received a grant of all such goods, chattels, and debtes, which ought to come to His Highness by the means of the attainder of Richard Bancks, late of Westness, in the county of York, attainted of manslaughter" (Patent Roll). In 1614 Sir Sigismund and Henry Alexander received a royal gift of £1000. Henry Zinzan was appointed harness maker to the Ordnance, with a salary of £10 per annum. He long retained office in the royal household, for there is an indenture, dated 1st May 1638,

* Lady Anne Clifford was successively Countess of Dorset and Pembroke. Her narrative is included in Nichols' Progresses of James I., vol. ii., p. 287.

between him and Joseph Zinzan or Alexander, one
of his sons, in which he is described as "one of the
equerries of the stable, son and heir of Robert
Zinzan, *alias* Alexander, long since deceased" (Patent
Roll, Charles I., xiv. 23, 26).

Sir Sigismund Alexander held a command in the
Low Countries in 1617 (Coates' History of Reading).
Among the undated State Papers of the reign of
Charles I., there is a list of captains recommended for
service in the Palatinate.   Among the lieutenants
is named Sir Sigismund Alexander ; he afterwards appears as a petitioner for a company under the name of
Sir Sigismund Zinzan, specially recommended " by the
Prince and Queen of Bohemia."   In a document containing a list of colonels and lieutenant-colonels con
nected with Ireland, he is named in a roll of captains.

Sir Sigismund Zinzan or Alexander married Margaret, daughter of Sir Philip Sterley, knight, of the
county of Nottingham, by whom he had five sons and
three daughters.   Margaret, one of the daughters,
married, first, Sir William Shelley, knight; and secondly, Robert Thomas, Esq.   On the 9th March
1640-1, along with her father, she presented to the
House of Lords a petition, praying for relief against a
sentence of the Judges Delegates, made upon an appeal
from the Ecclesiastical Court, touching the validity of
her marriage with Sir William Shelley (Manuscripts
in the House of Lords, quoted in Appendix to
Fourth Report of Royal Historical Commissioners).

Henry, son of Sigismund Zinzan or Alexander, married Jacoba, eldest of the three daughters, and co-heiress of Sir Peter Vanlore, Bart. of Tilehurst, Berkshire. Mary, Sir Peter's youngest daughter, had, as her first husband, Henry Alexander, third son of the first Earl of Stirling, who afterwards succeeded to the earldom. Among the Close Rolls is an indenture, executed on the 11th January 1661, between Sir Robert Crooke, who married Susan, second daughter of Sir Peter Vanlore, and his two brothers-in-law, Henry Zinzan or Alexander, and Henry, Earl of Stirling. Henry Zinzan or Alexander died in November 1676, and Jacoba, his wife, in the following year. Both were interred at Tilehurst, and are commemorated by a monument in the parish church.

By his wife, Jacoba Vanlore, Henry Zinzan or Alexander had three sons, Henry, Nicholas, and Peter; also five daughters. Henry, the eldest son, was born 2d January 1633. An indenture, dated 28th August 1704, between Peter Zinzan or Alexander of Reading, Berks, and Nicholas Zinzan, *alias* Alexander, of London, describes the former as "brother and heir of Henry Alexander, *alias* Zinzan, late of Tylehurst, in the county of Berks, deceased." Nicholas Zinzan was a member of St John's College, Oxford, and took the degree of M.A., 16th March 1694. He was ordained deacon by Bishop Hough in Magdalen Chapel, 22d May 1692.

Peter Zinzan or Alexander, third son of Henry

Zinzan, was vicar of St Lawrence, Reading.   His
grandson, Peter Zinzan, baptized 30th September
1705, was elected a demy of Magdalen College, Oxford, in July 1723, on the Berkshire foundation, and
took the degree of M.A. in 1729.   He resigned his
demyship in 1731, but became probation-fellow in
1735.   He afterwards held various offices in his
college, of which he became vice-president in 1746.

In a letter addressed by the magistrates of Leith
to the magistrates of Edinburgh, dated 17th October 1668, one Charles Zinzan is named as resident at
Leith, and as having had his house attacked by sixteen French soldiers (Analecta Scotica, vol. ii., p.
164); he may have been a son of Henry Zinzan or
Alexander.   Charles Zinzan, who practised medicine
at Reading, married, first, the widow of Charles
Hopson, Esq. of Beenham, and secondly, Sarah,
daughter of —— Matthews of Reading.   He died
at Reading on the 9th November 1781, and his
remains were deposited in St Mary's churchyard.
He is the individual referred to in Dr Bacon's "Kyte"
in *The Oxford Sausage*.   Describing his manners,
Mr Coates remarks: " Had he not retired from his
profession upon his first marriage, he would probably
have been distinguished in it; but wealth, as is frequently the case, checked the exertions of genius
(Coates' History of Reading, and Private Sources).

APPENDIX.

No. I.

TRANSLATION OF CHARTER IN FAVOUR OF SIR
WILLIAM ALEXANDER OF THE LORDSHIP AND
BARONY OF NEW SCOTLAND, DATED 10TH SEPTEM-
BER 1621.

> JAMES, by the grace of God, King of Great Britain, France,
> and Ireland, and Defender of the Faith, to all good
> men, clerical and lay, of his entire realm, greeting,

Know ye, that we have always been eager to embrace every
opportunity to promote the honour and wealth of our kingdom
of Scotland, and think that no gain is easier or more safe than
what is made by planting new colonies in foreign and unculti-
vated regions, where the means of living and food abound;
especially if these places were before without inhabitants, or
were settled by infidels whose conversion to the Christian faith
most highly concerns the glory of God.

But while many other kingdoms, and, not very long ago, our
own England, to their praise, have given their names to new
lands, which they have acquired and subdued, we, thinking
how populous and crowded this land now is by Divine favour,
and how expedient it is that it should be carefully exercised in
some honourable and useful discipline, lest it deteriorate through
sloth and inaction, have judged it important that many should
be led forth into new territories, which they may fill with

colonies; and so we think this undertaking most fit for this kingdom, both on account of the promptness and activity of its spirit, and the strength and endurance of its men against any difficulties, if any other men anywhere dare to set themselves in opposition; and as it demands the transportation only of men and women, stock and grain, and not of money, and can not repay at this time, when business is so depressed, a troublesome expenditure of the treasures of this realm; for these reasons, as well as on account of the good, faithful, and acceptable service of our beloved counsellor, Sir William Alexander, knight, to us rendered, and to be rendered, who first of our subjects at his own expense, attempted to plant this foreign colony, and selected for plantation the divers lands bounded by the limits hereafter designated.

We therefore, from our sovereign anxiety to propagate the Christian faith, and to secure the wealth, prosperity, and peace of the native subjects of our said kingdom of Scotland, as other foreign princes in such cases already have done; with the advice and consent of our well-beloved cousin and counsellor, John, Earl of Mar, Lord Erskine and Garioch, etc., our High Treasurer, Comptroller, Collector, and Treasurer of our New Revenues of this our Kingdom of Scotland, and of the other Lords Commissioners of our said kingdom, have given, granted, and conveyed, and by the tenor of our present charter, do give, grant, and convey, to the aforesaid Sir William Alexander, his heirs or assigns, hereditarily, all and single the lands of the continent and islands situated and lying in America, within the head or promontory commonly called Cape of Sable, lying near the forty-third degree of north latitude, or thereabouts; from this cape, stretching along the shores of the sea, westward to the roadstead of St Mary, commonly called St Mary's Bay, and thence northward by a straight line crossing the entrance or mouth of that great roadstead, which runs toward the eastern part of the land between the countries of the Suriqui and Etechemini, commonly called Suriquois and Etechemines, to the river generally known by the name of St Croix, and to the remotest springs or source from the western side of the same, which empty into the first-mentioned river; thence by an imaginary straight line which is conceived to extend through the land, or run northward to the nearest bay, river, or stream emptying into the great river of Canada; and going from that, eastward, along the low shores of the same river of Canada, to the river, harbour, port, or shore commonly known and called by the name of Gathepe or Gaspie, and thence south-south-east to the isles called Bacalaos or Cape Breton, leaving the said isles on the right, and the mouth of the said great river of Canada, or Large Bay, and the territory of Newfoundland, with the islands belonging to the same lands on the left; thence to the headland or point of Cape Breton aforesaid, lying near latitude 45° or thereabouts; and from the said point of Cape Breton toward the south and west to the above-mentioned Cape Sable, where the boundary began; including and containing within the said coasts and their circumference, from sea to sea, all lands of the continent, with the rivers, falls, bays, shores, islands, or seas, lying near, or within six leagues on any side of the same, on the west, north, or east sides of the same coasts and bounds: and on the south-south-east (where Cape Breton lies), and on the south side of the same (where Cape Sable is) all seas and islands southward within forty leagues of said seashore, thereby including the large island commonly called Isle de Sable, or Sablon, lying towards Carbau, in common speech, south-south-east, about thirty leagues from the said Cape Breton, seaward, and being in latitude 44° or thereabouts.

The above described lands shall in all future time bear the name of New Scotland, in America; and also, the aforesaid Sir William shall divide it into parts and portions as seemeth best to him, and shall give names to the same at his·pleasure. With all mines, both the royal ones of gold and silver, and others of iron, lead, copper, tin, brass, and other minerals, with the power of mining and causing to dig them from the earth, and of purifying and refining the same, and converting to his own use, or that of others, as shall seem best to the said Sir William, his heirs or assigns, or to whomsoever it shall have pleased him to establish in said lands; reserving only to us and

our successors a tenth part of the metal vulgarly known as
ore of gold and silver, which shall be hereafter dug or obtained
from the land; leaving the said Sir William and his aforesaids
whatever of other metals of copper, steel, iron, tin, lead, or other
minerals, we or our successors may be able in any way to obtain
from the earth, in order that thereby they may the more easily
bear the large expense of reducing the aforesaid metals, together
with margarite, termed pearl, and any other precious stones,
quarries, forests, thickets, mosses, marshes, lakes, waters, fisheries
in both salt and fresh water, and of both royal and other fish,
hunting, hawking, and anything that may be sold or inherited;
with full power and privilege and jurisdiction of free royalty,
chapelry, and chancery for ever: with the gift and right of
patronage of churches, chapels, and benefices; with tenants,
tenancies, and the service of those holding the same freely;
together with the offices of justiciary and admiralty within all
the bounds respectively mentioned above; also with power of
setting up states, free towns, free ports, villages, and barony
towns; and of establishing markets and fairs within the bounds
of said lands; of holding courts of justice and admiralty within
the limits of such lands, rivers, ports, and seas; also with the
power of improving, levying, and receiving all tolls, customs,
anchor-dues, and other revenues of the said towns, marts, fairs,
and free ports; and of owning and using the same as freely in
all respects as any greater or lesser baron in our kingdom of
Scotland has enjoyed in any past, or could enjoy in any future
time; with all other prerogatives, privileges, immunities, dignities, perquisites, profits, and dues concerning and belonging to
said lands, seas, and the boundaries thereof, which we ourselves
can give and grant, as freely and in as ample form as we or any
of our noble ancestors granted any charters, letters patent,
enfeoffments, gifts, or commissions to any subjects of whatever
rank or character, or to any society or company leading out such
colonies into any foreign parts or searching out foreign lands,
and in as free and ample form as if the same were included in
this present charter; also, we make, constitute, and ordain the
said Sir William Alexander, his heirs and assigns, or their

deputies, our hereditary lieutenants-general, for representing our royal person both by sea and by land, in the regions of the sea and on the coasts, and in the bounds aforesaid, both in seeking said lands and remaining there and returning from the same; to govern, rule, punish, and accept all our subjects who may chance to visit or inhabit the same, or who shall do business with the same, or shall tarry in the said places; also, to pardon the same, and to establish such laws, statutes, constitutions, orders, instructions, forms of government, and ceremonies of magistrates in said bounds, as shall seem fit to Sir William Alexander himself, or his aforesaids, for the government of the said region, or of the inhabitants of the same, in all causes, both criminal and civil; also of changing and altering the said laws, rules, forms, and ceremonies as often as he or his aforesaids shall please, for the good and convenience of said region, so that said laws may be as consistent as possible with those of our realm of Scotland. We also will that, in case of rebellion or sedition, he may use martial law against delinquents, or such as withdraw themselves from his power, as freely as any lieutenant whatever of our realm or dominion by virtue of the office of lieutenant has or can have the power to use; by excluding all other officers of this our Scottish realm, on land or sea, who hereafter can pretend to any claim, property, authority, or interest in and to said lands or province aforesaid, or any jurisdiction therein by virtue of any prior disposal or patents: and that a motive may be offered to noblemen for joining this expedition and planting a colony in said lands, we, for ourselves and our heirs and successors, with the advice and consent aforesaid, by virtue of our present charter, do give and grant full and free power to the aforesaid Sir William Alexander and his aforesaids to confer favours, privileges, gifts, and honours on those who deserve them, with full power to the same, or any one of them, who may have made bargains or contracts with Sir William or his deputies for the said lands, under his signature, or that of his deputies, and under the seal hereinafter described, to dispose of and convey any part or parcel of said lands, ports, harbours, rivers, or of any part of the premises; also of erecting machines of all sorts, introducing arts or sciences, or practising the same, in whole or in part, as he shall judge to be for their advantage: also to give, grant, and bestow such offices, titles, rights, and powers, make and appoint such captains, officers, bailiffs, governors, clerks, and all other officers, clerks, and ministers of royalty, barony, and town, for the execution of justice within the bounds of said lands, or on the way to these lands by sea, and returning from the same, as shall seem necessary to him, according to the qualities, conditions, and deserts of the persons who may happen to dwell in any of the colonies of said province, or in any part of the same, or who may risk their goods and fortunes for the advantage and increase of the same; also of removing the same persons from office, transferring or changing them as far as shall seem expedient to him and his aforesaids.

And, since attempts of this kind are not made without great labour and expense, and demand a large outlay of money, so that they exceed the means of any private man; and, on this account, the said Sir William Alexander and his aforesaids may need supplies of many kinds, with many of our subjects and other men for special enterprise and ventures therein who may form contracts with him, his heirs, assigns, or deputies, for lands, fisheries, trade, or the transportation of people and their flocks, goods, and effects to the said New Scotland: We will that whosoever shall make such contracts with the said Sir William and his aforesaids, under their names and seals, by limiting, assigning, and fixing the day and place for the delivery of persons, goods, and effects on ship-board, under forfeiture of a certain sum of money, and shall not perform the same contracts, but shall thwart and injure him in the proposed voyage, which thing will not only oppose and harm the said Sir William and his aforesaids, but also prejudice and damage our so laudable intention; then it shall be lawful to the said Sir William and his aforesaids, or their deputies and conservators hereinafter mentioned, in such case to seize for himself or his deputies, whom he may appoint for this purpose, all such sums of money, goods and effects, forfeited by the violation of these contracts.

And that this may be more easily done, and the delay of the law be avoided, we have given and granted, and by the tenor of these presents do give and grant, full power to the Lords of our Council that they may reduce to order and punish the violators of such contracts and agreements made for the transportation of persons. And although all such contracts between the said Sir William and his aforesaids, and the aforesaid adventurers shall be carried out, in the risk and the conveyance of people with their goods and effects at the set time, and they with all their cattle and goods arrive at the shore of that province with the intention of colonising and abiding there, and yet afterwards shall leave the province of New Scotland altogether, and the confines of the same, without the consent of the said Sir William and his aforesaids, or their deputies, or the society and colony aforesaid, where first they had been collected and joined together, and shall go away to the uncivilised natives to live in remote and desert places, then they shall lose and forfeit all the lands previously granted them, also all their goods within the aforesaid bounds; and it shall be lawful for the said Sir William and his aforesaids to confiscate the same and reclaim the same lands, and to seize and convert and apply to his own use and that of his aforesaids all the same belonging to them, or any one of them.

And that all our beloved subjects, as well of our kingdoms and dominions, so also any others of foreign birth, who may sail to the said lands or any part of the same for obtaining merchandise, may the better know and obey the power and authority given by us to the aforesaid Sir William Alexander, our faithful counsellor, and his deputies, in all such commissions, warrants, and contracts as he shall at any time make, grant, and establish for the more fit and safe arrangement of offices, to govern said colony, grant lands and execute justice in respect to said inhabitants, adventurers, deputies, factors or assigns, in any part of said lands, or in sailing to the same, We, with the advice and consent aforesaid, do order that the said Sir William Alexander and his aforesaids shall have one common seal pertaining to the office of justiciary and admiralty, which, by the said Sir William

Alexander and his aforesaids, or their deputies, in all time to come, shall be safely kept: On one side our arms shall be engraved, with these words on the circle and margin thereof, "Sigillum Regis Scotiæ, Angliæ, Franciæ, et Hiberniæ;" and on the other side our image, or that of our successors, with these words, " Pro Novæ Scotiæ Locum Tenente;" and a true copy of it shall be kept in the hands and care of the conservator of the privileges of New Scotland, and this he may use in his office as occasion shall require. And as it is very important that all our beloved subjects who inhabit the said province of New Scotland or its borders may live in the fear of Almighty God, and at the same time in His true worship, and may have an earnest purpose to establish the Christian religion therein, and also to cultivate peace and quiet with the native inhabitants and savage aborigines of these lands, so that they, and any others trading there, may safely, pleasantly, and quietly hold what they have got with great labour and peril; we, for ourselves and our successors, do will and decree, and by our present charter give and grant to the said Sir William Alexander and his aforesaids, and their deputies, or any other of our government officers and ministers whom they shall appoint free and absolute power of arranging and securing peace, alliance, friendship, mutual conferences, assistance, and intercourse with those savage aborigines and their chiefs, and any others bearing rule and power among them; and of preserving and fostering such relations and treaties as they or their aforesaids shall form with them, provided those treaties are on the other side kept faithfully by these barbarians; and unless this be done, of taking up arms against them, whereby they may be reduced to order, as shall seem fitting to the said Sir William Alexander, and his aforesaids and deputies; for the honour, obedience, and service of God, and the stability, defence, and preservation of our authority among them; with power also to the said Sir William Alexander and his aforesaids, by themselves or their deputies, substitutes, or assigns, for their defence and protection at all times, and on all just occasions hereafter, of attacking suddenly, invading, expelling, and by arms driving away as well by sea as by land, and by all means, all and singly, those who without the special licence of the said Sir William and his aforesaids shall attempt to occupy these lands, or trade in the said province of New Scotland, or in any part of the same; and in like manner all other persons who presume to bring any damage, loss, destruction, injury, or invasion against that province, or the inhabitants of the same: And that this may be more easily done, it shall be allowed to the said Sir William and his aforesaids, their deputies, factors, and assigns, to levy contributions on the adventurers and inhabitants of the same; to bring them together by proclamations, or by any other order, at such times as shall seem best to the said Sir William Alexander and his aforesaids; to assemble all our subjects living within the limits of the said New Scotland, and trading there, for the better supplying of the army with necessaries, and the enlargement and increase of the people and planting of the said lands: With full power, privilege, and liberty to the said Sir William Alexander and his aforesaids, by themselves or their agents, of sailing over any seas whatever under our ensigns and banners, with as many ships of as great burden, and as well furnished with ammunition, men, and provisions, as they are able to procure, at any time, and as often as shall seem expedient: and of carrying all persons of every quality and grade who are our subjects, or who wish to submit themselves unto our sway, for entering upon such a voyage with their cattle, horses, oxen, sheep, goods of all kinds, furniture, machines, heavy arms, military instruments, as many as they desire, and other commodities and necessaries for the use of the same colony, for mutual commerce with the natives of these provinces, or others who may trade with these plantations; and of transporting all commodities and merchandise, which shall seem to them needful, into our kingdom of Scotland without the payment of any tax, custom, and impost for the same to us, or our custom-house officers, or their deputies; and of carrying away the same from their offices on this side, during the space of seven years following the day of the date of our present charter; and to have this sole privilege for the space of three years next hereafter, we freely have granted, and by the tenor of our present charter grant and give, to the said Sir William and his aforesaids according to the terms hereinafter mentioned.

And after these three years are ended, it shall be lawful to us and our successors to levy and exact from all goods and merchandise which shall be exported from this our kingdom of Scotland to the said province of New Scotland, or imported from this province to our said kingdom of Scotland, in any ports of this our kingdom, by the said Sir William and his aforesaids, five per cent. only, according to the old mode of reckoning, without any other impost, tax, custom, or duty from them hereafter, which sum of five pounds per hundred, being thus paid by the said Sir William and his aforesaids to our officers and others appointed for this business, the said Sir William and his aforesaids may carry away the said goods from this our realm of Scotland into any other foreign ports and climes, without the payment of any other custom, tax, or duty to us, our heirs or successors, or any other persons; provided also that said goods within the space of thirteen months after their arrival in any part of this our kingdom may be again placed on board a ship. We also give and grant absolute and full power to the said Sir William and his aforesaids of taking, levying, and receiving to his own proper use, and that of his aforesaids, from all our subjects who shall desire to conduct colonies, follow trade, or sail to the said lands of New Scotland, and from the same, for goods and merchandise, five per cent.; besides the sum due to us; whether on account of the exportation from this our kingdom of Scotland to the said province of New Scotland, or of the importation from the said province to this our kingdom of Scotland aforesaid: and in like manner from all goods and merchandise which shall be exported by our subjects, leaders of colonies, merchants and navigators from the said province of New Scotland to any of our dominions, or any other places; or shall be imported from our realms and elsewhere to the said New Scotland, five per cent. beyond and above the sum before appointed to us: and from the goods and merchandise of all foreigners and others not under our sway, which shall be either exported from the said province of New Scotland, or shall be imported into the same beyond and above the said sum assigned to us, ten per cent. may be levied, taken, and received for the proper use of the said Sir William and his aforesaids, by such servants, officers, or deputies, or their agents, as they shall appoint and authorise for this business. And for the better security and profit of the said Sir William and his aforesaids, and of all our other subjects desiring to settle in New Scotland aforesaid, or to trade there, and of all others in general who shall not refuse to submit themselves to our authority and power, we have decreed and willed that the said Sir William may construct, or cause to be built, one or more forts, fortresses, castles, strong-holds, watch-towers, block-houses, and other buildings, with ports and naval stations, and also ships of war: and the same shall be applied for defending the said places as shall, to the said Sir William and his aforesaids, seem necessary to accomplish the aforesaid undertaking: and they may establish for their defence there, garrisons of soldiers, in addition to the things above mentioned; and generally may do all things for the acquisition, increase, and introduction of people, and to preserve and govern the said New Scotland, and the coasts and lands thereof in all its limits, features, and relations, under our name and authority, as we might do if present in person; although the case may require a more particular and strict order than is prescribed in this our present charter, and to this command we wish, direct, and most strictly enjoin all our justices, officers, and subjects, frequenting these places, to conform themselves; and to yield to and obey the said Sir William and his aforesaids in all and each of the above-mentioned matters, both principal and related; and be equally obedient to them in their execution as they ought to be to us whose person he represents, under the pains of disobedience and rebellion. Moreover, we declare by the tenor of our present charter to all Christian kings, princes, and states, that, if hereafter any one, or any from the said colonies, in the province of New Scotland aforesaid, or any other persons under their licence and command, exercising piracy at any future time, by land or by sea, shall carry away the goods of any person, or in a hostile manner do any injustice or wrong to any of our subjects, or those of our heirs or successors, or of other kings, princes, governors, or states in alliance with us; then, upon such injury offered, or just complaint thereupon, by any king, prince, governor, state, or their subjects, we, our heirs and successors, will see that public proclamations are made in any part of our said kingdom of Scotland, just and suitable for this purpose, that the said pirate or pirates who shall commit such violence, at a stated time to be determined by the aforesaid proclamation, shall fully restore all goods so carried away: and for the said injuries shall make full satisfaction, so that the said princes and others thus complaining shall deem themselves satisfied.   And if the authors of such crimes shall neither make worthy satisfaction, nor be careful that it be made within the limited time, then he or they who have committed such plunder neither are nor hereafter shall be under our government and protection; but it shall be permitted and lawful to all princes, and others whatsoever, to proceed against such offenders, or any of them, and with all hostility to invade them.

And though it is appointed that no nobleman and gentleman may depart from this country without our consent, yet we will that this our present charter be a sufficient permission and assurance to all engaging in the said voyage, save those who may be accused of treason, or retained by any special order; and according to our present charter, we declare and decree that no person may leave this country and go to the said region of New Scotland, unless they have previously taken the oath of allegiance to us, for which purpose we, by our present charter, give and grant the said Sir William and his foresaids, or their conservators and deputies, full power and authority to exact the said oath from, and administer it to, all persons proceeding into the said lands in that colony.   Moreover, we, for ourselves and our successors, with the advice and consent aforesaid, declare, decree, and ordain that all our subjects going to the said New Scotland, or living in it, and all their children and posterity born there, and all adventuring there, shall have and enjoy all the liberties, rights, and privileges of free and native subjects of our kingdom of Scotland, or of our other dominions, as if they had been born there.

Also, we, for ourselves and our successors, give and grant to the said Sir William and his aforesaids, the free power of regulating and coining money for the freer commerce of those inhabiting the said province, of any metal, in what manner, and of what form they shall choose and direct for the same.

And if any questions or doubts shall arise on the meaning and construction of any clause in our present charter, all these shall be taken and explained in their amplest form, and in favour of the said Sir William and his aforesaids. Besides, we, of our certain knowledge, proper motive, regal authority, and kingly power, have made, united, annexed, erected, created, and incorporated, and by the tenor of our present charter do make, unite, annex, erect, create, and incorporate the whole and undivided, the said province and lands of New Scotland, with all the seas and limits of the same, and minerals of gold and silver, lead, copper, steel, tin, brass, iron, and any other mines, pearls, precious stones, quarries, forests, thickets, mosses, marshes, lakes, waters, fisheries, as well in fresh waters as in salt, as well of royal fishes as of others; cities, free ports, free villages, towns, baronial villages, seaports, roadsteads, machines, mills, offices, and jurisdictions, and all other things, generally and particularly mentioned above, in one entire and free lordship and barony, which shall be called in all future time by the aforesaid name of New Scotland.

And we will and grant, and for ourselves and our successors decree and order, that one seisin now made by the said Sir William and his aforesaids upon any part of the soil of the said lands, and upon the province before described, shall, in all future time, be effective; and shall be a sufficient seisin for the whole region, with all the parts, appendages, privileges, accidents, liberties, and immunities of the same mentioned above, without any other special and definite seisin to be taken by himself or his aforesaids on any other part or place of the same: And concerning this seisin, and all things which have followed it, or can follow it, we, with the advice and consent above mentioned, for ourselves and successors, have dispensed, and by the tenor of our present charter, in the manner hereafter mentioned, do dispense for ever, *To hold and to possess* the whole and undivided, the said region and lordship of New Scotland, with all the bounds of the same within the seas above-mentioned, all minerals of gold and silver, copper, steel, tin, lead, brass, and iron, and any other mines, pearls, precious stones, quarries, woods, thickets, mosses, marshes, lakes, waters, fisheries, as well in fresh water as in salt, as well of royal fishes as of others, states, free towns, free ports, towns, baronial villages, seaports, roadsteads, machines, mills, offices, and jurisdictions, and all other things generally and specially mentioned above; with all other privileges, liberties, immunities, and accidents, and other things above-mentioned, to the aforesaid Sir William Alexander, his heirs and assigns, from us and our successors, in free covenant inheritance, lordship, barony, and royalty for ever; through all their just bounds and limits, as they lie in length and breadth, in houses, buildings, erected and to be erected, bogs, plains, and moors; marshes, roads, paths, waters, swamps, rivers, meadows, and pastures; mines, malt-houses, and their refuse; hawkings, huntings, fisheries, peat mosses, turf-bogs, coal, coal-pits, coneys, warrens, doves, dove-cotes, workshops, maltkilns, breweries, and broom; woods, groves, and thickets; wood, timber, quarries of stone and lime, with courts, fines, pleas, heriots, outlaws, rabbles of women, with free entrance and exit, and with fork, foss, sok, sac, theme, infangtheiff, outfangtheiff, wrak, wair, veth, vert, vennison, pit, and gallows; and with all other and singly, the liberties, commodities, profits, easements, and their rightful pertinents of all kinds, whether mentioned or not, above or below ground, far and near, belonging, or that can belong, to the aforesaid region and lordship, in any manner, for the future, freely, quietly, fully, wholly, honourably, well, and in peace, without any revocation, contradiction, impediment, or obstacle whatever.

Annually, at the festival of Christ's Nativity, on the soil of the said lands, and of the province of New Scotland, the said Sir William Alexander and his aforesaids shall pay to us, and our heirs and successors, under the name of quit-rent, one penny of Scottish money, if so much be demanded.

And because the tenure of the said lands, and of the province of New Scotland, and the quit-rent above-mentioned, may fail through want of the timely and lawful entry of any heir or heirs of the said Sir William succeeding him, a thing which they may not easily accomplish, on account of the great distance from our kingdom; and these same lands and province, on account of non-entrance, may come into our hands, and those of our successors, until the lawful entrance of the legitimate heir; and we, being unwilling that the said lands and region at any time should fall into non-entry, or that the said Sir William and his aforesaids should be thus deprived of the benefits and profits of the same, therefore we, with the advice aforesaid, have dispensed with the said non-entry whenever it shall occur, and by the tenor of this our charter, we, for ourselves and our successors, do dispense; and also we have renounced and exonerated, and by the tenor of our present charter, do renounce and exonerate, the said Sir William and his aforesaids in respect to the above-mentioned non-entrance of the said province and region, whenever it shall come into our hands, or by reason of non-entry may fall, with all things that can follow therefrom: provided, however, that the said Sir William, his heirs and assigns, within the space of seven years after the decease and death of their predecessors, or entry to the possession of said lands, and of other things aforesaid by themselves, or their lawful agents holding power for this purpose, do homage to us and our successors, and come to and receive through us the said lands, lordship, barony, and other things aforesaid, according to the laws and statutes of our said kingdom of Scotland. Finally, we, for ourselves and our successors, do will, decree, and ordain that this our present charter and infeoffment above written, of the lands aforesaid, lordship and region of New Scotland, and the privileges and liberties of the same, shall be ratified, approved, and established in our next Parliament of our said kingdom of Scotland, whenever it shall meet, so that it shall have therein the force and efficacy of a decree; and for this, we, for ourselves and our successors, declare that this our charter shall be a sufficient warrant; and, as a prince, we promise that the same shall be ratified and approved; and also we promise to alter, renew, increase, and extend the same into the most ample form as often as it shall seem necessary and expedient to the said Sir William and his aforesaids.

Moreover, it has seemed best to us, and we order and enjoin our beloved   our sheriffs, especially appointed on our part, on seeing this our charter under our Great Seal, so to give and grant to the aforesaid Sir William and his aforesaids, or their attorney or attorneys, possession and seisin, actual and real, of the lands, lordship, barony, and other things mentioned above: with all privileges, immunities, liberties, and other things above expressed; and this seisin we, by the tenor of our present charter, declare to be as lawful and regular as if he had a precept, under proof of our Great Seal, and in the most ample form, with all clauses requisite for the aforesaid purpose; with which we, for ourselves and successors, do for ever dispense. In witness whereof we have commanded our Great Seal to be affixed to this our present charter. Witnesses—Our well-beloved cousins and councillors, James, Marquis of Hamilton, Earl of Arran and Cambridge, Lord Aven and Innerdaill; George, Earl Marischal, Lord Keith, etc., Marshal of our Kingdom; Alexander, Earl of Dunfermline, Lord Fyvie and Urquhart, etc., our Chancellor; Thomas, Earl of Melrose, Lord Binning and Byres, our Secretary.—Our beloved familiar Councillors, Baronets; Sir Richard Cockburn, junior of Clerkington, Keeper of our Privy Seal; Sir George Hay of Kinfauns, our Register of the Rolls, and Clerk of the Council; Sir John Cockburn of Ormiston, Clerk of our Justiciary; and Sir John Scot of Scotstarvet, Director of our Chancery, Knights.

At our Castle of Windsor, the 10 day of September, in the year of our Lord 1621, and of our reigns the fifty-fifth and nineteenth years respectively.

By signature superscribed by the hand of our Sovereign Lord the King; and subscribed by the hands of our Chancellor, Treasurer, Principal Secretary, and of the other Lords, our Commissioners, and of our Privy Council of the said Kingdom of Scotland.

Written to the Great Seal, 29 *Sept.* 1621,

J. SCOTT, *Gratis.*

Sealed at Edinburgh, 29 *Sept.* 1621,

JA. RAITHE, *Grs.*

No. II.

CHARTER OF NOVODAMUS TO SIR WILLIAM ALEXANDER, DATED 12TH JULY 1625.

CHARLES, by the grace of God, King of Great Britain, France, and Ireland, and Defender of the Faith, to all good men of his whole land, clergy and laity, greeting.

Know ye, etc. [*Same as charter of 1621, up to "said kingdom of Scotland," p.* 180] . . . in which case the heirs and assignees of the said Sir William Alexander shall, notwithstanding the foresaid non-entry, enjoy and possess all and sundry the foresaid lands, country, and lordship of New Scotland, with all and sundry profits, as if the said non-entry had never happened, or as if they had never fallen into non-entry. Which lands, country, and lordship of New Scotland, as well mainlands as islands, within all and sundry the said bounds and seas thereof, with the woods, fishings, as well in salt waters as in fresh, of royal fishes as of others, with pearls, precious stones, veins, royal minerals of gold and silver, other minerals of iron, steel, lead, copper, brass, tin, mountain brass, and others whatsoever; and all privileges, liberties, immunities, prerogatives, offices and jurisdictions, and others, specially and generally above recited, formerly belonged to the said Sir William Alexander and his heirs and assignees, and were, by him and his procurators, in his name, duly and lawfully resigned into our hands, and that, for our new heritable infeftment of the same, to be granted in favour of the said Sir

William, or his heirs and assignees foresaid, in due and competent form, as accords, to be holden, as said is, with dispensation
of non-entry, in manner before written, when it shall happen.

Moreover, we, with advice before written, for the good, faithful, and willing service, performed and rendered to us by the said
Sir William Alexander, and respect being had to the great and
manifold expenses and charges bestowed and expended in the
plantation of the said bounds of the lordship and country of
New Scotland, and reduction of them under our obedience, and
for other weighty and onerous causes, have of new given, granted,
and disponed, and by our present charter, give, grant, and dispone, to the before-mentioned Sir William Alexander, and his
heirs and assignees heritably, all and sundry the foresaid lands,
lordship, and country of New Scotland, together with all and
sundry castles, towns, fortalices, manor places, houses, buildings,
built and to be built; gardens, orchards, planted and to be
planted; tofts, crofts, meadows, grazings, woods, shrubs, mills,
multures, mill-lands, fishings, as well of red as of other fishes,
salmon, large fish and small, in salt water as in fresh; together
with all and sundry teind-sheaves thereof included, as well great
as small; with the presentation, gift of benefices, churches, and
chapels, and rights of patronage thereof; annexes, connexes,
dependencies, tenants, tenandries, and services of free tenants of
the same; together with all and sundry precious stones, jewels,
crystal, alum, coral, and others, with all and sundry minerals,
veins, and quarries thereof, as well of regal and royal metals,
and minerals of gold and silver, within the said bounds and
lordship of New Scotland; as of other minerals of iron, steel,
tin, copper, brass, mountain brass, and other minerals whatsoever, with all and sundry parts, pendicles, pertinents, privileges,
liberties, and immunities of all and sundry the foresaid lands,
lordship, and country of New Scotland; with full power and
privilege to the said Sir William Alexander, his heirs and
assignees, of trying and searching, digging and examining the
ground for the same, and extracting, cleansing, refining, and
purifying them, and using, converting, and applying them to
their own proper uses (the tenth part of the royal metals, com-

monly called the ore of gold and silver, hereafter to be found
and extracted out of the said lands and country, only being
reserved to us and our successors), and the remainder of the said
metals, minerals, precious stones, jewels, and others whatsoever,
to belong to the said Sir William Alexander, his heirs and
assignees, to remain for ever with them, and be, with all profits
and duties thereof, converted to their own proper uses, with
power to the said Sir William Alexander, his heirs and assignees,
of building, constructing, and erecting upon and within all
the bounds of the said country, as shall seem to them expedient, cities, free boroughs of barony, towns, villages, harbours,
ports, and naval stations, and of appointing markets, as well
within the town as without, and imposing, levying, and receiving all and whatsoever tolls, customs, anchorages, and other
dues of said cities, boroughs of barony, towns, villages, fairs,
markets, free ports, harbours, naval stations, with all and sundry
casualties, profits, and duties whatsoever; and furnishing the
said cities and boroughs, as well within borough as without,
with sufficient and able magistrates, justices of the peace, pro-
vosts, bailies, aldermen, constables, and other officers, citizens,
free burgesses, and manufacturers, crafts of all kinds, with their
deacons and others thereto requisite, with full power, privilege,
and liberty, to them or their children, citizens and burgesses, to
sell wine and wax, salmon, herrings, and other staple goods and
merchandises, as well great as small, and constructing churches,
chapels, hospitals, maison-dieus, market-crosses, belfries, bells,
and all other ordinary ornaments thereto belonging, and planting
the said churches, and sufficiently providing them with sufficient
teachers, preachers, pastors, and ministers. And, in like manner,
of erecting, founding, and constructing common schools, colleges,
and universities, sufficiently provided with able and sufficient
masters, rectors, regents, professors of all sciences, letters, languages, and instruction; and of providing for sufficient maintenance, salaries, and living for them, to this effect. As also of
erecting prelates, archbishops, bishops, rectors, and vicars of
parishes and parish churches; and distributing and dividing all
the foresaid bounds of the said country into divers and distinct

shires, provinces, and parishes, for the better provision of the churches and ministry, division of the shires, and all other civil police; and, likewise, of founding, erecting, and instituting a senate of justice, places and colleges of justice, senators of council and session; members thereof, for the administration of justice, within the said country, and other places of justice and judicature. Further, of erecting and appointing secret and privy councils and sessions for the public good and advantage of said country, and giving and granting titles, honours, and dignities to the members thereof, and creating their clerks and members, and appointing seals and registers with their keepers. And also of erecting and instituting officers of state—a chancellor, treasurer, comptroller, collector, secretary, advocate, or attorney-general, clerk or clerks, register and keeper of the rolls, justice-clerk, director or directors of chancery, conservator or conservators of privileges of the said country, advocates, procurators, and pleaders of causes, and solicitors and agents thereof, and other members necessary. And likewise of gathering, collecting, and appointing meetings and assemblies of ecclesiastical persons and prelates, as well general, special or provincial meetings, as others; for ecclesiastical police and discipline, and authorising, ratifying, and confirming the said meetings, councils, and assemblies, with acts, statutes, and decrees thereon concluded, for the better authority of the same.

Further, we have made, constituted, and appointed, and by our present charter make, constitute, and appoint, the said Sir William Alexander, his heirs and assignees, our, and our heirs and successors', lieutenants-general, to represent our royal person, as well by sea as by land, of all and whole the said country and lordship of New Scotland, or to any judicature or jurisdiction heretofore, in virtue of any foregoing or subsequent right or title whatsoever. And with special power to the said Sir William Alexander, and his foresaids, of governing, ruling, and punishing and pardoning all our subjects, and others, inhabitants of the said bounds and country of New Scotland, or persons going thither, violators of the peace, or of the laws; and of making, sanctioning, and establishing laws there, as well civil as criminal, with laws of justiciary, admiralty, stewardship, regality, and sheriffship, at their good pleasure, provided the said laws be as conformable as possible to the laws of Scotland, respect being had to circumstances, place, country, persons, and their qualities. And likewise, of appointing rulers, commanders, and heads of all and sundry the foresaid cities, boroughs, ports, naval stations, and harbours, and also captains of castles, fortalices, and fort-resses, as well by sea and near the shore as by land, well and sufficiently provided, appointed, and fortified with troops of soldiers and forces for the maintenance, defence, and preservation thereof, and the repelling of all domestic as well as foreign in-vasions of the same: and of gathering, assembling, and making all the inhabitants of the said country meet together for the purpose before written, on all necessary occasions, for the repel-ling and resisting other force and violences whatsoever: And with power to the said Sir William Alexander and his foresaids, for the better fortifying of the said lordship and country of New Scotland, of transporting from the said kingdom, and other bounds convenient, all sorts of munitions, great and small, greater ordnance, cannons, demi-cannons of cast iron, swords, guns of brass and iron, and other instruments and engines of war, with small guns commonly called muskets, hagbuts, half haggs, pistols, powder, balls, and other necessary provision and arms, as well offensive as defensive; and wearing and using such arms, as well within the said country of New Scotland as in their passage and progress to the said lands, or from them, with their companions, associates, and dependants: Also, we, with advice aforesaid, have made, constituted, and appointed the said Sir William Alexander, his heirs and assignees heritably, our justices general, in all criminal causes within the said country and lordship of New Scotland; high admiral, and lord of regality, and admiralty within the said country, hereditary high steward also thereof, and of all and sundry such regalities, with power to him, and his heirs and assignees, of using, exercising, and enjoying all and sundry the foresaid jurisdictions, judicatures, and offices, with all and sundry privileges, prerogatives, immuni-ties, and casualties thereof; in like manner, and as freely as any other justice or justices general, high stewards, admirals, sheriffs, or lords of regalities, had, or can have, and possess, or enjoy, the said jurisdictions, judicatures, offices, dignities, and prerogatives in any of our kingdoms, bounds, and dominions whatsoever: With power to the said Sir William Alexander, his heirs and assignees, of constituting, erecting, nominating, and creating clerks, officers, macers, apprisers, and all other members of court, of all and sundry the foresaid judicatures and jurisdictions respectively, with all fees, dues, and emoluments thereto belonging as shall seem to them expedient: without prejudice always to all other infeftments, rights, or dispositions by us or our predecessors to whatsoever person or persons who are, or shall be, portioners of the said plantation of New Scotland, proceeding upon the resignation of the said Sir William Alexander only, and not otherwise, of whatsoever parts or portions of the said country and lordship of New Scotland, with the privileges and immunities mentioned in their infeftments.

And seeing, by reason of the great remoteness and distance of the said country and lordship of New Scotland from our said ancient kingdom of Scotland, both that the said country can neither easily nor conveniently be reached except in the summer time; and that the said country is altogether destitute of public scriveners and notaries, requisite for taking seisins; so that seisin at all times cannot conveniently be taken on the ground of the said country; and also respect being had to the great and manifold disadvantages which may result by default of timely seisin being taken upon this present patent; and upon other charters and similar infeftments granted, and to be granted, of the foresaid lands and lordship of New Scotland, or any part thereof; *Therefore*, that this our present charter may be more effectual, and that seisin thereupon may be more conveniently taken, it is necessary that seisin of all and sundry the foresaid lands of the said country and lordship of New Scotland be taken within our said kingdom of Scotland, and on the grounds and lands of the same in the most eminent place thereof; which can neither conveniently nor lawfully be done without an express union of the said country and lordship of New Scotland to the said kingdom of Scotland:

Wherefore, and for the advantage and readier convenience of the aforesaid seisin, we, with advice aforesaid, have annexed, united, and incorporated, and, by our present charter, annex, unite, and incorporate, with our said kingdom of Scotland, all and sundry the foresaid country and lordship of New Scotland, with the teinds and teind-sheaves thereof included, and all and sundry parts, pertinents, privileges, jurisdictions, and liberties of the same, and others generally and specially above mentioned: and by our present charter, will, declare, decern, and ordain that one seisin, now to be taken at our Castle of Edinburgh, as the most eminent and principal place of our said kingdom of Scotland, of all and sundry the said lands, country and lordship of New Scotland, or any part of the same, with teinds and teind-sheaves thereof included, respectively, is and shall be sufficient seisin for all and whole the foresaid lands, country, and lordship of New Scotland, with the teinds and teind-sheaves thereof included, or any parts of the said lands and country aforesaid, with all the privileges, jurisdiction, and liberties thereof respectively, and others specially and generally above mentioned, notwithstanding the said lands, country, and lordship of New Scotland are far distant, and lie discontiguous from our said kingdom of Scotland: as to which we, with advice and consent foresaid, have dispensed, and, by our present charter, for ever dispense, without prejudice and derogation, always to the said privilege and prerogative granted to the foresaid Sir William Alexander, and his heirs and assignees, of making and establishing laws, acts, and statutes concerning all and sundry the foresaid lands, country, and lordship of New Scotland, as well by sea as by land: And by our present charter we declare that, notwithstanding the said union, which is declared to be granted·solely for the advantage and convenience of seisin, the said country and lordship of New Scotland shall be judged, ruled, and governed by the laws and statutes made, and to be made and constituted and established by the said Sir William Alexander, and his heirs and assignees, relating to the said country and lordship of New Scotland, in like manner, and as freely in that respect as if the said union had never been made or hitherto granted: And further, notwithstanding the foresaid union, it shall be lawful to the foresaid Sir William Alexander, and his heirs and assignees, to give, grant, and dispone any parts or portions of the said lands, country, and lordship of New Scotland heritably belonging to them, to and in favour of whatsoever persons, their heirs and assignees, heritably, with the teinds and teind-sheaves thereof included, provided they are our subjects, to be holden of the said Sir William Alexander, or of us and our successors, either in blench farm, feu farm, or in ward and relief at their pleasure, and to entitle and denominate the said parts and portions, by whatsoever styles, titles, and designations shall seem to them fit, or be in the will and option of the said Sir William and his foresaids, which infeftments and dispositions shall be approved and confirmed by us or our successors freely, without any composition to be paid therefor. *Moreover*, we and our successors shall receive whatsoever resignations shall be made by the said Sir William Alexander and his heirs and assignees, of all and whole the foresaid lands and lordship of New Scotland, or of any part thereof in our hand, and [those] of our successors and commissioners aforesaid, with the teinds and teind-sheaves thereof included, and others generally and specially above-mentioned to and in favour of whatsoever person or persons (provided they are our subjects, and live under our obedience) : And they shall pass infeftments thereon, to be holden in free blench farm of us, our heirs and successors, in manner above-mentioned, freely, without any competition ; which lands, country, and lordship of New Scotland, with the teind-sheaves thereof included, and all and sundry parts, pendicles and pertinents, privileges, jurisdictions, prerogatives, and liberties of the same, and others specially and generally above-mentioned, together with all right, title, interest, claim of right, petitory as well as possessory (which we or our predecessors or successors had, have, or in any way could have, claim, or pretend thereto, or to any part of the same, or to the maills, farms, profits, and duties thereof, of whatsoever years or terms bygone, for whatsoever cause or occasion, we, with advice foresaid for the reasons above-mentioned, of new give, grant, and dispone to the foresaid Sir

William Alexander, and his heirs and assignees, heritably for
ever, renouncing and exonerating the same *simpliciter*, with all
action and instance heretofore, competent to and in favour of
the said Sir William Alexander, and his heirs and assignees, as
well for non-payment of the duties contained in their original
infeftments, as for non-performance of due homage conform
thereto, or for non-fulfilment of any point of the said original
infeftment, or for commission of any fault or deed of omission
or commission prejudicial thereto, and whereby the said original
infeftment may in any way be lawfully impugned or called in
question; for ever acquitting and remitting the same *simpliciter*
with all title, action, instance, and interest heretofore competent,
or that may be competent to us and our heirs and successors,
renouncing the same *simpliciter jure lite et causa cum pacto de
non petendo :* and with supplement of defects as well not named
as named, which we will to be held, as expressed in this our
present charter.

To be holden in free blench farm as said is, and dispensing
with non-entry whensoever it shall happen in manner aforesaid : *Moreover*, we, for us and our successors, with advice aforesaid, give, grant, and commit power to the said Sir William
Alexander and his heirs and assignees, of having and lawfully
establishing and causing to be coined current money in the said
country and lordship of New Scotland, and for the readier convenience of commerce and bargains among the inhabitants thereof,
of such metal, form, and fashion as they shall design, or appoint :
And for this effect, we give, grant, and commit to them, or their
heirs and assignees, lieutenants of the said country, the privileges
of coining money with iron instruments, and with officers necessary for that purpose: Further, we, for us and our successors,
with advice aforesaid, have given, granted, ratified, and confirmed,
and by our present charter give, grant, ratify, and confirm, to the
said Sir William Alexander, and his heirs and assignees, all
places, privileges, prerogatives, pre-eminences, and precedencies
whatsoever, given, granted, and reserved, or to be given, granted,
and reserved, to the said Sir William Alexander, his heirs and
assignees; and his successors, lieutenants of the said country

and lordship of New Scotland, over the knights-baronets, and remanent portioners and associates, of the said plantations, so as the said Sir William Alexander, and his heirs-male descending of his body, as lieutenants foresaid, shall and may take place, prerogative, pre-eminence, and precedency, as well before all esquires, lairds, and gentlemen of our said kingdom of Scotland, as before all the foresaid knights-baronets of our said kingdom, and all others before whom the said knights-baronets, in virtue of the privilege of dignity to them, can have place and precedency; for the advancement of which plantation and colony of New Scotland, and in respect of it especially, the said knights-baronets were, with advice foresaid, created in our said kingdom of Scotland, with their estate and dignity, as a special token of our favour conferred upon such gentlemen and honourably born persons, portioners of the foresaid plantation and colony; with this express provision always, that the number of the foresaid baronets never exceed one hundred and fifty. *Finally*, we, with advice aforesaid, for us, our heirs and successors, will, decern, and ordain that this our patent and infeftment, with all its contents, be ratified, approved, and confirmed in our next Parliament of our kingdom of Scotland; and that it may have the force, strength and effect, of an act, statute, and decree of that supreme judicatory, as to which we, for us and our successors, declare and ordain this our present charter, to be a sufficient warrant to the Lords of the Articles of our said Parliament, for the ratification and confirmation thereof in manner before written. *Moreover*, to our lovites   and each of you conjunctly and severally, our sheriffs in that part especially constituted, greeting : We charge and command you that ye give and deliver to the foresaid Sir William Alexander, or his certain attorney, bearer of these presents, heritable state and seisin, as well as corporal, actual, and real possession of all and whole the foresaid lands, country, and lordship of New Scotland, with all and sundry parts, pendicles, privileges, commodities, immunities, and others, generally as well as particularly above expressed, at our said Castle of Edinburgh, without delay, and this in no wise ye leave undone: Which to do, we commit to you and each of you conjunctly and severally, our sheriffs in that part foresaid, our full and irrevocable power by our present charter : which seisin we, with advice aforesaid, for us and our successors, by our present charter, will, declare, and ordain to be as lawful and sufficient as if precepts of seisin, separately and ordinarily to that effect, had been directed out of our Chancery upon our said charter, as to which we, with advice aforesaid, for us, our heirs and successors, have 'dispensed, and by our present charter for ever dispense.

In Witness whereof, we have ordered our Great Seal to be appended to this our present charter, the witnesses being our well-beloved cousins and councillors, James, Marquis of Hamilton, Earl of Arran and Cambridge, Lord Aven and Innerdaill, etc.; William, Earl Marischal, Lord Keith, etc., Marischal of our kingdom; our beloved councillor, Sir George Hay of Kinfauns, knight, our Chancellor; our well-beloved cousin and councillor, Thomas, Earl of Melrose, Lord Binning and Byers, our Secretary; our beloved familiar Councillors, Sir Richard Cokbourne of Clerkington, Keeper of our Privy Seal; Sir John Hamilton of Magdalens, Clerk of our Rolls, Register, and Council; Sir George Elphinstone of Blythswoode, our Justice-Clerk; and Sir John Scot of Scotstarvet, Director of our Chancery, Knights.—At our Palace of Oatlands, the 12th day of July, A.D. 1625, and the first of our reign.

No. III.

ANACRISIS; OR, A CENSURE OF POETS ANCIENT AND MODERN. By Sir William Alexander, Earl of Stirling.

AFTER a great travel both of body and of mind which (since not voluntary, but imposed upon me) was the more painful, by retiring for a time where I was born, of late gladly embracing this rarely offered opportunity to refresh myself, and being curious, as the most dainty kind of pleasure for such as are

capable of their delicacies, to recreate myself with the Muses
(I may justly say recreate, since they create new spirits, which
shaking off gross affections, diving into the depths, reaching the
heights, and contemplating both, are transported with these
things which are only worthy to entertain so noble a thing as the
mind of man). I began to renew my acquaintance there, having
of a long time been a stranger with them; so that at the first, I
could not begin to practise as one of their ordinary train, but
only to court with these whose credit might procure my access.
I conversed with some of the modern as well as with the ancients,
kindling my fire at those fires which do still burn out of the
ashes of ancient authors, to whom I find them in no way
inferior, though like affectioned patriots, by writing in the vulgar
tongues, seeking to grace their own country. I have pitied the
ignorance of some who might be admitted for versifiers and poets,
that would extol as an excellent piece of poetry, that which,
wanting life, had nothing but language, masking ignorance with
Greek and Latin, whose treasure long feeding upon, they had by
time digested, and converted to their own use, though venting it
but in excrements !

Language is but the apparel of poesy : which may give beauty
but not strength. And when I censure any poet, I first dissolve
the general contexture of his work in several pieces, to see what
sinews it hath, and to mark what will remain behind, when that
external gorgeousness consisting in the choice or placing of words
as if it would bribe the ear to corrupt the judgment, is first
removed, or at least only marshalled in its own degree. I value
language as a conduit; the variety thereof to several shapes, and
adorned truth or witty inventions, that which it should deliver.
I compare a poem to a garden, the disposing of the parts of the
one to the several walks of the other; the decorum kept in
descriptions and representing of persons, to the proportion and
distances to be observed in such things as are planted therein,
and the variety of invention, to the diversity of flowers thereof :
whereof three sorts do chiefly please me—a grave sentence by
which the judgment may be bettered; a witty conceit which
doth harmoniously delight the spirits ; and a generous rapture

expressing magnanimity, whereby the mind may be inflamed for great things. All the rest, for the most part, is but a naked narration or gross stuff to uphold the general frame: yet the more apt, if well contrived and eloquently delivered, to angle vulgar readers, who perchance can scarce conceive the other.

I condemn their opinions, who, as they would include all perfection in one, do prefer some one with whom they sympathise, or whom they have most practised, to all others. There is none singular in all, and yet all are singular in some things. There is none so excellent, that is not excelled in some pieces by some others; and every one hath his own particular grace, none being positively, but only comparatively to be praised, and that for parts, not in the whole—men's works, like themselves, not being all of one quality, nor ever alike.

I like the phrase, style, method, and discreet carriage of Virgil; the vigour and variety of invention in Ovid; the deep judgment and grave sentences of Horace and Juvenal; the heroical conceptions, showing an innate generosity, in Statius Papianus and Lucan. And I cannot wonder enough at that man (deservedly renowned and admirably learned), who, with a passionate kind of partiality (the more strange that it is against dead men, who have exceeded envy, having their just value set upon them by sundry ages), would advisedly vilify Lucan in so extreme a measure, saying, "Videtur potius latrare quam canere;" whom Statius Papianus and Martial (his superiors in poesy), both celebrating his birth by eternal testimonies, have magnified so much:

> " Hæc est illa dies, quæ magni conscia partus
> Lucanum populis et tibi Polla dedit ; "

and thereafter:

> " Vatis Apollinei, magno memorabilis ortu
> Lux redit, Aonidum turba favete sacris
> Hæc merita, cùm te terris Lucane dedisset
> Mixtus Castaliæ Boetis ut esset aquæ."

Julius Scaliger doth aggravate much any hyperbole wherein he hath seemed to exceed, and hath not remarked, at least will

not remember, the unmatchable height of his ravishing conceits
to provoke magnanimity.   If he had as narrowly sifted Virgil,
whom he will needs justify as without any blemish, without
reposing as by an implicit faith upon his sufficiency, he would
have found an error in him more gross than any that is in
Lucan; as this, where the praise of an epic poem is to feign a
person exceeding nature, not such as all ordinarily be, but with
all the perfections whereof a man can be capable—every defi-
ciency in that imaginary man being really the author's own,
whose unlimited invention, for lack of judgment, could reach
to no greater height.   He (seeking to extol the valour of Æneas,
which only could be done by the valour of some valorous enemy
whom he had vanquished) doth so extremely extenuate the
courage of Turnus at his death, leaving him no time to recover
it, that, where out of a poetic liberty he should have afforded
more than was ordinary, wanting nothing but fortune, and at
least inferior to none but to him whom he would grace with his
ruin, he doth make him die like a dastard; casting thereby
down all the glory intended for Æneas overcoming but a coward;
and, in a more abject manner than the lowest-minded man
could have descended to conceive, burdening the gods with his
cowardice, whose mind, in whatsoever state his body was, should
have continued free, not basely begging his life.

> " Ille humilis supplexque, oculos dextramque precantem
>   Protendens, ' equidem merui, nec deprecor ' inquit
>   Utere sorte tuâ; miseri te si qua Parentis
>   Tangere cura potest, **oro** (fuit et tibi talis
>   Anchises genitor), Donni miserere senectæ;
>   Et me seu corpus spoliatum lumine mavis,
>   Redde meis; Vicisti; tua est Lavinia conjux."

Thus would he unworthily ransom his life with loss of his
honour and of his lady, and I never read that part of Virgil but
I remember the speech of Paulus Emilius, when Perseus, King
of Macedon, came with tears, a suitor to him, that he might not
be led in triumph.   "Fie upon you, beast," said he; "you beg
that which you ought to give unto yourself, and have disgraced
my victory, who now, after all my travels, can have no credit,

having only overcome such a base coward as was not worthy to have been contended with." If I have been too bold in censuring Julius Scaliger, let me be excused by his example in censuring all his betters; and it is only to give Lucan his due, not to derogate from him.

There is no man doth satisfy me more than that notable Italian, Torquato Tasso, in whom I find no blemish but that he doth make Solyman, by whose overthrow he would grace Rinaldo, to die fearfully, belying the part that he would have personated during his life; as if he would choose rather to err in imitating others, than to prove singular by himself. Speron, thinking his exquisite work of "Godfred" to be too full of rich conceits, and more dainty than did become the gravity of such a work, said that it was an "heroic poem written in madrigals;" and yet when he wrote a "Week of the Creation" in emulation of Du Bartas, it did no way approach to the perfections of the other, which doth confirm me in my first opinion, that every author hath his own genius directing him, by a secret inspiration, to that wherein he may most excel, and, as I said, excelling in some things, and none in all.

Many would bound the boundless liberty of a poet—binding him only to the birth of his own brains; affirming that there can be no perfection but in a fiction; not considering that the ancients, upon whose example they ground their opinion, did give faith unto those fables whereby they would abuse our credulity, not only as to true history, but as to true Divinity, since containing the greatness of their gods and grounds of their religion, which they in their own kind did strive superstitiously to extol; so that hereby they would either make our religion or our affection thereunto inferior unto theirs, and imaginary matters to be more celebrated than true deeds, whose envied price, affectionately looked upon, must beget a generous emulation in any virtuous reader's mind.

The treasures of poesy cannot be better bestowed than upon the apparelling of truth, and truth cannot be better apparelled to please young lovers than with the excellences of poesy. I would allow that an epic poem should consist altogether of a

* o

fiction, that the poet, soaring above the course of nature, making
the beauty of virtue to invite, and the honour of vice to affright,
the beholders, may liberally furnish his imaginary man with all
the qualities requisite for the accomplishing of a perfect creature,
having power to dispose of all things at his own pleasure.

No. IV.

HISTORY OF ALEXANDER HUMPHRYS OR ALEXANDER, CLAIMANT OF THE EARLDOM OF STIRLING.

ALEXANDER HUMPHRYS, one of the claimants of the earldom of
Stirling, was son of William Humphrys, merchant, residing at
Fair Hill, Birmingham, by his wife, Hannah, younger daughter
of the Rev. John Alexander, who, on the 1st November 1743,
died minister of Plunket Street Presbyterian Church, Dublin,
and whose father, James Alexander, a solicitor at Dublin, was
descended from the family of Alexander, at Candren, near Paisley (vol. ii., chap. xxiii.).

Alexander Humphrys was born at Birmingham on the 21st
June 1783. Having accompanied his father to France during
the peace of Amiens in 1802, he was, on the outbreak of hos-
tilities, arrested by order of Napoleon. His father died at
Verdun, in France, on the 1st May 1807, but he personally continued a captive till 1814, when, on the restoration of peace, he
returned to England. The family resources being nearly ex-
hausted, he settled at Worcester, where he some time assisted
in Netherton House school, which he subsequently conducted
on his own account. Through his wife, Fortunata Bartoletti
of Naples, whom he married in 1812, he became acquainted
with Mademoiselle le Normand,* who, at Paris, conducted busi-

---

* Mademoiselle le Normand composed the following, among other works:
" Les Souvenirs Prophétiques d'une Sibylle," 8vo, 1814 ; " Memoires Historiques
et Sécrets de l'Impératrice Joséphine," 2 vols., 8vo, 1820, of which a second

ness as an authoress, book-vender, **and fortune-teller by cards**. This person predicted that, after encountering many trials and difficulties, he would attain distinction and opulence. Impressed with this prediction, he proceeded, on the death of his mother, which took place on the 12th September 1814, to institute inquiries as to his descent. There was, he learned, a dormant peerage in the House of Alexander; and in 1815, or the year following, he requested Mr Josiah Corrie, his family solicitor at Birmingham, to promote, on **his behalf**, a claim for **the** earldom of Stirling. Mr Corrie, in the absence of documents, declined to act.

In February 1819, some one, under the signature of "F. D.," communicated with the *Gentleman's Magazine,* desiring to receive some information respecting the family of Alexander. He specially inquired—"1. What descendants, **from** the **fourth**, fifth, sixth, and seventh sons, of Sir William Alexander, **were** existing in 1739? When the earldom became dormant? **and** who and what are the descendants now existing? 2. Whether any correct pedigrees of the family, comprising the younger branches down to 1740, or later, can be procured? 3. Whether it be possible to refer to the papers of the successive claimants of the honours?"

In the *Gentleman's Magazine* for April 1819, the editor refers to further inquiries by "F. D." in these words:

"'**F. D.**,' in addition to the inquiries respecting the Alexander family, inserted in our number for February last, p. 98, would be thankful for any particulars, through the medium of our miscellany, of **the descent of** the Rev. John Alexander, minister of the Presbyterian **church in** Plunket Street, Dublin, from 1730 till his death, **November 1, 1743**. Mr Alexander was a native of Londonderry, and nearest **male** heir to the earldom of Stirling on the demise of Henry, fifth earl, in 1739. He was author of **an** excellent work on Irenæus, **and** one **of** those men whose society was courted by the celebrated Dean Swift."

edition, **in** three volumes, **was** published in 1827; "Souvenirs de la Belgique Cent Jours d'Infortunes, ou le Procès Mémorable," 8vo, 1822; "Ombre Immortelle de Catharine II. au Tombeau d'Alexandre I.," 8vo, 1826 (Swinton's Report of Humphrys' Trial).

The statement by "F. D." that the Rev. John Alexander of Dublin composed "an excellent work on Irenæus" had been made in a letter, alleged by "one of Mr Alexander's descendants at Birmingham" to have been written by Dr Isaac Watts, to Mr Alexander "from the Lady Abney's in Lime Street, London, on the 18th April 1727." The supposed letter was printed in 1816 in the *Monthly Repository of Theology*, a religious serial published at Hackney (vol. xi., p. 193). The other statements, that Mr Alexander was a native of Londonderry, a friend of Dean Swift, and "nearest male heir to the earldom of Stirling," were altogether groundless.

With the signature "H. W.," a correspondent, in the *Gentleman's Magazine* for May 1819, presented the following note :

"The Rev. John Alexander was probably a descendant of Captain Andrew Alexander of Londonderry, whose name appears in the list of Protestants attainted by James the Second's Parliament, held in Dublin in 1689."

In 1823 Mr Humphrys entered into correspondence with Mr Thomas Christopher Banks of London, author of the "Dormant and Extinct Baronage of England." Having, "out of grateful respect to the memory of his maternal grandfather, John Alexander, as well as out of consideration for the wishes oftentimes expressed by his deceased mother," sought permission to adopt the surname of Alexander, he procured, on the 8th March 1824, a royal licence for that purpose. Without further process, he attended the election of a representative peer in Holyrood Palace on the 2d June 1825, and, answering to the name of the Earl of Stirling, tendered his vote. He claimed the peerage "under the destination of a royal charter of *novodamus*, under the Great Seal dated 7th December 1639, granted by Charles I. in favour of William, Earl of Stirling" (Reg. of Elections of Peers, vol. ii., fol. 228).

As "Earl of Stirling," Mr Humphrys Alexander proceeded to the town of Stirling, to visit a locality associated with his alleged progenitors. At the instance of Mr James Wright, his solicitor at Stirling, his arrival was welcomed by the ringing of the public bells, while the magistrates waited upon him at his hotel, to offer congratulations. His visit was chronicled in a local newspaper,* which described "the interest with which his lordship visited the castle, and every part of the town worthy of notice," adding that "he seemed to take peculiar interest in viewing Argyle Lodge, formerly the town residence of the Earls of Stirling."

At Stirling, Mr Humphrys Alexander confirmed to his solicitor, Mr James Wright, his claim to a place of sepulture adjoining the High Church (vol. i., p. 187); before leaving the place, he conveyed to the treasurer of the kirk session a donation of £5 for the parochial poor. In appreciation of his dignity and munificence, the town council placed him on their burgess roll, and apprised him of the honour in these terms: "At Stirling, the twenty-seventh day of June, one thousand eight hundred and twenty-five years.—Which day the magistrates and town council of the burgh of Stirling being convened, they resolve to elect and admit the Right Honourable Alexander, Earl of Stirling, to be a burgess *qua* guildbrother of the burgh; and authorise the provost to subscribe a proper ticket of admission, and transmit the same to his lordship, the expense being to be defrayed by the town, and authorise the chamberlain to pay the same accordingly. Extracted from the Records of the Town Council of the Burgh of Stirling by William Galbraith, Town Clerk."

From Stirling Mr Humphrys Alexander proceeded to Glasgow, where he was introduced to Mr John Dillon, a solicitor with whom, in relation to his claims, he subsequently corresponded. Under the designation of "Alexander Humphrys Alexander, Earl of Stirling," he was, on the 7th February 1826, served before the Bailie Court of Canongate "lawful and nearest heir-male in general of his mother," Hannah Alexander; he was thereafter retoured "Earl of Stirling and Dovan," † his mother being described as "Countess of Stirling." In this service was assumed the validity of the charter of *novodamus* of the 7th December

* *Stirling Journal*, 16th June 1825.

† The Dovan was the ancient name of the river Devon, which flowed near Menstry in its passage from the Ochil hills to the river Forth.

1639, on which he had in June recorded at Holyrood his claim
to the earldom ; it was made to re-grant to the first earl, on his
resignation of a former patent, the earldom of Stirling and
Dovan, with remainder to females, failing heirs-male. In the
service was presented a statement of pedigree, in which Mr
Humphrys Alexander's maternal grandfather, the Rev. John
Alexander, was described as son of John Alexander of Antrim,
son of John Alexander, fourth son of the first earl, by his wife,
Agnes Graham. At a subsequent stage he corrected his pedigree by alleging that his ancestor, John Alexander of Antrim,
was son of John Alexander of Gartmore by a second wife,
" Elizabeth Maxwell of Londonderry."

Mr Humphrys Alexander despatched to America Mr Thomas
Christopher Banks, there to assert his claim as Earl of Stirling
to the vast territories which had belonged to the first earl. To Mr
Dillon, his Glasgow correspondent, he, in a letter, dated the 24th
November 1826, wrote as follows : " I have been cruelly disappointed about ' the loan negotiation,' which has been twice broken
off and again renewed. The great news received from Mr Banks
by the last packet has made the prospect brighten up again, and
I am now once more flattered that the object of my wishes will
be accomplished almost immediately. By all he was received
in a most flattering manner. The British consul, Mr Buchanan,
had tendered his services to Mr Banks in a very handsome
manner, by a letter. With my second counsel, Mr Clark, whom
Mr B. describes as a man of high character, great soundness,
and perspicuity of judgment, and devoted to my interests with
an ardent zeal, he had had daily meetings and conversations,
for the purpose of examining the charters and documents, and
arranging the plan of proceedings. The cause will be conducted
in its proper time for hearing, by Mr Webster, as leading counsel, assisted by Mr Clark, and Mr Banks as my agent and representative ; and it is now confidently anticipated the Congress
will grant me a location of five millions of acres, which is found
to be not one-twentieth part of the lands originally granted, all
convertible at once, at common market prices, into cash, and will
be more than one million sterling." To Mr Dillon he reported,

on the 25th July 1827, that Mr Banks was using in America, " with complete effect, copies of charters obtained by the first Earl of Stirling," adding, " By degrees, all the valuable papers of which my grandfather was robbed, about the time that the General preferred his claims to the earldom, are finding their way back to me."

Mr Banks returned from America in the autumn of 1827, when " the loan negotiation " was vigorously renewed. In April 1828, on the recommendation of Mr James Wright, Stirling, Mr Ephraim Lockhart, Writer to the Signet at Edinburgh, undertook the office of law adviser in the case, and, under his direction, Mr Banks proceeded to Ireland to institute inquiries respecting the claimant's family. The materials which Mr Banks alleged he had procured in Ireland during his visit in 1828 did not include the charter of *novodamus*, and he accordingly undertook a second mission to Ireland early in 1829. From Carlow he communicated to Mr Humphrys Alexander on the 17th March, that, having " found, on his return to Dublin, on the 10th inst., a parcel, enclosing an old document, which appears to be an excerpt from the charter of *novodamus*, 7th December 1639, and bearing on it an indorsement, with the initials, as they seemed, of Mr Conyers," he had proceeded to Carlow to make inquiry about it of Mr Fairclough, who was possessor, he had ascertained, of some of Mr Conyers' papers.*

Deeming the " excerpt " genuine, Mr Lockhart proceeded to

---

* To Mr Conyers we shall refer subsequently. It may be stated meanwhile that Mr Banks afterwards acknowledged that the excerpt charter came into his hands at Carlow, having there reached him by post in a packet, which bore the postmark of Portsmouth or Falmouth. But the narrative which he transmitted to Mr Humphrys Alexander was intended for transmission to Mr Lockhart, whom it was necessary to satisfy as to the absolute genuineness of his discovery. On this subject we subjoin a MS. note of the late Mr William B. B. D. Turnbull, advocate, Edinburgh : " Mr Lockhart stated to me that Banks wrote to him, desiring to be informed of the style of a *novodamus*, supposing such had been granted to the first Earl of Stirling. Lockhart sent him a draft, and was surprised when he received 'the excerpt' three months afterwards, to find that Banks had made it in *ipsissimis verbis* of the copy sent him. Banks had at the same time procured from the Register House various copies of charters granted about the period founded on."

raise upon it, in the Court of Session, a process for proving the tenor of the *novodamus* charter. This action was raised against "Dr John Watts, physician, New York, and William Alexander Duer, Esq., residing in Albany, in the state of New York, grandsons and heirs-portioners of line of the deceased William Alexander, surveyor-general of the province of New Jersey," the summons setting forth that the alleged charter had, about the year 1758, been abstracted from Mrs Hannah Alexander, the claimant's grandmother, by "a servant of hers, at the instigation of the said William Alexander." As probably anticipated, Messrs Watts and Duer, who had no possible interest in the case, remained silent. The action was, however, resisted by the officers of State, and was dismissed on the 4th March 1830. It was followed by another action, directed against the officers of State, and Mr Graham of Gartmore, in which "the excerpt" of the alleged charter of *novodamus* was again founded on. This second action was dismissed on the 2d March 1833.

The alleged discovery of the excerpt charter took place in the spring of 1829, and thereafter Mr Humphrys Alexander was enabled to recommend his case to financial agents and money-lenders. In October 1829, he quitted Worcester for London, where, through a person named Morant, he was introduced to Mr John Tyrrell, a financial agent. Ascertaining from Mr James Wright, the claimant's solicitor at Stirling, that Mr Edward Alexander of Powis claimed descent from an ancestor of the first Earl of Stirling, Mr Tyrrell suggested to Mr Alexander's elder son, now Major-General Sir James Edward Alexander, that the honours and advantages of the earldom might be shared with him, on his abetting the claim. The proposal not being entertained, Mr Tyrrell introduced the claimant to several capitalists, who, on his granting them bonds for £50,000, handed him sums together amounting to £13,000. Mr Humphrys Alexander now rented a house in Baker Street, and set up his carriage.*

* Commenting on the evidence given by Mr Tyrrell at Mr Humphrys Alexander's trial in April 1839, the anonymous author of a pamphlet, issued on the

Procuring a brieve from Chancery, dated the 21st September 1830, Mr Humphrys Alexander was, on the 11th October of that year, served by a jury in the Burgh Court of Canongate, heir in general of William, first Earl of Stirling, described in the record as "his great-great-great-grandfather." Among the documents accompanying the claim were extracts from Douglas's Peerage, and from parochial and other records; also several documents, of which the genuineness was subsequently questioned. Of these last two were affidavits, dated 1722 and 1723. In the former, Sara Lyner, "residing at Bally-ryder, in the parish of Stradbally, Queen's County, Ireland, a widow, aged eighty-four," deponed that her mother was in the service of Lord Montgomery, in the county of Down, and that while there "Mr John Alexander of Garthmore, a son of the Lord Sterline in Scotland, came to see my lord, and brought with him his ounely son." In the family of this "only son," Mr John Alexander of Antrim, she subsequently served; she was present when in May 1682 he married Miss Mary Hamilton at Donagheady, and she nursed her mistress after the birth of her only son in September 1686, and which son was then (1722) residing at Stratford-upon-Avon, Warwickshire. This affidavit of Sara Lyner bore to have been sworn before Jonas Percy, an Extraordinary Commissioner of the Irish Court of Chancery.

The second affidavit proceeded in the name of Henry Hovenden of Ballynakill, in the Queen's County, and bore to have been sworn on the 16th July 1723, before the Hon. John Pocklington, one of the Barons of Exchequer in Ireland. In this instrument, Hovenden declared that the Rev. John Alexander, then residing in Warwickshire, was "grandson and only male representative of John Alexander of Gartmore, the fourth son of William, first Earl of Stirling;" he declared further that he had

claimant's behalf, has these words : "Of this money [£13,000], scarcely as many hundreds ever reached Lord Stirling's pocket. Only a portion of the money, less than a half, was ever paid, and of this his lordship was robbed at the moment of payment, by the very people who pretended to supply it" (Remarks on the Trial of the Earl of Stirling, by an English Lawyer, London, 1839, 8vo).

seen in the possession of Thomas Conyers of Carlow the charter
of *novodamus* of the 7th December 1639, the contents of which,
as presented in the alleged "excerpt," he minutely detailed.
Thomas Meredith, a notary-public, certified the signature of
Hovenden; and in a postscript Thomas Conyers declared that
"Lord Sterling's charter was trusted to his late father in troublesome times by y⁰ dec⁴ Mary, Countess of Mᵗ Alexander."

On the 30th May 1831, Mr Humphrys Alexander followed
up his service as heir-general to the first Earl of Stirling, by
effecting a service "as heir of tailzie and provision" to the first
Earl of Stirling, in different lands in Scotland, erected into an
alleged earldom of Dovan, but in which no investiture of the
ancestor was even alleged. Next, on the 10th June 1831, he obtained a brieve as heir of the first Earl of Stirling in the lands,
continents, and islands of Nova Scotia, and part of Canada; and
on the 2d July, conducted a special service before the Sheriff of
Edinburgh—the evidence consisting of the recorded charter in
favour of the first earl, dated 12th July 1625, and of the retour
of his previous service in the court of Canongate. The circle of
legal formalities was completed on the 8th July 1831, when, on
a precept from Chancery, he was infeft in the North American
territories within the Castle of Edinburgh.

While these proceedings were in progress, the claimant lost no
opportunity of asserting his alleged rights. He voted at the
general election of representative peers on the 2d September
1830, and at the general election on the 3d June 1831. On the
14th July 1831, he granted his agent, Mr Banks, 16,000 acres
of land in Canada, and created him a baronet of Nova Scotia.
On Mr Philippart, another of his agents, he bestowed similar
honours and privileges. As "lord proprietor of the province of
Nova Scotia, New Brunswick, and the adjacent islands," he
opened an office at 53 Parliament Street, London, for the sale
of lands, and for debentures on his American possessions. In a
prospectus, dated 12th July 1831, he offered his lands in Nova
Scotia at prices varying from two to twenty shillings per acre.
"He especially recommended for purchase by colonists a million
of acres of most excellent land in New Brunswick."

In January 1831 the claimant approached the throne. He addressed a memorial to King William IV., praying that in his character as a peer he might be admitted to the royal presence. The memorial being referred to Lord Chancellor Brougham, his lordship reported to the king the decision of the Court of Session adverse to the memorialist, and his own opinion that his pretensions were untenable. Mr Humphrys Alexander renewed his memorial in August, when he claimed the privilege, as Hereditary Lieutenant of Nova Scotia, of rendering homage at the coronation. This application was unheeded. To the public authorities of Nova Scotia, he, on the 28th October 1831, addressed a manifesto, in which he refused to recognise any allotment of territory made otherwise than by his alleged ancestor, but offering, in matters of purchase or lease, to allow "the native inhabitants of Nova Scotia or Canada every preference over persons emigrating from Great Britain." To Earl Grey, as First Commissioner of His Majesty's Treasury, he sent a protest against any interference with his rights on the part of Government. In June 1832 he petitioned Parliament against a charter being granted to the Land Company of New Brunswick and Nova Scotia. These proceedings attracted general attention. In 1832 the Marchioness-Dowager of Downshire, as heir of line of the fourth Earl of Stirling, presented a memorial to the House of Lords, complaining that the title of Earl of Stirling had been unlawfully assumed, and setting forth that if the charter of *novodamus* were a genuine document, its effect would be to vest the earldom in her person. On the 19th March of the same year, the House of Lords, on the motion of the Earl of Rosebery, appointed a select committee to consider the subject of persons claiming dormant peerages voting at elections of Scottish representative peers, with a view of preventing the facility with which titles might be unlawfully assumed. To this committee the memorial of the Dowager Marchioness of Downshire was referred.

Mr Humphrys Alexander strongly resisted interference with his assumed rights. To the committee of the House of Lords he presented a protest, in which he maintained that the Marchioness of Downshire was only entitled to compete with him in the Scottish courts, by which, he maintained, his title had been duly recognised. On his behalf, in 1832, Mr Banks, assuming the title of "Sir Thomas Christopher Banks, Bart. N.S.," issued an octavo volume, entitled, "An Analytical Statement of the Case of Alexander, Earl of Stirling and Dovan, containing an explanation of his official dignities and peculiar territorial rights and privileges in the British Colonies of Nova Scotia and Canada." In this work, which was dedicated to the king, Mr Banks entreated his Majesty to recognise his client as *de facto* Earl of Stirling and Dovan; he added, in "an advertisement," that he regarded his own title of baronet as being perfectly as legal and efficacious as if it had been conferred by the Crown itself. Against the claims of the Marchioness of Downshire he urged his client's services in the court of Canongate, and his votes at the peers' elections at Holyrood. On his client's behalf, he further pleaded that, as a peer, he had been exempted from arrest by an English judge. Connected with the matter of arrest, he referred to certain proceedings instituted against his client at the instance of Vice-Admiral Sir Henry Digby, K.C.B., who had advanced him £500, and had demanded payment of his bond. The admiral, he declared, had acted against his client in a manner which "the lowest Jack in the service would disapprove," by becoming "a cat's-paw of his enemies," designating his lordship as a commoner, employing against him "Janus-like solicitors," and a barrister who "had perverted facts," and dragging him into a court "which admitted of pettifogging malice," viz., the Court of Common Pleas. Mr Banks' "Statement" was accompanied with several pedigree charts, and a map entitled, "The largest and most valuable portions of the territories in America granted to the Earl of Stirling."

On the 1st January 1833, Mr Humphrys Alexander addressed to the Scottish peers a printed letter, in which he intimated his intention not to vote at the approaching election at Holyrood, lest he should thereby expose himself to misrepresentation or insult. Having remarked that, "if not checked in their reckless course," his opponents might "give a death-blow to the privileges of all Scots peers who have not seats in the House of Lords," he concluded: "The day of retribution is not far off, and then I may act a part which, I have no doubt, will cause me to be differently respected and considered by those who are now pleased to cavil about straws, and who would deny me all but what they cannot give nor take away, namely, a rectitude of conscience and principle, which, in point of honour, stands as high and uncontaminated as that of the proudest of my opponents."

The printed letter addressed to the Scottish peers was followed by a series of anonymous communications in the *Times*, the *Morning Post*, and other newspapers, asserting and upholding Mr Humphrys Alexander's claims.

In his "Analytical Statement," Mr Banks expressed himself as "not doubtful" that the Crown would concur in confirming him as a baronet of Nova Scotia. Having failed to obtain recognition, he raised in the Court of Session an action of declarator, with the view of enforcing it. To this action the Scottish officers of State lodged defences, which Mr Banks, in a second pamphlet, hastened to criticise. His new publication was addressed to the sovereign. It bore the following title: "A Letter to the King's most excellent Majesty, respecting what are called 'the defences of the officers of State' to a certain action of declarator now sisted before the Court of Session at Edinburgh, showing the uncandid, covert, and invidious assertions therein unnecessarily introduced, which, having been printed, tend, as doubtless meant, to the prejudice of the pursuer, in the merits of his action, and of his public character, before trial of the cause.

> " ' Which rogue ought most to be condemn'd to shame,'
> Who *steals* my purse, or he who *saps my name!*'

Edinburgh, 1834, 8vo."

"It was unfortunate," wrote Mr Banks, "for monarchs, who might wish to live and reign in the hearts of their subjects, that they seldom knew anything of the conduct of their official servants." "This ignorance," he added, "occasioned them execrations when blessings would otherwise be given." The Scottish officers of State he characterised as worthy of his notice "only from their official character," "not from nobility of blood;" they were "Satanites," "imps of the fallen angel;" their "intents" were "demon-like;" they "practised insolence;" "worshipped the golden calf;" abused their authority; were miserable satellites; and wrote "as the lowest English scribbler in Grub Street."

Only a few weeks after the appearance of his second pamphlet, Mr Banks differed seriously with his client; he withdrew his publications, abandoned his action of declarator, and renounced his title! Henceforth he was personally subjected to denunciations and epithets of reproach similar to those he had, in the supposed interests of his client, dealt so unsparingly to others. In a quarto publication issued by him in 1836, Mr Humphrys Alexander characterises his former agent as "a traitor," "an impostor," "an extortioner," "a detractor," "a low-minded ruffian," "a companion of the foul fiend." He denounced his services as having been "detrimental to him," and his pamphlets as having "created animosity." In a future pamphlet, issued under his sanction, Mr Humphrys Alexander described Mr Banks as "a notorious character," through whom "he had been involved in all his difficulties."

The pretensions of Mr Humphrys Alexander had become portentous; and as his various services, if unchallenged, might lead to serious complications, it was deemed advisable to adopt against him decisive measures. By the Scottish officers of State, an action of Reduction Improbation was raised in the Court of Session to set aside his services, both general and special, along with the retours, precept, and instrument of sasine following thereon.

By a portion of the newspaper press, Mr Humphrys Alexander's movements, as "Earl of Stirling and Dovan," were duly chronicled. The following paragraph relative to the marriage of his daughter appeared in April 1835 in various journals : "*Runaway Match in High Life.*—The gossips of Edinburgh have experienced considerable excitement from the circumstance of an Englishman having eloped with the fair daughter of a Scotch peer.

The young lady is the beautiful A. A., only daughter of the Earl of S——g (who has recently claimed the title), and the bridegroom is W——e P——n, Esq., a person of good property in Cheshire. The parties were married yesterday at St James's, by the gentleman's brother, and instantly departed for Paris."

In the action of Reduction Improbation, Lord Cockburn, as Ordinary, granted, on the 26th November 1835, at the instance of the defender, a commission for receiving additional evidence on his behalf. Under authority of that commission, witnesses were examined at Birmingham, Dublin, and Rathgael, in the county of Down. At Rathgael, Margaret M'Blain, a widow, residing at Newtonards, aged about eighty, deponed that "she remembered the last Countess of Mount Alexander, who resided in Donaghadee, and died sixty-four years past last April; that she was ten years and upwards in Lady Mount Alexander's service, till the time of her ladyship's death; that she has often heard Lady Mount Alexander speak of a John Alexander, who had a son also called John Alexander, who married Mary Hamilton; that the said John the second and Mary Hamilton had a son, who was the Reverend John Alexander; that John the first was called of Gartmore, and John the second lived in Antrim, and the Reverend John Alexander was a minister in Dublin, and died there."

Mary Lewis in Newtonards, a widow, aged about eighty-six, deponed that she had "heard of a person of the name of Alexander who married a woman called Mary Hamilton."

Samuel Battersby, weaver, Newtonards, aged fifty, deponed that one John Pew, clerk of the church at Newtonards, deceased, told him that the ancient parish registers were destroyed. His wife, Eleanor Battersby, daughter of Mary Lewis, a previous witness, said she had heard her grandmother, Sophia Monk, state that Mary Hamilton, sister of James Hamilton, of Bangor, was married to John Alexander of Antrim, and bore him an only son, John, who afterwards became a clergyman in Dublin; and that she had heard "her grandmother say that she had heard her father say that the said John of Antrim was descended from the Alexanders of Scotland, and was nearly related to the Earl of Mount Alexander in

Ireland ; and that she had heard her grandmother also say that she had heard from her father that John of Gartmore was the Honourable John Alexander, and was father of John of Antrim."

In further evidence, Mr Humphrys Alexander lodged in process a paper described as a leaf torn from the family Bible of his late uncle, the Rev. John Alexander, son of the Rev. John Alexander of Dublin ; it contained the following legend :

" Inscription on my grandfather's tomb at Newton, copyd for me by Mr Henri Lyttleton.

"Here lieth the Body of Iohn Alexander, Esquire, late of Antrim, the only son of the Honourable Iohn Alexander, who was the fourth son of that most illustrious and famous statesman, William, Earl of Sterline, Principal Secretary for Scotland : who had the singular merit of planting, at his sole expense, the first colonie in Nova Scotia. He married Mary, eldest daughter of the Rev. Mr Hamilton of Bangor, by whom he had issue, one son, Iohn, who, at this present time, is the Presbyterian minister at Stratford-on-Avon, in England, and two daughters, Mary, who survives, and Elizabeth, wife of Iohn M. Skinner, Esquire, who died 7th January $17\frac{10}{11}$, leaving three children. He was a man of such endowments as added lustre to his noble descent, and was universally respected for his piety and benevolence. He was the best of husbands ; as a father, most indulgent ; as a friend, warm, sincere, and faithfull. He departed this life at Templepatrick, in the county of Antrim, on the 19th day of April 1712.

"This leaf, taken out of poor John's Bible, is put up with other family papers for my son Benjamin.—Done this sixteenth day of December 1776, in the presence of my friends and Mr John Berry, who, at my request, have subscribed their names as witnesses.

" HANNAH ALEXANDER.

" Abel Humphrys.
Ann Humphrys.
John Berry."

Neither the tombstone at Newtonards nor the Bible said to have contained its inscription were forthcoming, but certain persons at Birmingham vouched the handwriting of Abel Humphrys and John Berry, two of the three persons attesting the signature of Hannah Alexander attached to the inscription. Respecting the tombstone, the witness Margaret M'Blain deponed that she had been informed by her deceased husband, a mason, that "a tombstone with the name John Alexander, Esq., Antrim, formerly stood in the old church at the east end of Newtoun House, alongside the tombstone of Lady Mount Alexander;" while Eleanor Battersby, another witness, affirmed that she learned from Andrew Kelly, coachman, that Richard Monk, her great-grandfather, "had attended the funeral of Mr John Alexander of Antrim in Newtonards church."

Other efforts were put forth on the claimant's behalf. On the 26th May 1836 Mr Richard Broun, a solicitor, eldest son of Sir James Broun, Bart. of Colstoun, convened a meeting at London of the baronets of Nova Scotia, to consider the privileges of the order, but with the subsidiary object of acknowledging "the Earl of Stirling" as their chief. After several adjournments, the baronets met at Edinburgh on the 21st October, when Mr Broun submitted a lengthened report. He was allowed to print and circulate it; but certain resolutions which he had prepared for adoption were ignored or negatived. The report, which was founded on materials supplied by Mr Lockhart, Mr Humphrys Alexander's solicitor at Edinburgh, bore the following title: "Case of the honourable the Baronets of Scotland and Nova Scotia, shewing their rights and privileges, dignitorial and territorial.

> "Retinens vestigia famæ
> Virtutis præmium Avorum."

Edinburgh, 1836, 8vo, 69 pp.

To Mr Humphrys Alexander, the reporter refers in these words: "At the Peace of Paris in 1763, the right of inheritance to the first Earl of Stirling was in the person of his great-great-grandson, John, seventh earl. He died three years thereafter, and was succeeded by his brother Benjamin, eighth earl. This nobleman did not live to institute proceedings for his rights in America, but died in 1768, when his titles devolved on females till the 12th September 1814, when Alexander, the present Earl

* P

of Stirling and Dovan, succeeded by the decease of his mother. His lordship completed his titles in 1831, when, having been proved heir to the property, he obtained a precept from his Majesty, as overlord, for giving him seisin of Nova Scotia. This precept was directed to the Sheriff of Edinburgh, who, on his Majesty's behalf, gave the earl hereditary state and seisin of Nova Scotia, with its dependencies, on the 8th of July 1831, at the Castle of Edinburgh, in the manner prescribed by the foundation charters of the province."

The defection of Mr Banks probably led Mr Humphrys Alexander to apprehend that the officers of State had availed themselves of his services and possible disclosures. In the Edinburgh newspapers he published the following advertisement :

"*Intimation.* — Lord Stirling respects the motives which have induced T. W. C. to withhold his own name and address ; and, having ascertained, by the reference to Sir G. M., the perfect truth and correctness of T. W. C.'s information, he feels bound in gratitude for so generous and well-timed a disclosure of important facts on the part of a stranger, to comply with his request of a short acknowledgment in either the Edinburgh or London newspapers. Lord S. begs to assure T. W. C. that all his statements respecting the amissing charter of 1639 have been verified by the search, and will soon completely effect its discovery. The information sent respecting dark intrigues of the opposite party will be useful ; but T. W. C. will be glad to hear that, as might have been expected, those men who seek the overthrow of a family by treachery, whose plans are supported by fabricated papers and defamatory statements, have *traitors in their own camp*, to whose revelations Lord S. is indebted for ample means of exposing and punishing the chief conspirators."

In September 1836, Mr Humphrys Alexander, conjointly with Mr Lockhart, his solicitor at Edinburgh, issued a quarto volume, with the following title : " Narrative of the Oppressive Law Proceedings and other measures resorted to by the British Government, and numerous private individuals, to overpower the Earl of Stirling, and subvert his lawful rights, written by himself ; also, a genealogical account of the family of Alexander,

Earls of Stirling, etc., compiled from MSS. in the possession of the family, followed by an historical view of their hereditary possessions in Nova Scotia, Canada, etc., by Ephraim Lockhart, Esq.; with a copious appendix of royal charters and other documents. *Rien n'est beau que le vrai.*" In this "Narrative," which is dedicated to the king, Mr Humphrys Alexander requests his Majesty to grant him full compensation for the "grievous injury inflicted upon him" by his ministers. The charge of forgery he repudiates "with indignation," and intimates that he had detected a wicked design at the colonial office "to entrap him, by means of a forged letter, into the hands of a merciless enemy."* He denounces the king's ministers as having pursued him with "intrigue, deadly hate, envy, and accursed villainy." Because "he was entitled to a princely fortune with vice-regal powers and privileges," he had, he maintains, "been pursued with despicable falsehoods, animosities, and aspersions;" described as a "ruffian," and assailed by "lovers of defamation." The recognition of his claims as Lieutenant of Canada would, he believed, "stop an impending revolution in that colony, while, were his claims resisted, he would publish his "Narrative" in French as well as English, and circulate copies throughout America and Europe. Though declining "to satisfy his enemies, at a time when such explanations were unnecessary," as "to how or when he made a discovery," which he "reserved to be made available hereafter," he declared that he had recently made in support of his claims

---

* In a lengthened appendix, Mr Humphrys Alexander presents a correspondence between Mr J. J. Burn of Gray's Inn, his solicitor in London, and Lord Goderich, Secretary for the Colonies, respecting a letter which he alleged was handed to his wife on the 22d August 1832, in which the writer, who subscribed himself "B. T. Balfour," expressed a desire that, in his character of Lord Stirling, he would attend at the Colonial Office to meet Lord Goderich on the following day. Through his solicitor, Mr Humphrys Alexander charged Lord Goderich's private secretary as the writer of the forged letter—which he alleged was intended to entrap him into being arrested for debt on a judgment procured against him by Sir Henry Digby. His solicitor subsequently charged Lord Goderich's secretary with joining in a conspiracy "to end Lord Stirling, his case, his cares, and his claims, by doing an act not likely to be discovered that would apparently be acceptable to his principals."

"important discoveries both in France and America—one most important document for establishing his descent having been restored to him." Referring to the charter of *novodamus*, he said he had recently ascertained that duly authenticated copies were extant, "which all these years have been purposely withheld by the persons who have them in their keeping."

The action of Reduction Improbation came before the Court of Session in November, but Mr Humphrys Alexander did not avail himself of his alleged discoveries by adding to the evidence offered to the commission in January. On the 10th December, Lord Cockburn as Ordinary issued a proposed judgment reducing the services. In an exhaustive note, his lordship declared the affidavits of Lyner and Hovenden to be inadmissible, while the genuineness of the latter he held as open to suspicion. The tombstone inscription he pronounced worthless as evidence in the absence of the Bible, from which the leaf containing it had been procured. The evidence of M'Blain and Battersby as to the existence of the tombstone at Newtonards was, he held, negatived by the testimony of other witnesses intimately acquainted with the locality, who deponed that no tombstone, such as that described, had occupied a place in the church. Instructing his solicitor to appeal to the Inner House against the proposed judgment (which was pronounced on the 20th December), Mr Humphrys Alexander proceeded hastily to Paris. His family remained in London.

On the 22d April 1837, one of his sons wrote to him from London in these terms: "At ¼ to seven to-night, I write a few hasty lines to say that I received *   new evidence yesterday, and ever since have so occupied as not to be able to do anything —not write a letter. It contained 4 documents and a beauti-

---

* On the 22d December 1838, the Court of Session directed the letters addressed to Mr Humphrys Alexander by his son relative to the De Porquet packet to be examined by Mr Thomas Thomson, clerk of court. The order was executed, and a report thereon presented to the court on the 3d January 1839. "In reference to the blank between the words 'I have received,' and the words 'new evidence yesterday,' Mr Thomson reported that one word of three or four letters had been lost, in consequence of a perforation made by tearing or rubbing out the substance of the paper at the spot."

ful portrait of John of Antrim . . . haste. I will write on Monday full particulars. Your affectionate son, E."

To Mr Humphrys Alexander, his son, on the following day, wrote more fully. He stated that having, on the 21st inst., called at the shop of the family booksellers, Messrs De Porquet and Co., 11 Tavistock Street, he was informed by a young man at the counter that the firm had about an hour before received, by the twopenny post, a packet, which, being addressed to them, they had opened. It was found to contain an enclosure addressed, "To the Right Honble the Earl of Stirling," along with a card inscribed in these terms: "Mrs Innes Smyth's compliments to Messrs De Porquet and Co. She had fully intended calling in Tavistock Street when she arrived in town yesterday from Staffordshire; but another commission she had to execute having prevented her, she is induced to send the enclosed packet to them by the twopenny post, with her particular request that they will forward it *instantly* to the Earl of Stirling, or any member of his lordship's family, whose residence may be known to them. Hackney, *April* 19*th*." On receiving the packet, he consulted with his father's solicitors as to the manner of opening it, and they suggested that it should be opened before a public notary, which was accordingly done. Within the packet was found a parchment, inscribed, "Some of my wife's family papers," the handwriting, according to the young gentleman, being that of his maternal grandfather. The packet was impressed with three black seals, "the opening of which the notary could not venture to witness." Consequently the young gentleman, accompanied by one of his father's solicitors, proceeded to Doctors' Commons, where, in presence of proctor Thomas Blake and other three witnesses," he "cut the parchment over the middle black seal," and drew out the contents. The several documents were then examined and numbered by the proctor, who inscribed his initials upon each, as did the three persons who were present as witnesses.

In an unsigned note, dated 17th April 1837, the sender of the packet described the papers as stolen from the house of William Humphrys, the claimant's father, by a young man, lately deceased, at the instance of whose family they were returned. They were sent anonymously, to avoid "disgrace and infamy "

Among the documents enclosed in the packet was an emblazoned pedigree of the Earls of Stirling, "reduced to pocket size by Thomas Campbell on the 15th April 1759, from the large emblazoned tree in the possession of Mrs Alexander of King Street, Birmingham." This document presented a statement of pedigree corresponding with that adduced by the claimant in his different services; it represented John Alexander, fourth son of the first Earl of Stirling, as having settled in Ireland in 1646, and as having died there in 1665, leaving, by his second marriage* with Elizabeth Maxwell of Londonderry, a son, John. "W. G.," a lawyer, writing from Edinburgh on the 14th January 1723 to the Rev. John Alexander of Dublin, refers to the charter of *novodamus*, and suggests that though it is not in the Register of the Great Seal, it may have occupied a portion of the 57th volume of that Register, where several leaves are now wanting;† he adds that Mr Thomas Conyers of Catherlough in Ireland held the original, while Mr Conyers adds a certification that he did so.

A letter from the Rev. John Alexander describes his correspondent, "W. G.," as Mr William Gordon of Edinburgh. A miniature portrait of the alleged John of Antrim was on the back inscribed, "John Alexander, Esq., of Antrim, died April 19, 1712. From the original painting done at Versailles in his fortieth year: now in the possession of P. Denison, Esq., of Dublin. Thos. Campbell, pin^x." A letter, dated Dublin, Sep-

---

* John, fourth son of the first Earl of Stirling, died about the year 1641, without male issue. He did not contract a second marriage (see vol. i., p. 257).

† Mr George Robertson, one of the deputy keepers of the Records of Scotland, at the trial of Mr Humphrys Alexander for forgery, produced the following certificate: "I, George Robertson, do certify that I have searched the Principal Record of the 57th volume, and that at the beginning of the said 57th volume, twelve leaves have been destroyed or lost. The charters originally recorded on these missing leaves are, however, ascertained with precision from two ancient indices of the Great Seal Record. I have examined these, and can state as the result that the twelve leaves now lost did not contain any charter, diploma, patent, nor other grant in favour of William, Earl of Stirling, nor of any Earl of Stirling, nor of any person of the name of Alexander."

tember 16, 1765, and subscribed, "A. E. Baillie," informs Mr John Alexander of Birmingham, son of the Rev. John Alexander of Dublin, that the family tombstone at Newtonards had been destroyed by the American claimant of the Stirling peerage. Letters subscribed "B. Alexander" (Benjamin Alexander), in 1765 and 1766, also refer to this event, and enter into details conforming to the statements in the pedigree.

On the 12th July 1837, Mr Humphrys Alexander (as he afterwards deponed), was surprised by having exhibited to him at Paris, by his friend Mademoiselle le Normand, a map of Canada, or New France, which she had found in her cabinet, where some unknown person had left it, accompanied by a letter. The letter, written in French, set forth that the sender, being a person in office, had concealed his name, and that he had sent the map to Mademoiselle le Normand on account of certain autographs attached to it, which, he hoped, would prove useful to her friend, the Earl of Stirling.

The map was one of a series prepared by the celebrated French geographer, Guillaume de L'Isle. It was dated 1703, and to the back of it were attached letters and certifications specially adapted to the exigencies of Mr Humphrys Alexander's claim. One Philip Mallet certified that the charter of *novodamus* granted to the first Earl of Stirling, and which could not be found in Britain, was in the register at Port Royal in 1706. This charter Caron Saint Estienne, writing from Lyons on the 6th April 1707, stated he had read; while Esprit Flechier, Bishop of Nismes, certified that he had seen a transcript prepared by M. Mallet. To the map was attached a letter, dated Antrim, 25th August 1704, and subscribed John Alexander, in which the writer claimed to be the only son of John Alexander, fourth son of the first Earl of Stirling, and stated that he was then educating his son John for the Scottish Church at the University of Leyden.* That letter, in its turn, was certified as

---

* The Scottish Church has never recognised attendance at foreign universities as part of a theological curriculum. In 1704 Mr John Alexander, latterly Presbyterian minister at Dublin, was a student at the University of Glasgow (see vol. ii., p. 149).

authentic, under date 16th October 1707, by the celebrated François Fénelon, Archbishop of Cambray. A copy of the inscription on the alleged tombstone at Newtonards was also affixed to
the map, accompanied by a note bearing that it had been communicated by Madame de Lambert, an alleged patroness of the
Rev. John Alexander.

On the 13th August 1837, Mr Humphrys Alexander left
Paris, and proceeded to Edinburgh, "to attend the election of
peers." In October he despatched one of his sons to Paris to
receive from Mademoiselle le Normand the map and other documents of July, which, if genuine, would, along with the contents of
the packet of the preceding April, have fully established his claims.

To sustain his appeal in the action of Reduction Improbation,
Mr Humphrys Alexander produced in court, on the 25th November 1837, the documents discovered at London and Paris,
the latter under the seal of Mademoiselle le Normand. The
genuineness of these productions being impeached by the officers
of State, the court authorised a commission to make the necessary inquiries. The commissioners made a searching examination at Paris, and on their report the officers of State moved
that the claimant should be judicially examined. This motion
being acceded to, the examination of the claimant was, in the
Second Division of the Court of Session, conducted by the Lord
Advocate, on the 18th December 1838. The claimant admitted
that Mademoiselle le Normand told fortunes by means of cards,
and was paid by those who consulted her. For revealing his
own fortune, he had paid her five napoleons. This, he said, was
"a long time ago," but he afterwards recollected that it was in
1837. Not long before the discovery of the map of Canada, he
had granted to Mademoiselle le Normand a bond for 400,000
francs; it was for borrowed money, and in reimbursement of
outlays for researches made on his behalf in France, Germany,
and Holland.*

---

* In a pamphlet published at Paris in 1845, Mr Humphrys Alexander condemns Mademoiselle le Normand, then deceased, for "creating a prejudice against
him in having the map of Canada, covered with her sealed envelope, carried to
the Court of Session, and opened in the presence of the judges."

On the 14th February 1839, Mr Humphrys Alexander was, on a charge of forging seventeen documents, committed to prison at Edinburgh. Judicially examined by one of the sheriffs of Edinburgh on the 14th and 18th February, and again on the 6th March, he stated that during his late residence at Paris, "he was engaged in literary pursuits;" and in particular, was concerned in supplying information with regard to the state of society in England to a friend who was engaged in publishing a work on the subject; he was also occupied in writing a memoir of his own life. He expressed a "strong suspicion" that the map of Canada was brought to Mademoiselle le Normand from one of the administerial departments in the archives of France, and that it was sent her "through the intervention or direction of a person high in office." On the 18th March he was served with an indictment. It embraced five counts, embodying charges as to forging and uttering the excerpt charter of *novodamus*, the writings on the back of the map of Canada, and the various papers contained in the packet addressed to the care of his bookseller.

The trial was fixed to take place in the High Court of Justiciary at Edinburgh, on the 3d of April, but was adjourned from that day to the 29th of the same month, to enable the prisoner better to prepare his defence. The trial continued four days. The prosecution was conducted by Lord Advocate Rutherfurd, Solicitor-General Ivory, and Messrs Cosmo Innes and Robert Handyside, Advocates-Depute. Messrs Patrick Robertson, Adam Anderson, and John Inglis, advocates, were counsel for the prisoner. At the bar, he was accompanied by his early friend, Colonel D'Aguilar, Deputy Adjutant-General of the Forces in Ireland, who also advanced £500 to aid his defence.

In support of the charge relative to the excerpt charter of *novodamus*, it was proved that Archbishop Spottiswoode of St Andrews, whose name as Chancellor of Scotland was appended to it as a witness, ceased to hold office as chancellor on the 13th November 1638, and died on the 26th November 1639,* eleven days before the date assigned to the instrument.

* In Craufurd's "Lives of the Officers of State," it is stated that Archbishop

It was also proved that the words "*Gratis* per signetum" at the end of the excerpt could not have been attached to a completed charter, the proper words being "per preceptum secreti sigilli." Further, at the commencement of the excerpt were the words, " Reg. Mag. Sig., lib. lvii."—meaning Register of the Great Seal, 57th volume, while it was shown that the charter of *novodamus* was not contained in the volume so indicated, and that the formula, Reg. Mag. Sig., was not used prior to the year 1806.

Respecting the map of Canada, it was proved that though bearing date 1703, it could not have been printed till subsequent to the 24th August 1718, when its author was appointed " Premier Geographe du Roi," as which he is described upon the map itself. It therefore followed that the inscriptions attached to it were spurious, since at the date assigned to them the map was non-existent. In the defence strong testimony on behalf of the prisoner's character was borne by Mr Josiah Corrie, his family solicitor at Birmingham, Mr Charles Hardinge of Bole Hall, near Tamworth, Mr Roger Aytoun, Writer to the Signet at Edinburgh, and Colonel D'Aguilar. In giving his evidence, Colonel D'Aguilar said : " Nothing on earth would have induced me to stand where I now do before this court, if I did not believe Lord Stirling to be incapable of doing a dishonourable action. If the correspondence of an individual can, in any case, be relied on, as an index to his mind and character, I have in my possession—in the letters of Lord Stirling—what will afford the best proof of his uprightness and integrity. His early letters to me I have not preserved; but latterly, and especially since he has had the misfortune to be placed in his present situation, I have heard from him regularly." Mr Patrick Robertson, the prisoner's senior counsel, thus concluded an ingenious argument in his defence :

Spottiswoode died on the 27th December 1639 ; but in the Latin inscription on his monument in Westminster Abbey, contained in the same work, the date of the archbishop's death, is thus indicated : " Ex hac vita in pace migravit anno domini 1639, sexto calendas Decembris." At the trial, Mr Robertson, on the part of the prisoner, admitted that the words *sexto calendas Decembris* denoted the 26th of November.

"When I look back on the life of this unfortunate man, I see nothing but anxious days of heart-sickening hope and sleepless nights of feverish rest, disturbed and chequered by golden dreams that were speedily dissipated by the rays of the morning sun—a rising family, taught to look on nobility and wealth as their birthright, yet seeing nothing but penury and distress before them—calling to their parent for bread, and lo! he has nothing to give them but a stone.

> 'Lo! poverty to fill the band
> That numbs the soul with icy hand,
> And slow consuming age.'

And when I look forward to the future, I trust I see a prospect that his mind shall be directed to pursuits more solid, and to the attainment of objects more consolatory and enduring. Let the visionary coronet be plucked from his bewildered brow—let the prospects of wealth and of courtly titles and honours vanish into air; but oh, gentlemen, leave him that best and highest title to nobility—his good name; let his character remain to solace him on retiring from the fatigues and bustle of this vain and transitory world. Gentlemen, I am one of those who venerate the memory of the illustrious dead—of those whose prejudices, feelings, and principles unite in admiration of hereditary rank and high title, conferred as the reward of patriotism and virtue upon those whose names adorn the page of history, and who are enrolled amidst the nobles of the land; and I also venerate those of more recent name, who, from their valour, their piety, or their learning, have been added to grace that august assembly. But without truth, integrity, and honour, titles and distinctions are worse than nothing. Without these, the glitter of the coronet hath no splendour in my eye—the rustling of the silken robe hath no music in my ear. On the tarnished ermine I trample with contempt. Do not, gentlemen—do not add to the pangs of this man more than he deserves. Leave him in possession of that character which he has hitherto enjoyed, as his only solace under· his heavy trials. Leave him that, without which the crown itself is but a bauble, and the sceptre a toy; for, in my conscience, I believe him innocent of the crimes here charged, and to have been merely the dupe of the designing, and the prey of the unworthy."*

* Mr Humphrys Alexander was dissatisfied with the manner in which his defence was conducted. He considered Mr Robertson's appeal to the jury as "ill-judged," and his entire speech as doing him "more harm than all the accusing, surmising, and guessing of the Crown lawyers."

After deliberating five hours, the jury brought in the following verdict:

"The jury unanimously find it proved that the excerpt charter libelled on is a forged document; and by a majority find it not proven that the pannel forged the said document, or is guilty art and part thereof, or that he uttered it, knowing it to be forged. They unanimously find it proved that the documents on the map libelled are forged; and by a majority find it not proven that the pannel forged the said documents, or is guilty art and part thereof, or that he uttered them, knowing them to be forged. They unanimously find it not proven that the documents contained in De Porquet's packet are forged, or were uttered by the pannel as genuine, knowing them to be forged. They unanimously find it not proven that the copy letter to Le Normand, in the fifth and last charge of the indictment, is either forged, or was uttered by the pannel as genuine, knowing it to be forged."

When the chancellor of the jury had read this verdict, the prisoner fainted and was borne from the court. The following judgment was put on record: "The Lords Commissioners of Justiciary, in respect of the foregoing verdict of assize, assoilzie the pannel *simpliciter*, and dismiss him from the bar." * A few months subsequent to the trial appeared an octavo pamphlet of 134 pages, entitled, "Remarks on the Trial of the Earl of Stirling at Edinburgh, by an English Lawyer." In this publication the writer expressed dissatisfaction with the verdict of the jury, and denounced both the judges and the officers of State.

On the 4th June 1839, Mr Humphrys Alexander presented a note to the Court of Session, requesting delay, in order that he might determine whether he should abide or not by the documents pronounced forgeries by the jury. The request was refused, and the Court, on the 9th July 1839, affirmed the judgment of Lord Cockburn, reducing the defender's services. Against this decision Mr Humphrys Alexander offered to appeal to the House of Lords. It was now contended by the Scottish officers of State that the summons in their action of

---

* From a return presented to Parliament in May 1840, the expenses incurred in conducting Mr Humphrys Alexander's trial were set down at £2585.

Reduction Improbation contained declaratory as well as reductive conclusions, and they accordingly craved a remit of the process to the Lord Ordinary to dispose of the former. On the 29th May 1840, the Court issued an interlocutor, remitting the process to Lord Cunningham, as Ordinary, who, on the 2d June, affirmed the declaratory conclusions. Against this judgment, confirmed by the Inner House, and against the former interlocutor, Mr Humphrys Alexander in August 1841 appealed to the House of Lords, but the final hearing and disposal of the case were suspended. In December 1842 an advertisement appeared in the *Edinburgh Evening Post*, and other Scottish newspapers, inviting applications to the Rev. J. C. Helm, Worthing, Sussex, who undertook to satisfy inquirers that the map of Canada, with its autographs, was now proved to be genuine and authentic. Messrs Swinton & Turnbull, advocates, who had published reports of Mr Humphrys Alexander's trial, accordingly communicated with Mr Helm, who forwarded to each a tract of four duodecimo pages, in which it was set forth that, since the trial, " the Earl of Stirling has discovered that an Englishman named Rowland Otto Baijer, a prisoner of war in France during the empire, died at Verdun in 1805, and that in an account of writings found in his apartments, and delivered to a Monsieur Gorneau, was a copy of De Lisle's map of Canada, with an epitaph in English, an autograph letter of John Alexander, with a marginal note by Fénelon, a note by the traveller Mallet, and other attestations." This, maintained the writer, was " absolutely the identical map which figured in the court at Edinburgh." In 1845 Mr Humphrys Alexander issued a further publication ; he printed at Paris an octavo pamphlet of 75 pages, entitled, "Two Letters addressed to the Right Hon. Thomas, Lord Denman, Lord Chief Justice of the Court of Queen's Bench." In this publication he insisted on his rights as Earl of Stirling and Lieutenant of Canada, maintained the genuineness of the impugned documents, including those on the map of Canada, and begged that in his impending appeal to the House of Lords, Lord Denman would " act as a mediator between him and the Government." He referred to his " undeniable grievances," and hoped that, under his lordship's auspices, he would no longer be oppressed and persecuted.

On the 6th March 1845 the appeal of Mr Humphrys Alexander was heard in the House of Lords, when their lordships found that the interlocutor of the Court of Session, of the 2d June 1840, not having been reclaimed against, the process was asleep. The appellant thereupon raised a process of "wakening" before the Lord Ordinary, but after certain proceedings, and an order in the case by the House of Lords, on the 19th February 1846, procedure was sisted.

Mr Humphrys Alexander now removed to the United States, and establishing his residence at Washington, presented to the American Government a statement of his claims. By General Pierce, President of the United States, an application on his behalf was, about the year 1854, addressed to the British Government, which was followed by a correspondence.

Mr Humphrys Alexander died at Washington on the 4th May 1859, aged seventy-six. By his wife, Fortunata, daughter of Signor Giovanni Bartoletti, of Naples, he had five sons, Alexander William Francis, Charles Louis, Eugene, William Donald, and John, and a daughter, Angela; she married, in April 1835, William Wilberforce Pearson, Esq. of Scraptoft Hall, Leicestershire, with issue.

On the 11th February 1864, Alexander William Francis Alexander, eldest son of Alexander Humphrys Alexander, was served heir in general to his father by the Sheriff of Chancery at Edinburgh. He thereupon revived, in the Court of Session, the process of wakening. The competency of the proceeding was resisted by the officers of State, but by an interlocutor, dated 29th June 1864, the Court repelled the objections, and, on payment by the appellant of costs incurred by the officers of State prior to the 2d June 1840, permitted the raiser to reclaim. On the 25th May 1866, the Court found the action raised by the officers of State, as regarded its declaratory conclusions, incompetent; and in respect of these conclusions, dismissed it, with costs to the appellant. But on the 19th June of the same year, the Second Division pronounced the following judgment: "In respect of the interlocutor of Lord Cockburn of the 20th December 1836, and of the interlocutor of the Second Division of the 9th July 1839, reduce the precept from Chancery, the instrument of seisin, and procuratory of resignation, and decern." Thereupon Mr William Francis Alexander petitioned the House of Lords for leave to revive his former appeal, and on the 7th June 1867 the required permission was obtained. The appeal was heard in the House of Lords on the 20th February 1868, and subsequently it was argued for the appellant that it was incompetent for the Crown to reduce his services, inasmuch as there was not a competing claimant. The case was also argued on its merits, the appellant being represented by Sir Roundell Palmer, Q.C., and the Lord Advocate appearing for the officers of State. By the Lords Chelmsford, Westbury, and Colonsay, judgment was delivered on the 3d April 1868. Their lordships held that the action of Reduction was competent, disallowed further proof on account of the circumstances of suspicion under which the former evidence was rejected, and affirmed eight interlocutors appealed against. In an opinion extending to forty-one folio pages, Lord Chelmsford entered into a minute and careful criticism, showing the defective character of the evidence, which, he remarked, solely rested on forged documents.

On the 15th April 1872, Mr Charles Louis Alexander, second son of Mr Humphrys Alexander, made a claim on behalf of his brother, as Earl of Stirling, to the British American Fisheries. A portion of his printed appeal to Congress is subjoined:

"The Fisheries, now under Treaty consideration, are private property. They have become *irrevocably so* since the 30th May 1871. The Crown of Great Britain, in attempting, nearly forty years ago, to suspend, 'for political reasons,' as it stated apologetically, the exercise of the rights established by law, and confirmed by seisin granted by King William IV. on the 8th of July 1831, brought an 'illegal' action against the late Earl of Stirling in January 1833. One of the services of heirship, dated *May* 30*th*, 1831, by which the earl, under an order of the Court of Session, was served nearest lawful heir of tailzie and provision to William, first Earl of Stirling, was never questioned by the Crown, and is now for ever prescribed in favour of his heirs.

" ' According to Act of Parliament, a service of heirship to an ancestor, *which remains unchallenged by any other heir*, shall, *after a lapse of twenty years*, become *absolute* in the heir so served ; and that, in all cases between the *Crown and a subject*, such service *shall become absolute if it remains unchallenged by the Crown after a lapse of forty years.*' The service above named, being dated May 30th, 1831, the forty years expired on May 30th, 1871, and the Government of Great Britain is bound, on demand, to give a new charter in accordance with said service. This fact, in addition to the *want of title* in the Crown to interfere at all in an heirship, established by law, *nullifies all the litigious proceedings commenced in January* 1833, during the political agitation in the Canadas, which resulted subsequently in rebellion.   .   .   .

· " These rights are founded upon a charter, granted 10th September 1621, of Nova Scotia, etc. ; a *novodamus* of the same, dated 12th July 1625 ; and a charter of the Dominion of Canada, dated 2d February 1628. *These charters were formally ratified by Act of Parliament, 28th of June* 1633. They are all on file in the Record Office at Edinburgh, Scotland. Their present validity has been proved by their use on various treaties, and on questions of boundary ; and, further, their legal force was established by their renewal in the Act of seisin (quoting them at length), in Lord Stirling's favour, by King William IV., on the 8th of July 1831.

" Litigious proceedings, worthy only of the barbarous ages—an unholy system of law practice grown out of feudal conquest—have been pursued for forty years. They have been condemned in strong terms by British lawyers and judges, and never more so than in the House of Lords in April 1845, on appeal from decisions (*two of them actually made in secret*) in Scotland, when Lord Chancellor Cottenham and ex-Chancellors Brougham, Lyndhurst, and Campbell heard the case, and expressed their opinions that the whole proceedings of the Crown ' *were wrong, illegal, unconstitutional, and arbitrary*'— ' *unheard of in British Courts,*' etc. This course of illegality, however, was persisted in because, as Lord Advocate Murray stated in the Court of Session, in 1837, ' the case had political consequences.'

" This opposition led to a succession of crimes, commencing with the celebrated forgery at the Colonial Office in 1833, to inveigle and carry off Lord Stirling, details of which were published in a quarto volume at Edinburgh, 1837 (containing all the self-convicting letters from the Government, and final confession of the Solicitor of the

Treasury, Mr Maul), to the forgery trial in Edinburgh, *in revenge for the publicity given to the official forgery;* wherein a map of Canada, with writings upon it, stolen by a British agent from the Office of Foreign Affairs in Paris, was in a disreputable way *forced* on Lord Stirling, and then *secretly* withdrawn from the Court, and a *copy or forgery substituted for it.*

" The charge fell through, the rebutting testimony proving that the Crown witnesses were a *set of criminals.* The Lord Advocate, *finding that Mr Mark Napier, an eminent Crown Counsel, and other reliable witnesses,* could prove the substitution before *named,* referred the case to the Home Office in London. After consultation, the Government decided that the Crown had gone too far to retract ; that the case must proceed at all hazards, and every effort be made ' to save the honour of the Crown, compromised by ITS AGENTS !' etc.

" *As one forgery naturally required others to sustain it,* so ALL the official and newspaper reports of the sham trial were but a series of misrepresentations of the testimony ' to save the honour of the Crown' by calumniating the heir. It was considered necessary not only to falsify evidence, *but passages in letters were interpolated in imitation of Lord Stirling's handwriting* and *read to the jury by the chief judge, after the case closed, to carry, if possible, a verdict by surprise.* In short, a ' powerful and proud Government was not too proud or too powerful to allow itself *to be* the tool of *petty-fogging lawyers,* and *cover up their crimes* because Lord Stirling had ' obstinately refused' (a Crown Counsel's words) to arrange (i.e., '*share*') *with them,* and so ensure to them enough to cover the fortunes promised if they could destroy the established right.

" That the British Government had no doubts of Lord Stirling's rights, and knew well the weak course it was pursuing, is shown by the fact that at the severe contest for election of sixteen Peers at Edinburgh, in 1838, it commissioned the Earl of Buchan to offer Lord Stirling an English Barony (enabling a Peer to sit in the House of Lords without form of election), if he would vote the whole Government ticket. But Lord S. refused to change his politics or abandon his friends, arguing that his rights should be settled independently of party questions.

" But to leave this revolting view of official imbecility on one side and greed on the other, I will add, that on June 1, 1854, Lord Stirling forwarded to Hon. William L. Marcy, then Secretary of State, a letter and protest against any interference with his established rights in the Fisheries. The Hon. Reverdy Johnson, in a lengthy opinion, dated May 5, 1854, confirming English and Scotch opinions, together with those of Hon. R. J. Walker, John L. Hayes (author of 'Vindication' of Lord Stirling, published in this city in 1854), and A. H. Lawrence, Counsellors of Law in this country, says : 'It is evident that those proceedings were originally instituted for immediate political effect in the Canadas, and with no expectation of finally disturbing the foundation of Lord Stirling's title.' Lord Stirling died at my house, May 4th, 1859. A few years later a settlement of the case was talked of in England, but procrastinated until the 'arbitrary decisions,' etc., had been rescinded. Accordingly, the present earl, my eldest brother, by decree of the Court of Session, after decision of a jury, was in the usual form declared heir to his father, etc., etc., and in February 1864, the 'arbitrary decisions' were reversed, and finally the Court of Session *dismissed the Crown case* on the ground of '*illegality*' in May 1866.

"It is but justice to a few honourable men to state that Earl Grey, Reform Prime Minister in 1830, the late Earl Derby, Sir Robert Peel, and other British statesmen, protested against the persecution into which the opposition commenced 'from political reasons,' drifted through the action of lawyer swindlers, who wanted a compensating share in the case. Years ago, a London journal, commenting on this case, remarked that the Government 'ought to interfere and indemnify Lord Stirling,' and 'spare the poor earl from being worried to death by the wolf-dogs of the law.'

"I leave this case in the hands of Congress, trusting that with a view to protect its citizens in their rights, it will countenance no measure damaging to them, but cause a thorough investigation of the whole subject before taking final action in regard to the matter of the Fisheries."

On the statements put forth in this "appeal," commentary is useless, differing as they essentially do with the facts and circumstances of the case.

INDEX.

A.

* R

M'Farlane & Erskine, Printers, Edinburgh.

www.ingramcontent.com/pod-product-compliance
Lightning Source LLC
Chambersburg PA
CBHW020346030726
47496CB00007B/2017